THE LOVER

DOCTOR #3

E. L. TODD

Hartwick Publishing

The Lover

Copyright © 2019 by E. L. Todd

CONTENTS

1

PEPPER

I FELL ASLEEP ON THE COUCH, LEAVING MY SOAKING CLOTHES ON the bathroom floor. I never made it to the bedroom because I opened a bottle of wine and drank my sorrows away. It was the only way I could stop thinking about Finn and Layla and fall asleep.

A knock sounded at the door. "It's me." Colton's distinct voice made it through the wood.

I pulled my hair out of my face and glanced at my appearance in the mirror by the door.

I looked terrible.

There wasn't enough time to fix myself, and since Colton had already seen me at my worse last night, I opened the door. "Hey..." Everything came flooding back to me, the rain, the tears, and the truth. In a moment of catharsis, I'd told Colton the truth...a truth that I didn't even realize until that moment.

That I loved Finn.

"Hey." He let himself in and shut the door. "Sleep alright?"

"Other than the kink in my neck and the belly full of wine, yeah."

"Good." He looked at me with those compassionate blue eyes,

as if he loved me just as much as he had before. It seemed ridiculous in hindsight to think he would have had a problem with me seeing Finn since he was so calm and accepting about it now.

I felt like I should apologize. "I'm sorry about everything. It was wrong and it shouldn't have happened, but it just...kept happening. We agreed we should only be friends, but somehow... I don't know."

He bowed his head and slid his hands into his pockets.

"Finn had said he was going to talk to you about it, but he changed his mind."

He lifted his gaze and met my eyes once more. He rubbed the back of his neck before he released a quiet sigh. "He did talk to me, actually."

"Ooh..." That wasn't the story Finn had told me.

"He asked my permission to ask you out. He said he really liked you and wanted to see if it would go somewhere. I told him no."

I crossed my arms over my chest, my breath coming out shaky.

Colton shrugged. "It made me really uncomfortable. You're the one woman who's off-limits, but he went after you anyway. It's not like you're my ex-girlfriend or something. You were my wife, and you're still my best friend. I was pissed he would even think about making a move. He argued that it shouldn't matter because I'm gay, but that pissed me off more because it's irrelevant if I'm gay or straight. I told him when a relationship between you two ended, it would affect my relationship with both of you. Neither of you would be able to be in the same room together, and that'd affect my life drastically. He tried to change my mind, but it was no use. My answer was final."

So, our prediction was right. Colton would never be okay with this.

"But after seeing you last night...I've changed my mind."

I knew this was hard for Colton, but he loved me too much to stand in the way.

"I just wanted you to know he ended things with you because of me...not because he wanted to."

"And he didn't want me to know that was your answer... because he didn't want to affect our friendship."

He shrugged.

"He's a good guy, Colton. I know you're probably upset with him right now, but he's still loyal to you."

Colton wouldn't look at me.

"There's something I've never told you..."

His eyes flicked back to me.

"The reason Jax and I broke up was because he didn't like our relationship. He told me I had to choose—you or him. When I chose you, he dumped me."

His eyes slowly fell, filling with a mixture of guilt and sadness.

"I told Finn not to tell you. He could have used that in his argument, but he never did. I know you feel betrayed by him right now, but he's still one of the best guys I know. I hope you can cut him some slack."

Colton's silence was a sufficient answer. "If you want to be with him, I won't stand in the way. But as your best friend, I feel like I should warn you. Finn is a good man—there's no argument against that. But he's got a lot of issues. Even before he went into the military, he was the way he is now. He's not the commitment type."

In the limited time I'd known Finn, I'd seen the way he was with women. He was heartless and unattached. His life was a series of one-night stands, of women whose names he would never remember.

"He doesn't stay in one place very long. He's been in Seattle for a few months, but I can't see his residence being permanent."

"He bought a house."

"And he can sell that house. It's a good piece of real estate. He'll easily get what he paid for it. He was in the military for so long because he likes moving around. He's never been the kind of guy to be stationary. I'm not sure why he's like that, but he is."

"I'm sure all of that is true, Colton. But he's different with me..." I felt naïve saying that out loud, like a stupid girl who believed a man would really change for her. But I believed it nonetheless.

"I never said he wasn't. But that won't last long. I hope I'm wrong, Pepper. But I really don't think I am..."

If I weren't already in love with Finn, logic would tell me to turn away and run. But I was so deep in this relationship, I had nothing more to lose. I was already betting everything.

"He said he never wants to get married or have a family. I doubt he's changed his mind about that. I doubt he'll *ever* change his mind about that."

I'd already had my heart broken once, and I didn't want to go through it again. But the idea of walking away sounded too painful. "When we got married, I thought we wanted the same things. I thought we would be together forever and have a family..."

He sighed guiltily.

"You know how that turned out, Colton. You were the safest bet in the world...and that fell apart. I understand how Finn is. I understand he's a risky choice. But I'm already in so deep, I lose whether I stay or leave."

"It'll hurt a lot more in the end if you stay."

Maybe he was right, but I wanted to deal with that later.

When Colton realized I wouldn't change my mind, he gave

up. "I had to warn you to ease my conscience...but I support whatever you want to do."

"You're sure you're okay with this?" I whispered.

He stared at me for a long time. "I love you, Pepper. I want you to have whatever you want. If Finn is what you want, then have him."

"I'm surprised you aren't angry with me..."

He shrugged. "After what I did to you, I should cut you some slack."

"I've forgiven you, Colton. Stop beating yourself up over it."

"Thanks...but I don't think I can."

I moved into his chest and hugged him. "I love you."

He squeezed me back. "I love you too, Pepper." He kissed my forehead.

"You know your brother loves you too, right?"

He remained silent as he hugged me, his chest rising and falling at a slow pace. When an answer didn't arrive, I knew it wasn't coming.

It would never come.

———

I ARRIVED at Finn's doorstep, my heart in my throat with a tremor in my fingers. Now that Colton was on board, there was nothing standing in our way. We could be what Finn wanted to be without repercussions.

I tried not to think about what had happened with Layla last night. If he did sleep with her, I couldn't be angry about it because we'd broken up. Colton had said he would never be okay with our relationship, so Finn drowned himself in an easy lay. It broke my heart, but it wouldn't stop me from being with him, from having what we were supposed to have.

Finn opened the door, his blue eyes reflecting the sunlight

that pierced through the clouds for just a moment. In just his sweatpants, he looked like the man of my dreams. He pushed the door farther open as he stared me down, the longing deep in his gaze.

Soldier sat at his side, looking at me with his tongue slightly hanging out.

I kept my eyes on the man in front of me, the person my heart screamed for. Being heartbroken over him was somehow worse than the night Colton had told me he didn't want to be with me anymore. My relationship with Finn seemed to make more sense than mine ever did with Colton. Now that I'd been with the right man, I could see that clearly. "Colton told me the truth."

With one hand on the door, he kept looking at me.

"That you only broke up with me because he said we couldn't be together."

His shoulders lowered slightly.

I kept staring at him, unsure what else to do. This didn't happen the way I wanted, but now that all the obstacles were out of the way, we could finally be together. Was that what he still wanted? Or was it more exciting when we were sneaking around?

He dropped his hand from the door. "Get your ass in here."

My lips softened into a smile, and I moved into his chest, reconnecting with that powerful physique I'd missed sleeping with every night. My cheek felt the warmth, and I wrapped my arms around his waist and closed my eyes, relishing the smell of his body soap.

He shut the door then wrapped his powerful arms around me. His soft lips brushed against my hairline, and then he kissed my forehead. He hugged me a little tighter and released a quiet sigh, one full of contentment and peace.

I felt at home. This was the place where I belonged, the only place that made sense. I felt terrible for lying to Colton, but the guilt didn't outweigh the happiness. Maybe we had no future, but right now, this was all I wanted.

He pulled away so he could look into my face. "I missed you."

A man like Finn didn't say sweet things like that often, if ever. He was honest to a fault, so he meant every single syllable of that phrase. It melted my entire body until I was a puddle on the floor. "I missed you too..."

His hand cupped my cheek, and he rested his forehead against mine. He closed his eyes and stood there with me, as if my presence soothed his soul. He didn't crush his mouth to mine and whisk me off to the bedroom right away. He missed me as the person who made his heart beat, who brought peace to his damaged soul.

THERE WAS NO BETTER feeling than being pressed into a mattress by a heavy man. His muscular body was so hard against mine. His powerful thighs brushed against the softness of my legs as he thrust inside me. His rock-hard chest rubbed my nipples as he moved up and down.

My ankles locked together around his waist, and I clawed at his back, moaning because this man drove me crazy. Every inch inside me made me feel like a woman, made me feel like the most desirable woman on the planet.

His hand dug into my hair and turned it into a mess as his eyes locked on mine. Sometimes, he kissed me, and sometimes, he just breathed with me, enjoying the perfect way our bodies fit together.

Finn ruined me for all other men. If I ever found someone else, I would always compare the sex to this...because it was so damn good. He wasn't just sexy and good in the sack. He was passionate and shared a deep connection with me.

He'd already made me come the second he was inside me. It didn't take much work on his part after the week of solitude and sadness. He seemed to be holding on by a thread the entire time, his dick so thick inside me with imminent explosion. He wanted this to be one of those sessions that went on forever.

But we had all the time in the world to have those kinds of nights. "Let go." I grabbed his ass and pulled him deep inside me, wanting to catch every drop of that come. I missed how heavy it felt, how warm it was as it dripped from my opening and down my thighs.

He grunted as his hips bucked automatically, shuddering noticeably as he finished. "Baby..." With his length buried deep inside me, he gave me everything he had, an entire load of arousal and affection.

My thighs squeezed him harder because the face he made while climaxing was something I could touch myself to. My fingers slid through his hair, and I released a satisfied breath, happy to be back in bed with the man I adored.

He gave me a soft kiss before he pulled out of me, his come immediately flowing to my entrance. He lay beside me, his naked body outstretched on the bed as he caught his breath. A sheen of sweat reflected the light coming through the blinds of the bedroom window. Head to toe, he was the perfect man, strong, lean, and covered in ink.

I turned into his side and wrapped my arm around his waist, feeling at peace with the world. All the heartache I felt last week disappeared like a bad dream. My breathing matched his pace, and I tucked my leg between his thighs, cuddling with him just the way I used to. It was so peaceful; I almost fell asleep a few times.

When Soldier realized we were resting, he jumped on the bed and curled up on the edge.

"He never leaves your side, huh?"

"Only when I kick him out of the bathroom."

I chuckled. "Does he whine when you leave?"

"No. He knows better than that."

"But what about when you come home?"

He smiled as he thought about it. "He does this thing where he spins around in a circle really fast, like he's chasing his tail. Then he pounces on me and paws at my chest. Sometimes, he barks a little."

"Because he's so happy to see you."

"Yeah...he's a cool dog. I stayed home all week, and he stayed by my side..." His smile diminished when he reflected on the week we'd stopped seeing each other. "He seemed to know something was wrong."

"Dogs can sense things."

"He's a good comrade. And he's a good jogging buddy."

"You jog?"

He nodded. "Around the neighborhood."

"That's pretty cute."

"Me or Soldier?"

"Both," I said. "But mainly Soldier."

He smiled slightly, understanding I was joking. "Colton told me you don't like to jog."

"No. Exercise in any form, really."

"Why is that?"

I shrugged. "I'm pretty lazy, I guess. I'm on my feet all day at work, and then I walk home. The idea of going to the gym after that sounds terrible." I studied his face. "You'd better not be judging me for that."

"I'm not."

"Then why are you staring at me?"

"I guess I wonder how you got such a nice ass if you never work out."

I rolled my eyes. "My ass is not that nice…"

"I disagree. I'm the one who gets to stare at it while I fuck you from behind."

I slapped his wrist playfully. "Crass, much?"

"You know that's how I am, baby." He kissed my forehead then rested his arm over mine. "And you like it."

"I like you—even when you're crass." I rested my cheek on his chest and tried to absorb the moment, relish the fact that this was real. No more hiding and no more lying. I didn't have to make up an excuse not to be set up on a date. I didn't have to watch free drinks appear in front of Finn since it would be obvious he was claimed. A burden of stress left my shoulders, and I felt so relieved.

Layla kept popping back into my mind, but I was too scared to ask him. We'd just made love without a condom, so I should have asked him before that happened, but being caught up in the moment, I didn't think about the obvious concern.

If he said it happened, I would feel sick to my stomach. So maybe it was best if I didn't ask.

Nothing good could come of it.

We sat in silence for a while, letting the rare sunlight stretch across the bed and keep us warm. Soldier kept shifting into the patch of sun as it moved, wanting to enjoy the rays as much as possible. He might be a military dog, but he was still a regular dog at heart.

Finn's face was tilted toward the window when he spoke. "Did Colton give you a hard time?"

The mention of Colton sucked away all my happiness.

Finn slowly turned back to me. "We had to talk about him sometime, right?"

I didn't want Colton to be a sore subject, not when he was

my best friend and Finn's brother. We would just have to break through this awkward stage until it was normal for Colton to see us together. "He was supportive." I considered telling Finn about the warning Colton gave, that Finn was a drifter and wouldn't settle down for anyone—not even me. But that felt like a cold thing to say. Finn and I had never had a serious conversation about our relationship, and I wanted to hear his intentions from him, not from Colton. "He said it was a little uncomfortable, but he wants me to be happy. If you make me happy...then he wants you to keep making me happy." I rubbed his hard torso, feeling his chest rise and fall softly as he continued to breathe.

"Good. I'm glad he was understanding toward you."

"Why do you say that? Was he not understanding toward you?"

Finn stared at the ceiling.

The sound of footsteps sounded in the hallway, accompanied by voices. "How much shit do you have?" Zach's voice was audible. "Because I got the small U-Haul. The rest of your stuff is in storage, so it shouldn't be too much, right?"

"Just my bed, a nightstand, and some clothes." Colton's voice grew louder as he passed the door.

"That shouldn't be too bad," Zach said.

"But I have a lot of clothes. You know me." Colton didn't sound like himself. There was a definite tone of displeasure, like he was dragging his feet as his mood sagged behind him.

Zach sighed. "Sometimes I hate that you're gay..."

I turned to Finn. "Colton is moving already?"

Finn shrugged slightly.

I got out of bed and started to pull on my clothes.

He eyed me without getting up. "What are you doing?"

"Going to talk to them."

He sat up, propping his body on his elbows. "You think that's a good idea? He's going to know what we were doing in here."

"He said he was fine with it, and I'm done hiding." I put on my clothes then checked my hair and makeup in the mirror. By the time I came out of the bathroom, Finn had pulled on his sweatpants and run his fingers through his hair.

Soldier knew something was going on, so he raised his head and pointed his ears.

I opened the door and heard them in Colton's bedroom.

"You brought the frame too?" Zach asked incredulously. "You knew you were only going to be here for like a month. Now we have to move it again." He lifted one side of the mattress.

"If we moved it to the storage center, we would have had to move it again anyway." He helped Zach maneuver the mattress and lean it against the wall so they could access the box spring.

Zach straightened then dragged his hand down his face. "Well, you aren't moving ever again. You're going to die in that apartment."

"What if I get married and have kids?" Colton asked.

"Then you'll all live in that two-bedroom apartment."

I stepped into the room with my arms crossed over my chest. "You guys need a hand?"

Colton turned his gaze on me, and instead of being happy like he usually was, there was a slight hint of disappointment. Then he turned rigid as the tension settled in. He quickly figured out exactly where I'd come from and what I'd been doing before he walked into the house. "I think Zach and I can take care of it."

Zach glanced back and forth between us, clearly uncomfortable with the situation. He didn't even look at me.

"Let's keep going." Colton nodded to the box spring, and he and Zach both bent down and lifted it up. They maneuvered it against the wall.

I felt Finn behind me, so I glanced at him over my shoulder. With his hands in his pockets, he leaned against the doorframe, not offering to help like he usually would. Soldier stayed at his side.

"Are you sure?" I asked. "Finn and I could help you save a lot of time."

Colton didn't look at me when he answered. "I said we're fine."

Last time we'd spoken, Colton had been restrained but supportive, but now he was blatantly hostile. Maybe seeing us leave Finn's bedroom together unnerved him. "I'm surprised you could get into your new apartment so soon. I think Damon just moved out."

Zach walked to the other side of the room and started taking clothes out of the closet and tossing them into boxes, keeping his back turned to us.

Colton placed his hands on his hips and finally lifted his chin to look at me. "I'm living with Zach for a week until it's open."

I continued to stand there with my arms over my chest, my eyebrow raised. "That seems like a lot of work."

"Couldn't agree more," Zach said, tossing a pile of t-shirts into a box.

Colton didn't look at him. "Shut up, Zach."

"I don't understand." I found it hard to believe Colton would move out prematurely just because he was uncomfortable with Finn and me sleeping together. "I really hope you aren't doing this just because you're uncomfortable with Finn and I sleeping together. Because we can always stay at my place."

He rubbed the back of his neck then looked at his night-stand. "That isn't why. You guys should enjoy your day while we finish this." He bent down and emptied the drawers of his nightstand.

I glanced at Finn, who continued to stand there with a stoic expression. His defined arms were crossed over his chest, his bulging muscles making the ink pop out. I turned back to Colton. "You said you would be supportive. You said you wanted me to be happy. I understand it may take some time to get used to, but moving out early is just dramatic. You should enjoy your time with your brother."

Colton released a sarcastic laugh. "I'll pass."

When I detected the disdain in his tone, I knew this was bad. "What's that supposed to mean?"

He rose to his full height and looked at me again. He opened his mouth to say something, but then he changed his mind and shut it again. "I don't want to live with Finn anymore. That's what it means."

I stepped forward. "Why? You said you were okay with this."

"I am okay with it. I said I won't get in your way, and I won't."

"Then why are you acting like this?" I came closer to him, the disappointment flooding my veins. "This isn't being supportive. When you told me you were gay, I was supportive. I didn't kick you out of the apartment and avoid you. I was by your side every step of the way. I didn't run the way you are now."

"Not the same thing," he said. "You know that."

"I think it's pretty similar…"

When the tension increased further, Zach cleared his throat and left the room. "I'm gonna go to the bathroom." He moved past Finn into the hallway.

Colton raised his gaze and looked at his brother. "Give us a minute."

Finn held his ground, like he was about to make a smartass comment. Instead, he obeyed and walked out with Soldier behind him.

I turned back to Colton. "What's your problem?"

"Finn. He's my problem." Now that we were alone, he was blunter. "If you guys want to be together, that's fine. But when he asked my permission, he had already slept with you. He had already been sneaking around behind my back. Our man-to-man conversation was meaningless. He betrayed me. He slept with my ex-wife and then had the balls to pretend it never happened. That's unforgivable." He stepped back, as if our positions were too close. "So no, I don't want to live with him. I don't want to see that asshole's face every day. He's an arrogant prick who doesn't give a damn about anyone but himself. I want nothing to do with him." With eyes filled with rage and mixed with despair, he was a man deeply wounded by Finn's actions. The betrayal ran deep, far inside his soul. His anger stemmed from broken trust, from a violation of safety.

"Why do you forgive me and not him?"

"It's different..."

"How?" I pressed. "I was equally responsible for this."

"Do you want me to be mad at you?" he asked incredulously.

"No. But I think you're being unfair."

"He's my brother. He crossed a line. You're my ex-wife. Our marriage ended because of my mistake. I can't dictate what you do and how you find happiness. It would be wrong of me to deny you something that you want."

"Then isn't it wrong to deny him what he wants?"

He raised an eyebrow. "Do you really not see where I'm coming from?"

"I do. I just think you need to cut him some slack—"

"Why?" he hissed. "I'm not overreacting. When he asked for my permission, it made me uncomfortable, but I got over it in a few days. It wasn't anything we couldn't forget about. But sleeping with you this entire time... It's wrong." He shook his head. "He lied to me. He fucking lied."

"Colton, I'm sure your imagination is far worse than what actually happened."

"No," he snapped. "Because I don't imagine anything. He's my brother, and he should have been honorable. He fucked the one woman on this planet who was off-limits. So fucking disrespectful. We haven't even been divorced for a year. What kind of asshole does that?"

"Look, Finn and I agreed that nothing was going to happen. We kissed one night, and after that happened, Finn said we couldn't go any further. He said he didn't want to betray you. He said he was too loyal to you. But then...it was unavoidable. We're like two magnets, Colton. I can't explain it."

"Every woman is a magnet to Finn," he snapped. "You really think you're any different?"

The insult stung.

He rolled his eyes. "There were hundreds of women before you, and there will be hundreds after you."

That stung even more.

"Why would you even want to be with a guy who would screw over his brother like that?" He threw his arms up. "Doesn't sound like the honorable man everyone describes him as. He sounds like a jerk who can't keep his dick in his pants."

"Please don't say that..."

"It's true. And I have every right to say it." He dropped his hands and turned back to his stuff.

"I know you're upset right now, but running away isn't the solution."

"I'm not running away. I just don't want to live with the guy."

"You really can't wait a week?" I asked.

"I can't wait a minute." He rose to his full height again. "You should get back to Finn so I can finish up. I want to get out of here as quickly as possible."

My heart slowly started to crack from the pain throbbing in my chest. "So, what? You're just never going to be in the same room together? What about us?"

"We'll be fine, Pepper."

"How can we be fine if the three of us never see each other?"

"I'll see Finn because of you. But don't expect me to talk to him like everything is fine."

My jaw was practically on the floor. "And you don't think that will make it uncomfortable?"

"Why would I care about making it uncomfortable? He didn't care about making me uncomfortable when he slept with you."

My arms tightened across my chest as the weight of the situation fell on my shoulders. This was really terrible, terrifying. Finn and Colton were the closest people to me, and I didn't want to choose between them.

"He didn't even tell me the truth, Pepper. I found out from you. The guy didn't have the balls to do it himself."

"Because he knew how you would have reacted. You would have flipped out and not listened to another word he said."

"And I would have had every right to. But he's a coward who didn't have the courage to face me. That kind of bravery must have been really useful in the military…"

Colton did have every right to be angry, but I couldn't let a comment like that slide. I knew Finn was in the wrong for what happened, but I couldn't allow the defamation of his character. "I understand you're upset right now, but don't say anything like that ever again. I mean it, Colton. I'll never forgive you if you do."

His eyes narrowed on my face, but he didn't repeat those horrifying words. "You're defending him now?"

"I defend everything he's done for our country. He's a veteran and a hero. Don't insult his service or his sacrifice. That's completely below the belt, and you know it. It's fine if you have a problem with him, but keep that part of his life out of it."

Colton's anger remained, but he didn't argue.

"He's your brother. You need to work this out."

"I don't have to work out anything. The guy has never been a part of my life anyway. He's been gone since I was sixteen. He didn't even come to our wedding. So why do I have to be close with him now?"

"Colton."

"What?" he asked, dead serious.

"You don't mean that."

"I do mean it. He's only been here for a few months, and he's already slept with my ex-wife. That's the kind of guy we're dealing with."

"That's not how it happened," I argued. "It wasn't like he took one look at me and just decided to go for it. Our relationship built through our friendship. It became stronger and stronger with every interaction. Our chemistry was crazy. I'm telling you, our relationship means something. I know you think I'm just the flavor of the week, but I'm not."

He crossed his arms over his chest. "Even if that's true, it doesn't matter. I don't want to be friends with someone who would do that."

"Colton, he's your brother." Finn had let Colton live with him when he needed a place to stay. He marched into Colton's former boss's office and punched him in the face after he'd treated Colton badly. Finn tried to stay away from me even though he wanted me so much. He was much more than what Colton gave him credit for.

"Yeah, he is," he said in agreement. "But he's not my friend."

2

COLTON

Zach had a one-bedroom apartment, so I was stuck sleeping on the couch.

It was still better than staying with Finn.

I sat on the couch with a beer in my hand while Zach sat in the armchair with Stella sprawled across his lap. It was difficult getting used to seeing them together, especially when they were affectionate all the time.

"I can't believe Finn and Pepper are together," Stella said in surprise. "I had no idea. She didn't tell me anything."

"Yeah," I said bitterly. "She didn't tell me either." After I'd packed up my things, I walked out the front door without looking back. Finn didn't try to change my mind. He didn't bother saying goodbye to me.

I wished I could take Soldier with me.

"Now it all makes sense," Stella said. "Finn turned me down because he was already seeing Pepper."

"You think they've been seeing each other that long?" Zach asked in surprise. "That would be a long time."

"I have no idea." I'd never asked.

"I've never dated a set of brothers before," Stella said. "That must be interesting."

The thought crossed my mind. Would Pepper compare the two of us? If Finn had a bigger dick, would she tell everyone? I'd been compared to my brother my entire life, and now my best friend would compare me as well.

Zach watched me while his hand rested on her thigh. "You okay, man?"

I dragged my hand down my face and ignored the game on the TV. "Not really. Pepper acts like I'm ridiculous for being upset."

"You have every right to be upset," Zach said in my defense. "That would be like me sleeping with Pepper. It's just something you don't do. But it's worse because Finn is your brother."

"I agree," Stella said. "But I also think you shouldn't be mad at him forever."

I looked at her. "It's one of those things you do stay mad about forever..."

"But he's your family."

I took a long drink of my beer then looked at the TV. "He's no friend of mine."

Stella pouted her lips. "That's sad."

"I don't think so," Zach said. "The guy comes back to town and screws his brother's ex-wife. Who the fuck does that?"

"You're just mad because you know I think he's hot," Stella argued.

"No," Zach said defensively. "Well...I'm kinda mad about that. But I'm mostly mad about what he did to Colton."

"I feel so stupid," I added. "I thought I saw something between them this entire time, but I brushed it off. I believed my brother wouldn't do that to me...but he did. Just goes to show you can't trust people...even your own family."

"That's not true," Zach said. "You can trust people. You just have to trust the right people."

"Well...Finn is definitely not the right kind of people."

"I have a question." Stella took the beer out of Zach's hand and helped herself to a sip. "Why are you so pissed at Finn but not at Pepper?"

"Because it's a different situation." I finished my beer then grabbed another one from the fridge. "She's not my brother."

"But she's your friend," she countered. "Didn't she cross a line too?"

"Not the same thing," I said as I shook my head. "After what I did to Pepper, she gets a free pass. This is her free pass. Besides, it's not going to last forever. It'll be over in a few weeks or months, and then he'll break her heart. He'll be out of the picture, and the whole thing will blow over. He'll relocate somewhere else, and I'll never have to see him except on the occasional holiday."

"You seem confident," Zach said. "You really think Finn would do that to her?"

"He does it to everyone else," I countered. "Why would she be any different?"

Zach shrugged. "Maybe she is different to him. I doubt he would put your relationship on the line for a woman who didn't mean anything to him."

I looked back at the TV screen and refused to believe that. Pepper believed it to be true, but she was too blinded by love to see logic. If Finn was capable of ruining his relationship with his only brother, he was capable of anything. I hoped I was wrong, for her sake.

But I knew I wasn't.

I SAT across from Tom while we had dinner together at a steak house. Our relationship had been going really well until the news about Finn and Pepper hit me hard in the face. I always imagined my partner and I would do double dates with Pepper and her guy, but now that wouldn't be possible.

He sipped his wine and kept his eyes on me, his blond hair perfectly styled with gel and hair spray. He was meticulous with his looks, always wearing the best clothes and maintaining the best hygiene. His apartment was spotless. He reminded me of Finn in some ways. "You seem down."

"Sorry...this whole Finn and Pepper thing has been on my mind a lot."

"It makes you that uncomfortable?"

I shrugged. "I guess. There are so many reasons I'm against this relationship, but I guess my brother's betrayal hurts me the most. We've never been close, but when he moved back to Seattle, I was really excited to spend time with him. I've always looked up to him. He's always been the cool, handsome, popular guy...and he was my hero. We really started to click, and I felt like I had another best friend. But then all of this happened... It makes me wonder if he ever felt the same way."

"Maybe he did."

"I find that hard to believe."

"What did he say when you told him you were gay?"

I shrugged. "He didn't care."

"That's something."

"Finn isn't the kind of guy to have strong opinions about other people...or what other people believe."

"He minds his own business."

"Yeah, I guess." I drank my wine then watched the waitress set our dishes in front of us. I had a sizzling steak, and he got the salmon. It was nice to have a relationship that was molding into a comfortable friendship. The physical desire was still there, but our relationship was deepening into something better than sex.

"So you're never going to talk to him again?"

"That's not possible, unfortunately."

"You're never going to be close to him again, then?"

"I wasn't close with him in the first place..." As his actions indicated.

Instead of grabbing his silverware and digging into his food, he gave me a strong stare across the table. "I've been gay my whole adult life, and I've lost a lot of people along the way because of that. Sometimes, it's for the best. Sometimes, it's not. But if your brother has been supportive of you during the most difficult time in your life...maybe he deserves a second chance."

"So he's vindicated because he doesn't have a problem with me being gay?" I asked incredulously. "So, if he murdered Pepper, that would be okay too?"

"I'm just giving you some perspective." He grabbed his knife and cut into his salmon.

My phone started to vibrate in my pocket, so I pulled it out to check the screen.

Finn was calling me.

Just looking at his name pissed me off. I didn't want to hear his voice or his apologies. If he said I'd left something at the house, then he could keep it. I'd rather lose my possessions than have to talk to him. I declined the call and slipped the phone back inside my pocket.

"Do you need to get that?" Tom asked.

"No...it was no one important."

———

A WEEK LATER, I woke up to an empty apartment. Zach had spent the night at Stella's, so I had the place to myself. My new apartment would officially be available on Monday, so Zach and I would move everything then.

I had some coffee and turned on the TV. I was in my sweatpants and t-shirt, still tired after sleeping on the old couch all night long. I'd stayed at Tom's on Thursday and Friday, and I didn't want to overstay my welcome.

A knock sounded at the door.

I took another sip of my coffee then peeked through the peephole.

It was Finn.

He'd ditched his sweatpants and put on real clothes, jeans and a dark blue hoodie. His head was tilted down slightly, and his hands rested in his pockets, his gaze directed away from the peephole. With a perfectly shaved jawline, he looked like he'd showered before he came over here on a Saturday morning.

I wondered if Pepper had spent the night.

Jealousy moved through me, a sensation I couldn't explain. I wasn't exactly sure why I was jealous at all. Was I jealous of her? Because I'd been married to her for so long? Or was I jealous of him? Jealous that my ex-wife had fallen in love again so quickly...with my brother.

"I'll stand here all day if I have to." Finn must have heard my footsteps or the sound of the TV in the living room.

I knew exactly why he was there, but I was surprised anyway. I'd assumed he would let this go, let our relationship fall into ruin because it couldn't be repaired. No act of contrition would make me look at him the same.

I opened the door, my eyes locking on to his. We had the same eye color, and that defining characteristic made it obvious we were related. I kept my hand on the doorknob because he wasn't welcome inside. "Can I help you?" I tried not to sound like such an ass, but my rage took on a life of its own.

Finn stared at me with his stoic expression, always

appearing confident and masculine without saying a single word. It used to be an attitude I admired, but now that I had no respect for him, I thought it was just obnoxious. He rubbed the back of his head, showing the ink that peeked out from underneath his sleeve. "You gonna let me in?"

"Why would I do that? They say never let a stranger into your apartment."

His eyes narrowed slowly, clearly wounded by that smartass remark. "They also say you shouldn't start a fight with a stranger." He pushed my arm down and let himself inside.

I didn't push him back out. Finn was an opponent I could never defeat. I shut the door behind him. "Yes...please come in."

Finn turned around and faced me. "I've given you space for the past week. But now, I want to talk."

"What's there to talk about?"

He tilted his head slightly, his blue eyes full of a hostile sheen. "Us."

"There is no us, Finn. You made your choice. Live with it."

He pulled his hands out of his pockets and took a deep breath, his powerful chest rising with the motion. "I apologized."

"An apology doesn't exonerate your crime."

"You're going to punish me forever?"

"I'm going to punish you longer than a week," I snapped.

He rubbed his palm along his jaw, smoothing out his annoyance. "Colton, I want to make this right—"

"If you wanted to make it right, you wouldn't have fucked my ex-wife. If you wanted to do this the right way, you would have talked to me first. You wouldn't have snuck around behind my back for god knows how long. You had plenty of chances to make it right, but you never did. You could have even told me what was going on, but instead, you asked for my permission as if nothing had happened." I shook my head. "It's crazy that I used to look up to you... Now I have no respect for you."

As if my brother had been stabbed in the gut, he dropped his eyes to where the stab wound would be.

"I don't want to make this right, Finn. I want you to leave me alone."

"It was a complicated situation, alright? I never would have done something like this in a million years. I've never slept with another's wife, even when I could have gotten away with it. I would never sleep with a friend's ex either. With Pepper...it was different."

"And that makes it right?"

"No. She's just...amazing. She's different from other girls I've met. The second she came into my life, I stopped wanting anyone else. There's something about her that turned me into a different man. I can't explain it—"

"Yes, she's incredible," I said in a bored voice. "Why do you think I married her? Why do you think she's still my best friend?"

"Colt, I said I was sorry, and I meant it. Meet me halfway here."

"I don't have to meet you anywhere, asshole."

He slid his hands back into his pockets. "I don't know what else to do."

"There's nothing for you to do. I just feel stupid for trusting you."

"I'm not a bad guy, Colt. This is a special circumstance—"

"Yeah, it is. Because you screwed over your brother."

He shut his mouth and clenched his jaw, the irritation visible in his eyes.

"I was excited when you moved back to Seattle because I thought we could get close. I never really got to know you after I turned sixteen. Maybe it's stupid, but I looked up to you. You were my big brother, the war hero and the doctor...but now it's obvious you never cared about me. You never cared about getting close to me."

"That's not true."

"It seems that way," I said coldly. "You did the worst thing a man could possibly do to his brother."

"No," he said firmly. "The worst thing I could have done was sleep with your wife while you were married to her. That never would have happened."

"Why not?" I demanded. "What's the difference?"

"You know what the difference is."

"And what would have stopped you then if you couldn't stop yourself now?"

"Let's not play this game, Colton," he argued.

I stepped away, getting angrier the longer I looked at him. "I'm done with this conversation."

Finn didn't move an inch. "We need to work this out."

"No."

"We're family."

"Pepper is more of my family than you are. Zach is my family. You were here for just a few months before you got into bed with Pepper. Zach never would have done that to me."

"Because he wouldn't have what I have with her."

I rolled my eyes. "She could be your damn soul mate, and it wouldn't make a difference. You totally crossed the line and ventured into unforgivable territory. What would you do if I slept with your ex-wife?"

"I don't have an ex-wife."

"Then pretend it's Pepper. Pretend you loved each other, and then I came along and got naked with her."

He did his best to keep a straight face, but his cheeks were starting to turn red.

"That's what I thought. Now get the fuck out."

Finn stood his ground even though he was livid. "What's your plan? What if Pepper and I are together for years? You're just not going to talk to me at all? What if we get married?"

I scoffed. "It won't last that long. You'll be gone in the next three months. Trust me on that."

His eyes narrowed. "You're hoping I'll break Pepper's heart?"

"No. But I know it's going to happen anyway."

3

PEPPER

I WALKED ACROSS THE HALL AND STEPPED THROUGH THE OPEN doorway into the apartment where I used to live. I remembered where the Christmas tree went every December, where we used to keep the mail until the pile started to fall over. Now there were boxes everywhere as Colton prepared to move back in.

Our relationship wasn't the same, and there was a palpable tension between us. But he didn't seem angry with me, and since this situation was so critical, I didn't mention Finn. That would just stir the pot—when the water was already boiling.

I opened one of the boxes on the floor and pulled out a stack of dishes. "Feels good to be back?"

"Yes." He pulled out the coffeemaker and placed it on the kitchen counter. "It'll be nice to have my own space again. I'm always crashing at Tom's because he doesn't have any roommates. Now I can have him over for dinner."

"That'll be nice."

He plugged in the machine then moved to the next box. "And it'll be nice to be close to you again. You'll eat all my food, but I always buy extra because I know that will happen."

I rolled my eyes. "You act like I'm a garbage disposal."

"That's a good term for it."

"You know, I could just let you unpack on your own..."

"No. You need to work for all that free food you're going to get from me."

I carried the stack of dishes to the counter and started to put them away in the cupboard. "I think that's fair, as long as you're cooking something good." I put everything away then shut the door. The longer we worked together, the less tense it felt. When we engaged in playful banter, we started to forget about the uncomfortable truth dividing us. "So, Stella and Zach...that's still going."

"He's over the moon." When he finished emptying a cardboard box, he broke it down so he could drop it in the recycling bin. "He's wanted Stella since I can remember, and thanks to me, he got her."

"Thanks to you?"

"I told him to tell her off when she was using him. When he stopped being a pushover, she finally respected him. A woman like Stella needs to be with a man she respects."

"That's good advice."

"And it worked. He's getting laid because of me."

I opened another box and found an assortment of picture frames. There was a picture of him and his parents, him and Zach, and the two of us on our wedding day. I'd worn a strapless sweetheart neckline dress with a mermaid bottom. I stared at it as I remembered that day, remembered how perfect it was.

Colton walked over to me. "Let's put those on the entryway table."

"You're going to put this picture up?" I asked in surprise. I'd taken all my stuff down because it was too difficult to look at.

"Why wouldn't I?" He took the picture out of my hand and set it on the table. "Still the happiest day of my life."

Comments like that reminded me why I fell in love with him

in the first place. And why it was so hard to get over him when we signed those papers. He had such a big heart, the kind that wouldn't fit on his sleeve because it was just too heavy. "Why wasn't it up before?"

"It was in my bedroom. I took it from the living room because..." He never finished the sentence.

But I could fill in the blanks. He'd taken the picture down because it would be too difficult for me to look at it, at least at the start of our breakup. The memory of our wedding day was so heartbreaking that I packed all my stuff away and dropped it off at the storage center. Looking at those photos only reminded me of everything I'd lost.

He cleared his throat then moved to the next box. "Are you happy I'm back, or do you prefer Damon?"

"Well, Damon didn't ask me to help him unpack so..."

He chuckled and pulled out his silverware and coffee mugs. "Sounds like a good neighbor."

"Yes. And he was quiet."

"But he was hot."

I shrugged, not finding any other man nearly as hot as Finn.

He carried his things to the kitchen and started to put them in the correct drawers and cabinets.

Finn wasn't open about his feelings, but I could tell his strained relationship with Colton was killing him. Finn was trying to earn Colton's forgiveness, but it didn't seem possible. I wanted to talk to Colton myself, but since I also wanted to keep our brittle relationship intact, I didn't want to risk making it worse. "How are things going with Tom?" It felt strange not to mention the most important thing going on in my life right now—Finn. I didn't see how this could work, because I couldn't pretend Finn didn't exist anytime Colton was around.

"Really good. I know he's my first, so I don't have a lot of experience, but it feels right. We can talk about anything, and we have a strong physical relationship. It's perfect..."

That was exactly how I felt about Finn. "I'm happy for you. Think you'll introduce him to your parents?"

He shrugged. "I don't know. We buried the hatchet, but that still seems weird right now. My mom will probably start sobbing when she realizes you've officially been replaced."

If she knew I was dating Finn, maybe she would feel better about it. Or maybe she would think that was weird. I really didn't know.

"I feel bad for Tom because he has impossible shoes to fill."

"Well, I'm sure his feet are bigger than mine, so that shouldn't be too hard. You guys ever talk about moving in together?"

"Not yet. Seems too soon for that."

If Finn asked me to move in, I would probably jump at the opportunity. "We should all go to dinner. I've met Tom a few times but haven't really spent any time with him."

"Yeah, that would be cool. What about tomorrow?"

"I'm free."

"Great. The three of us can go to that Italian place we like."

I stiffened when he mentioned the number of people in the party. Did he really think I would exclude Finn from everything? "Well, I would assume it would be four people..."

Colton stopped and looked at me, his eyebrow raised. Slowly, it came down again, disappointment replacing his surprise.

"I know you have your issues with Finn, but he's the man I'm seeing. I can't exclude him from things just because you don't like him." I wanted to be there for Colton, but if Colton controlled all the parameters of my relationship, then it would never last.

Colton turned away and then finished putting the mugs in the cabinet. "I guess I understand."

At least he wasn't completely irrational.

"Let's skip the dinner."

I stopped my lips from making a sigh, but my irritation was still conspicuous. "Colton, if you really want me to be happy, you're going to have to make this work. Because if you keep acting like this, you're going to make me choose between you two all the time. Don't force me to decide between the two men I love."

He shut the drawer and finally looked at me again. "Fine."

"Finn feels really terrible about—"

"Let's not do this. I don't want to talk about him. It's hard enough not to think about him when I'm with you as it is."

"I just think you should cut him some slack."

"I don't think I should do anything," he snapped. "Just drop it, Pepper. I don't want to fix the relationship. He's still my brother, so I'll see him on holidays and go to his funeral when he dies. But I don't have to be his friend. I opened my home to him when he came to Seattle, and he repaid me by sneaking around with you. The guy is an asshole. Other than his looks, I don't know what you see in him."

I should have dropped the conversation and tried to recover whatever was left of the afternoon, but I couldn't keep my mouth shut. "I see a lot of amazing things in that man. You're destroying his character based on one wrongdoing, which isn't fair."

"It's a big wrongdoing."

"He's still a good man, one of the best men I know. When your old boss was being a dickhead to you, Finn marched down to his office and punched him in the face. I know it happened because I was there."

Colton didn't react right away. It took a moment for the

words to pierce his hard exterior before reaching his heart. His tense expression slackened slightly.

"I need you to work this out, Colton. And if not for you and Finn, then at least for me. Because I love this man, and I love you. You're making it impossible to love you both at the same time."

He bowed his head then turned away. "I'll think about it."

That was the most improvement I'd seen so far, so I would gladly take it. "Alright...thanks."

I'D JUST GOTTEN home from work when my phone vibrated. *Where are you?* Finn's demanding tone was audible through the text.

At home.

And why are you over there?

I enjoyed Finn's house because it was so spacious and comfortable. With vaulted ceilings, trees outside the windows, and elegant furniture, it didn't feel like a place where he lived. It felt like a home. Plus, he had a really cute dog. *Because I live here.* I pretended to have an attitude, but in reality, I loved it when he asked me to come over. And I loved the way he asked...without actually asking.

Get your ass over here.

Bossy, aren't we?

NOW.

Ooh...busting out the caps.

He stopped typing. His silence was somehow more formidable.

I pulled on a jacket and grabbed my purse, a smile stretching my lips far and wide.

He messaged me again before I walked out the door. *Bring lingerie.*

I almost made a smartass comment back, but I let it slide. I was happy to have a man who wanted me to wear lingerie all the time, who found me so sexy that he ripped off my clothes the second I walked in the door.

———

HIS LARGE HANDS gripped my cheeks as he lowered me down onto his length. At over six feet with arms so strong he could hold me without difficulty, he fucked me in the middle of his bedroom, standing tall and proud like I weighed nothing.

My arms wrapped around his neck, and I felt my pussy slide down to his base then back up again. I didn't know what I enjoyed the most. The enormous cock that was hitting me deep and hard, the muscular physique that had no problem lifting me up and down for fifteen minutes, or the sexy look on his face as he stared at me.

All of those things together kept making me come—over and over. "Finn..." This was better than any fantasy I'd ever had. It was definitely better than any reality I'd had either. If he fucked all women like this, it was no surprise he got free drinks everywhere he went. The man was a walking vibrator—but better.

"You like this a lot, don't you?"

I bit my bottom lip as I felt his cock thicken inside me.

He slowed down his movements so he could kiss me on the mouth and steal my breath away. His long fingers dug deep into my ass as he held me on his length. "Tell me."

My hand cupped the back of his neck. "Yes." I looked into his blue eyes and fell deeper than ever before, forgetting about all the complicated issues surrounding this relationship. This was what I was fighting for, to have a deep and passionate romance with this special man.

He lifted me up and down a few more times before he released, wearing the sexiest expression as he dumped inside me. He groaned in fulfillment, flooding me for the second time that night.

I could fuck this man all night long and never go dry. He was the sexiest man in the world, hands down. If I could picture the perfect man, he would be identical to Finn.

He carried me to the bed then laid me down before he got off me.

The second he was gone, I felt the come drip between my thighs and pool at my entrance. I was in black lingerie with stockings, and my panties were somewhere on the bedroom floor.

"I'm gonna take a shower. You want to start dinner?"

"Sure. I can order a pizza."

He smiled slightly, the affection reaching his eyes. "I'll make something when I'm done. But you're going to have to learn sometime."

"Why would I when I have you?"

He leaned down and kissed me on the mouth before he stepped into the shower.

I stripped off my lingerie and pulled on one of his t-shirts before I went downstairs, Soldier in tow. "I got you something on my lunch break today."

His ears perked up, almost like he understood exactly what I was saying.

I opened my purse and pulled out the toy I'd picked up at the store. I ripped off the packaging and tossed it to him.

He immediately snatched it from the ground with his big teeth and started to play with it, jerking his neck back and forth and then digging his teeth deeper into the material.

"You like it?"

He growled as he jerked the toy around again.

"Good." I opened the fridge and pulled out a beer. I had to use a towel to twist off the cap before I could take a drink. When I took a seat on the couch and turned on the TV, Soldier jumped up on the couch beside me, bringing his toy along.

Finn came downstairs moments later, his sweats low on his waist. He eyed both of us on the couch and focused on the red toy in Soldier's grip. "Where did that come from?"

"I bought it for him." I grabbed one end and gently played tug-of-war with him.

He growled louder and sank his sharp teeth deep into the material.

Finn shook his head. "Spoiled."

"Spoiled?" I asked incredulously. "This is the only toy he has other than those tennis balls in the backyard."

"Because he's a dog, not a puppy." Finn went into the kitchen and started dinner.

"What are you making?"

"Tacos."

"Ooh...I'm down with that." I pulled the blanket over my legs and watched TV as I listened to Finn work in the kitchen. The smells grew more potent, and soon my mouth was salivating. "That smells good."

Soldier kept chewing on his toy.

When Finn was finished, he set up the table. "Come eat."

"Yay." I took a seat at the table, and Soldier lay on the ground at my feet, the toy still in his mouth.

Finn laid off the scotch and had a beer instead. He ate across from me, the muscles of his body moving every time he lifted the taco toward his mouth.

Eating with him reminded me of my married life, how nice these simple rituals were. Finn and I didn't talk as much as

Colton and I had, but conversation didn't feel necessary. We were just comfortable with each other.

His phone was on the table and lit up with a text message. His notifications were set to private, so the name of the person was on the screen but not the message. And the name on the screen was Layla.

Ugh, I hated that bitch.

I kept eating like I hadn't noticed, but her name made my stomach do a slight somersault. There was nothing to worry about because Finn was an honest guy who wouldn't cheat on me, regardless of how much she wanted him, but knowing he might have already slept with her made me fiercely jealous. And insecure.

Finn must have noticed the change in the air around us because he addressed it. "What is it?"

"Nothing. These tacos are perfect. I've always been a fan of hard shells."

He stopped eating and just stared at me. "Baby."

"What?" I asked, doing my best to feign innocence.

His eyes narrowed.

"I just... I don't like Layla." That was the truth, and I decided to drop it like a bomb. Maybe it was catty and petty, but any other woman would despise someone who wanted to sleep with her man. Maybe they already had slept together, and she was trying to make it happen again. Her beauty, ink, and intellect didn't make me feel better. I owned a store that barely broke even. I wasn't some badass woman who saved lives for a living.

He grabbed his phone and swiped across the screen so the message thread was open. Then he pushed it across the table so I could see. "I'm a transparent guy. Read anything you want."

I didn't look. "That's not what I want. I don't want a relationship where there's any need to check each other's phones."

He left it there. "I didn't sleep with her."

My body tightened before it gave a big release. The relief made every muscle in my body relax, made everything feel better. "You didn't?"

He shook his head. "I thought Colton already told you that. I guess he didn't."

"No...he didn't mention it."

"That night at the bar, she'd drunk too much. Asked me to take her home."

So I'd been sobbing my eyes out for nothing.

"She tried to make something more happen when I dropped her off, but that didn't go anywhere."

I hated the idea of her trying to drag him into her apartment, but at least he was honest about what happened. "Do you see her a lot at work?"

He shrugged. "Sometimes our shifts overlap."

"She's pretty."

"Yeah, she is," he said without hesitation. "But I've seen better." He held my gaze for a long time, not blinking as he shared his affection with me through just his eyes.

I would always be threatened by that woman, but at least I was a little less paranoid now. "Is that why you didn't sleep with Stella when she made a move on you?"

"Yes." He still had a taco on his plate, but he didn't reach for it. "I didn't think anything would ever happen between us, but I knew if something went down with Stella, then nothing ever could happen with us. So I steered clear."

That was sweet. "I'm sorry I told Colton the truth... I saw you leave with Layla, and I was hysterical. I wasn't thinking clearly, and everything just came pouring out. I threw you under the bus, and I feel so terrible about it."

"Don't."

"But it's my fault that you and Colton are like this."

"No. We're like this because of my decisions. It doesn't matter who told him or how it happened. It was the truth, and he was going to find out anyway. It's not your fault, baby. Don't feel bad."

Even when he soothed my feelings, I still felt guilty. "Things will work out between you. It'll take some time, but it'll happen."

"I don't know." He sighed then looked down at his food. "Colton is pretty upset. Every time I try to talk to him about it, he's just as angry. I can't say I blame him. I understand where he's coming from. There's nothing I can really say to justify it."

"I told him we tried to fight it, but it just happened."

"I don't think that matters to him."

"I know Colton is mad, but I also know he has a big heart. Once the sting wears off, he'll come around."

"I don't know...he's pretty stubborn."

Everyone told me I should hate Colton for what he did to me, but my anger couldn't overpower the love. "I forgave Colton for what he did to me. He really hurt me—more than I can explain. But I knew he would never hurt me on purpose. It just happened that way. And I forgave him. So I know he'll forgive you...when he's ready to."

"That sounds nice in theory, but the two instances aren't the same. You don't sleep with your brother's ex."

"No, the situations can't be compared. But you aren't a bad guy, Finn. I think Colton is taking it too personally, as if your attraction to me means you like him less. That if your love for him were greater, you wouldn't have crossed the line."

He looked out the back window behind me, his eyes filled with endless thoughts.

"I think that's why it bothers him so much."

"Yeah, I think so too."

"He was really excited to reconnect with you when you first moved in. He reminded me of a child, actually."

He bowed his head slightly.

"He looks up to you."

"No. He *looked* up to me. Now...he can't stand me."

"The fact that he was so fond of you gives you a strong chance to recover."

"Maybe...but I doubt it."

"I told him what you did to his old boss."

He looked up. "What did he say?"

"Nothing. But he seemed touched by it."

He picked up his fork and dragged it through the black beans on his plate.

"I asked him to try to keep an open mind, if not for you, then for me. He said he would..." Even though Colton's response had been barely audible. His heart definitely wasn't in it either, despite his call earlier agreeing to eat with Finn. "We're going to dinner with them tomorrow night."

"He knows I'll be there?" Finn asked incredulously. "And he still agreed?"

"Yes. I told him he can't make me choose between the two of you. It's not fair to me."

He nodded slowly. "So, you forced him."

"We won't make any progress unless I force him. He's too stubborn."

"In this instance, I don't think he's being stubborn. He just wants nothing to do with me."

I chose to believe they would find a way back to each other. It might not happen overnight, but it would happen eventually. It would take a lot of work and a lot of forgiveness. But I'd seen greater miracles happen. "Do you regret all of this?"

He looked up at me again, a slight look of confusion in his eyes. "Regret?"

"Yes, because of everything that's happened with Colton."

He stared me down, his fork still in his grasp. "No. I wish things had unfolded better, but I don't regret it. You?"

I hated being the cause of their turmoil, but Finn made me happier than I'd ever been. It was painful to think about a reality in which I never experienced this, if I'd ended up with someone else with a mild and tame passion. "No. But I wish things were different..."

"That makes two of us. Maybe my mom could help."

"You'd get her involved in this?"

"No," he said quickly. "But if my parents are thrilled to see us together, it'd force his hand. He couldn't keep up this charade forever, not when everyone else is supportive of this relationship."

"But she also might think it's weird...because it kinda is."

He shrugged. "Colton says it's irrelevant that he's gay, but I think it matters. He doesn't want you, can't have you, but he doesn't want anyone else to have you. Some people might assume he would be happy to see you with his brother. But he doesn't think that way, apparently."

"It's more complicated than that."

"Yeah, I know." He finished his food then downed his beer. He rested his arms on the table and stared at Soldier on the floor, where he still had the toy sitting on his paws. "He really loves that thing, huh?"

"Probably because it's the only toy he's got." I gave Finn a nasty look as I cleared the plates and carried them to the sink. Since Finn did the cooking, I did the cleaning. I scrubbed the pans and put them in the dishwasher before I wiped down the counter.

"You want to watch TV or go to bed?"

"Depends. What time do you work tomorrow?"

"Morning shift." His eyes narrowed in annoyance. "I hate the morning shift."

"Why?"

"It's quiet. People don't start rolling in until after noon."

"Since you have to be up early, let's go to bed."

"At least I can give you a ride home on my way to work tomorrow."

"True."

He started to turn all the lights off in the living room before he set the alarm. Together, we went upstairs with Soldier in tow, like a family that did this on a regular basis. We got into bed, and Soldier lay at the foot of the bed, taking up a big chunk of space with his size. Fortunately, he slept on my side, and since my legs were shorter, it worked.

Finn turned off the lights, and we lay there together, our faces close to each other on our pillows. He didn't cuddle with me as he usually did. Instead, he watched me with those brilliant eyes, like he could look at me forever. "If only I'd met you first..."

Our lives would be much easier if that had been the case, but I still wouldn't erase my time with Colton for anything. We had a bond that ran deep into our roots, a connection that existed beyond time and space. He was the closest thing I had to family, the gravity that kept me tethered to the earth. I needed both men in my life—not just one or the other. "It'll work out, Finn. Have faith."

He sighed quietly. "I feel bad for hurting my brother. But I don't feel bad for having you."

"It's perfectly okay to feel both things at once."

"Maybe. I just wish I could have both of you at once."

STELLA STOPPED by the shop during her lunch break. She strolled to the counter, wearing that knowing look on her face and decked out in her sexy workout clothes. She rocked a high pony with an 80's neon-color sweatband in her hair.

I knew what that look meant.

She sauntered to the counter then tapped her hand against the surface. "I can't believe you didn't tell me about Finn."

I'd known this conversation was coming, and I was prepared for it. "I didn't tell anybody."

"Obviously. You bagged the hottest piece of man candy in this city. Congratulations."

I rolled my eyes. "He's more than just a pretty face."

"Yes. He's a pretty body too. How big is he? Like, anaconda or garden snake?"

I narrowed my eyes. "I'm not answering that."

"Oh, come on."

"I respect his privacy, okay? I don't ask how big Zach is."

"Well, he's actually pretty well-endowed down there..." She tilted her head to the side and smiled. "I was pleasantly surprised."

I made a disgusted face. "TMI."

"We always talk about this stuff. You told me about Jax's junk."

"But that was different."

"How?" she asked incredulously.

"I don't know... It's different with Finn."

"It is?" She leaned farther over the counter. "Ooh...spill it."

I'd anticipated Stella would confront me with anger because I'd kept my relationship with Finn a secret for so long. She wanted him in the first place, and then I got him. That probably made things uncomfortable too. "I was expecting you to be angry with me."

"I was at first, but then I understood why you kept it a secret. If you'd told anyone, word might have gotten back to Colton. Besides, I wouldn't have felt comfortable keeping a secret like that anyway."

Stella could be surprisingly pragmatic at times. "You aren't upset with me, when you wanted Finn first?"

She rolled her eyes. "Girl, don't be ridiculous. It's not like anything ever happened with him. Now I know why..." She pointed her finger into my wrist. "Because he already had his eyes set on you. Kinda romantic."

"Well, I'm glad you aren't mad at me."

"Absolutely not. How can I get mad at my best friend for getting laid?"

I smiled when I realized we were finally okay. "I'm glad you're on board."

"So." She slapped her hand on the desk. "How is he? Come on, you can answer that, right?"

My cheeks immediately turned red.

"That looks like a good sign."

"He's as good as you would expect him to be."

"Ooh...that sounds nice."

"It is nice." It was the nicest thing in the world.

"Is he a slow and gentle lover? Or is he always a sailor on leave?"

"Both."

"Ooh...even better." A dreamy look appeared in her eyes. "There's nothing better on this earth than good sex."

"Are you getting that from Zach?"

She flipped her ponytail over her shoulder. "Yep. I didn't realize the garden growing in my own backyard."

"I'm glad things are working out. He's been after you for a long time."

"I know." She brushed off the compliment like it meant nothing. "I don't know where it's going to go, but I'm happy where we are. We agreed to stay friends if it doesn't work out."

"I hope so. Finn is already a wedge between Colton and me. We don't need another wedge in the group."

"Yeah...Colton has expressed his unhappiness."

"I'm sure he has." Colton made his disapproval clear to everyone. "Do you agree with him?"

"Who?" she asked, playing dumb.

"Colton."

She shrugged then looked at the lingerie piece sitting on the counter. "This is cute. Did you get this for Finn?"

I knew she was trying to sidestep the question. "That's a yes, then?"

She turned back to me and sighed. "Well...kinda."

That meant Zach agreed with Colton too.

"Look, how would you feel if you and Finn got divorced and then I started sleeping with him six months later?"

"Not the same thing—"

"It is the same thing. Doesn't matter if you're gay or straight, it's still a really awkward betrayal. It would make you sick to your stomach. And if I really did that behind your back, you would question our friendship. Don't pretend you wouldn't."

I couldn't deny any of that.

"I'm sure you guys are great together. You seemed to get along really well the second you met, but that doesn't make it right. You should just be grateful Colton is only mad at him and not at you."

"I feel like I deserve a punishment too."

"After what he did to you, he thinks you're even now."

"That doesn't make me feel better. I want them to be brothers again, to be friends again."

She shrugged. "I'm not sure that's going to happen."

"I have a little more faith than that."

"I don't know. Colton is pretty hurt."

Just when my relationship was supposed to bloom, it was overshadowed by this painful rift between the two men. Could Finn ever truly be happy with me if his brother wouldn't speak to him anymore? Were we doomed from the start?

4

COLTON

Pepper walked inside. "Ready for dinner?"

I'd been dreading this all day. Spending the evening with my brother across the table from me sounded like the most awkward evening ever. At first, I had been excited to spend time with Pepper and Tom, for them to get to know each other better so the three of us could be friends. But then I remembered Finn was part of the package...unfortunately. "I'm hungry. I'll say that."

"So, Stella has been telling me every little detail about her and Zach." I made a disgusted face. "We share everything, but since Zach is her guy, it's pretty gross."

"And I've heard everything about Stella, from the freckle on her right hip to the piercing in her navel. Welcome to the club." I grabbed my keys and wallet and stuffed them into my pockets. "Ready?"

"I skipped lunch today, so I'm starving."

"Finn isn't with you?" I'd rather spend the evening pretending he didn't exist, but I assumed the three of us would walk or drive together.

"He's meeting us there. He got called in to work."

"If he's too busy, he doesn't have to come at all."

Her eyes filled with a look of heavy disappointment, like she'd expected my venom to have disappeared by now.

Not even close.

"He wants to come," she said. "He'd like to get to know Tom better."

"He's been to the house many times. Finn never bothered then."

"You weren't as serious at the time."

Anytime Finn was mentioned, it always turned into an argument. Neither one of us could talk about him without getting our feathers ruffled. "Let's go."

She sighed under her breath, clearly disappointed we'd gotten off on the wrong foot. "Alright..."

We left the apartment together and walked down the street. It'd been a warm afternoon, but the cold quickly settled in. Though, thankfully, rain wasn't in the forecast. "How was work?"

"Busy, actually. Now that spring is almost here, weddings are around the corner."

"That's good."

"Yeah, but I'm a lot busier at this time of year. That means I have to work more." She pouted her lips.

And that meant less time with Finn. "But that's more money."

"But not enough for the number of hours I put in."

"Do you ever think about selling it and doing something else?"

She considered the question as she walked beside me. "It's crossed my mind before, but I can't picture myself doing anything else. The shop is a lot of time and work, but I'd rather do that than anything else...even if I don't make a ton of money."

We arrived at the restaurant and found Tom sitting in the

waiting area. His eyes brightened like the rising sun, and he rose to kiss me in greeting. "Hey, babe. Late as always."

"Pepper made me late." I kissed him back, feeling at peace with the world because I could be myself. I felt like the luckiest person alive, to have that kind of freedom. I'd been lying to everyone for so long that it felt overwhelming to be myself, to have Pepper smile and be happy for me.

Tom turned to Pepper. "You look beautiful." He hugged her and kissed her on the cheek.

"Thank you." She hugged him back and smiled in a genuine way, like she really liked Tom and wasn't pretending just for me. "You guys starving? Because I am. Stella visited me on my lunch break, and since she talks so much, I didn't get to eat the peanut butter and jelly sandwich I packed."

"Should we wait for Finn?" Tom asked.

I was hoping my brother had been forgotten.

"He told me we should sit and order some drinks," Pepper said. "Not wait in the lobby without any alcohol."

"Alright." Tom led the way, and we moved to a table near the window. The restaurant was close to the coast, so we could see the harbor in the distance. Tables around us had garlic bread and marinara sauce, and the walls were decorated with unique paintings of pasta in various dishes.

Pepper sat across from us, her hair in curls and her teal blouse fitting her frame perfectly. She was a stunning woman. Even though I preferred men, that truth couldn't be denied. Makeup or no makeup, it didn't make a difference. I almost couldn't blame my brother for losing his self-control. "What are you going to order?" She stared at the drink menu. "I know this is an Italian place, but I'm skipping the wine and getting a pomegranate mojito."

"Ooh, that sounds good," Tom said. "I'll do the same."

When the waiter came over, we ordered our drinks.

Pepper ordered for Finn. "And my boyfriend will have a scotch."

I looked out the window, painfully reminded that I would have to stare at that asshole for a couple of hours.

Tom put his hand on my thigh under the table.

Pepper stared at the menu. "I already know what I'm getting. The lasagna. Finn usually makes healthy food, so this is a real treat for me."

There was no escaping it. Even when Finn wasn't here, he was still the center of attention.

"I'm glad Colton is a good cook," Tom said. "I'm not talented in the kitchen."

"But you have a car, so it's an even trade," I responded. "You pick up groceries, and I cook them."

"Having a car would be nice," Pepper said. "But that costs a fortune."

"Doesn't Finn have a car?" Tom asked.

"Yeah, he does," Pepper blurted. "But we never leave the house, so we don't really use it much..." She seemed to realize the error of her words halfway through the sentence, but she finished it anyway because the damage was already done. She looked away and took a big drink of her mojito to wash away the embarrassment.

The thought of them together grossed me out enough to ruin my appetite.

Tom kept talking because he was the only one who wasn't uncomfortable. "How's Soldier?"

"He's great." Pepper grabbed on to Tom's question like it was a life raft. "Finn uses him as a workout buddy and guard dog, so I'm the one who gets him toys. I got him this little teddy bear to chew on, and he adores it. Makes him look like a puppy."

The only thing I missed about staying with Finn was that

dog. He was fun to play with, and I'd always looked forward to seeing him when I walked in the door.

"Does he sleep with Finn?" Tom asked.

"Yeah," Pepper answered. "He curls up into a little ball at the end of the bed. He's so cute."

We kept talking about Soldier, the safest subject we could all discuss, and then Finn approached our table minutes later. He'd changed out of his scrubs into a t-shirt and jeans, and his hair was still slightly damp as if he'd jumped out of the shower in a hurry. But of course, there was nothing my brother could do to look less attractive.

He greeted Tom first. "Hey, man. How's it going?" He extended his hand.

Tom smiled as he took it. "It's great. Nice to see you." Unlike me, Tom seemed to actually like my brother. It felt like a betrayal in many ways, but since I couldn't control his opinions, I let it go. "How was work?"

"A nightmare," Finn said honestly. "But it's rarely not." His eyes lifted to look into mine, and the charismatic energy died away like a collapsing star. He held my gaze as his lips tightened, like he could see my rage before he even tried to talk to me. "Hey, Colt."

I drank from my glass and ignored him.

Both Tom and Pepper looked at me.

I didn't care what their opinion was.

Finn stared at me for a moment longer before he sat down beside Pepper. "Hey, baby." He didn't lean in and kiss her like he probably usually did. His hand moved to her back, and he gave her a gentle rub before he lowered his hand again. "You got me a scotch?"

"Yes, I know you well." When her eyes settled on him, there was a distinct light in her gaze, noticeable affection everyone could see. As with any other straight woman, her hormones betrayed her as she stared at this man the entire world found beautiful.

It was one of the only times I'd been in their presence since I'd found out they were together. Now there were so many cues and hints I couldn't unsee. She looked at him the way she used to look at me—but with an intensity a million times stronger. There was no doubt that Pepper wasn't exaggerating when she described her feelings. She was head over heels in love with this man.

Finn looked at her in a special way too. And instead of letting his eyes wander around the room for other women or signs of danger, he was only interested in the brunette beside him, the woman who was as beautiful on the outside as she was on the inside.

I hated this so much.

I hated the fact that they seemed to really care about each other, but I still couldn't stand it. I'd loved this woman for years, and I'd never imagined us ending up like this, sitting across from each other while my brother was the one she was screwing.

Of all the men in the world, she had to pick my brother.

My player, heartbreaker brother.

Since I wasn't in the mood for conversation, Tom did all the talking. "We were just talking about Soldier and his new toy."

"Oh," Finn said. "You mean, how Pepper spoils the hell out of him?"

"I got him one toy," she said incredulously. "You act like I bought him a collar made out of diamonds."

"I'm sure that will be next on the list," he jabbed.

"I can't even afford to buy myself diamonds," Pepper said. "You think I'm going to buy them for a dog?"

Finn turned to Tom. "Soldier was supposed to stay on the floor at night. Then he moved to the end of the bed. And now he's moving to the spot right between us...all because of her." He nodded in her direction. "So when she's not there, he still expects to sleep right beside me, and I can't tell him otherwise."

Tom chuckled. "That doesn't sound so bad."

"It is when he hasn't had a bath," Finn said. "And he snores."

Pepper smiled. "It's so cute."

"But when I snore, she kicks me," Finn said. "And she kicks me hard."

"Well, you're super loud," Pepper said. "It's like a plane flying overhead."

Finn shrugged and kept drinking.

Tom laughed, finding Finn charismatic like everyone else.

The waiter arrived and took our order. Finn ordered another scotch right away, then got the chicken Marsala. The rest of us ordered pasta-based dishes before the waiter walked away.

I tried not to be too uncomfortable imagining them sleeping together, but it was hard. I'd slept beside Pepper for five years straight. She used to talk in her sleep, even laugh. She was the biggest blanket hog in the world. And she did that annoying thing where she kept snoozing her alarm clock until it went off three times. When I got to sleep in, that habit was the most obnoxious thing in the world.

But I missed it.

And knowing Finn got to experience that when he didn't deserve it felt wrong to me. He'd stabbed me in the back to get what he wanted, and in the end, he would break her heart like everyone else. He didn't treasure her the way I did, the way she deserved to be treasured. The only reason he was in this relationship was because he didn't have any other choice. It was the only way they could be together because Pepper wouldn't be some hit-it-and-quit-it kind of woman.

I stared into my mojito and swirled the alcohol around, seeing the mint leaves float with the movements. Maybe I needed to get used to evenings like these, but I also knew this wouldn't last forever. They would never get married and have a family. He was just the last guy to break her heart before she found the man she was really supposed to be with.

Finn was just a stepping stone.

Pepper looked at me. "How's it going at the office?"

I was so stubborn, I almost didn't answer just because Finn was there. "Good. I really like it there. A lot more than my old office." When Pepper had told me what Finn did for me, it was impossible not to be touched by the gesture. Finn had my back even when he never told me about it. But when it came to pussy, that was something he couldn't have my back for. "It's a big company, but there's still plenty of work for everyone. My job is salaried, so it doesn't matter how many minutes I clock or how many cases I take, which is nice. I'll be in court next week."

"For what?" Finn asked, his fingers around his glass.

I stared at him, feeling angry all over again. Sitting there with both of them made it seem like I approved of this situation, when I hated it just as much as I always had. I was tempted to throw my drink in his face. "There's a shipping company here in Seattle that's violating air pollution regulations. They're technically exempt because of a clause they were grandfathered under, but since they are way over the limit, something needs to be done. We'll see how it goes..."

"Sounds like a big deal," Finn said. "Nerve-racking."

I didn't appreciate him kissing my ass. "You've never cared about my work before, so no need to start now."

"Because you worked in real estate law," Finn said calmly. "That's boring. This isn't." He drank from his glass.

The table went silent with tension.

Pepper's eyes shifted back and forth between us. "This woman came into my shop yesterday and asked for handcuffs and whips and chains. I had to tell her I didn't run that kind of store." She blurted it out like she didn't know what to say, she was just desperate to change the topic.

But nothing could dispel the discomfort between Finn and me. I was pissed at him, and he was pissed that I was pissed. Both stubborn and aggressive, neither one of us would yield. When I was an ass to him, it was impossible for him to lie there and take it.

"Did she have a copy of *Fifty Shades* too?" Tom asked with a laugh.

"No," Pepper said. "But she asked if I had a copy for sale."

Tom laughed again.

Finn and I were still caught up in our silent battle while Pepper and Tom carried on. Maybe it made more sense for the two of them to have this dinner together and leave Finn and me out of it. We clearly couldn't be in the same room together.

The waiter brought the food, and a rock fell into my stomach. We still had a long way to go until this meal was officially over. There would be more heated looks and catty exchanges. It was hard to believe I'd actually liked my brother at one point. Now he just seemed like an enemy, someone I couldn't stand.

I turned to my food and started to eat even though I wasn't hungry.

Not the least bit.

———

WE WALKED OUTSIDE and stood on the sidewalk in front of the restaurant to say goodbye.

Tom hugged Pepper. "Thanks for having dinner with us. Colton always speaks so highly of you. You'll have to tell me some embarrassing stories one of these days."

"Oh, definitely," she said. "I have a lot of those."

I stood with my hands in the pockets of my jacket and felt

my brother staring at me. I continued to look away like the empty street was far more interesting than the blue color of his eyes.

"Soldier misses you," he said. "Maybe you should come by the house and visit him."

I missed the dog too, but I hated Finn more. "Pepper can bring him by the apartment sometime."

"No place for a dog of his size."

"We'll take him to the park." I kept my gaze directed away.

Finn stepped closer to me. "So, what are we going to do for the holidays? You're going to pretend I don't exist, and Mom and Dad are going to watch our relationship fall apart? Yeah...that sounds like a nice Christmas."

"When they figure out what you did, they'll understand."

"You forget that Mom wants Pepper to be happy more than anything. If I make Pepper happy, then Mom's happy. Maybe you're too selfish to understand that."

I slowly turned my head back to him. "What the fuck did you just say?"

"I said you're selfish."

"I'm selfish?" I pointed my finger in my chest. "I told Pepper she could do whatever she wanted because I want her to be happy. But that doesn't mean I won't hate you. You're the selfish asshole who couldn't keep your dick in your pants, even around your brother's ex-wife. No, asshole. You're the selfish one."

Pepper sighed as she watched us tell each other off. "Maybe this was a bad idea."

Tom nodded in agreement.

"Hate is a strong word, Colton." Finn stared me down with his arms by his sides.

"In this case, it's not strong enough." I turned to walk away, knowing Tom would come with me to his car in the parking lot.

"What do you want me to do, Colton?" Finn yelled as I

walked toward the lot. "Stop seeing her? Is that what it's going to take?"

I turned back around, hating my brother for not understanding my feelings at all. "No. I want you to go back in time and actually give a shit about me. I want you to go back in time and figure out what it means to be a brother, what it means to be loyal, what it means to be family. Because you have no fucking idea how important that is."

5

PEPPER

INSTEAD OF DRIVING TO HIS HOUSE OUTSIDE THE CITY, FINN pulled up to the curb outside my building. Then he rested his arm on the steering wheel and stared straight ahead, like he expected me to hop out of the truck without saying a word.

I didn't undo my seat belt. "What are you doing?"

"Dropping you off."

I slept at his place most nights of the week, so this was out of the ordinary. "I'm only going into my apartment if you're coming with me."

He sighed as he looked at the empty road in front of him. "And be across the hall from the man who hates me? I'll pass."

"Then let's go to your place."

He sighed again, like that was the last thing he wanted to do. "I want to be alone."

"No, you don't."

"Trust me, I do. I've been alone my whole life."

"But you aren't alone anymore." I kept my hands in my lap as I watched him on the other side of the truck. "So we can keep arguing about this while the engine runs and we waste gas, or we can go to the house where Soldier is waiting for us."

He ground his teeth together slightly before he hit the gas and pulled away from the apartment complex.

I looked out the window, relieved I won the standoff. "He doesn't hate you."

"That's not what I heard."

"He didn't mean it."

"I think he did, Pepper."

"I know that man better than anyone. Trust me, he doesn't hate you. He's just struggling to internalize the pain he feels. Seeing us together reminds him what you did, and he feels that betrayal all over again. He doesn't know how to control his emotions, how to accept what's going on right in front of him."

He drove down the streets until he left the city and entered the suburbs. "And what am I supposed to do about that?"

"I don't know...give him time."

"I don't think there's enough time in the world."

"I know it's hard, but you need to be patient with him. It's difficult for him. We were married for three years. Seeing me with his brother is probably really weird for him, even if things had run more smoothly."

He turned down the dark streets and approached the front of the house. He pulled into the garage then shut the door behind him.

Soldier's barks could be heard coming from inside the house.

Finn got out without waiting for me and entered the kitchen, ignoring Soldier when he whined for attention.

It was impossible for me to ignore him, so I leaned down and gave him a good rubdown before I joined Finn in his bedroom.

He was already stripped to his boxers and in bed, and judging from the fact he wasn't naked, he wasn't in the mood for sex. With one hand behind his head, he looked up at the ceiling.

I got ready for bed in the bathroom then joined him a

moment later, Soldier getting comfortable at the foot of the bed. The three of us crammed together on the single mattress, one large man and one big dog taking up most of the space.

I didn't cuddle with Finn because he didn't seem interested.

With his eyes glued to the ceiling, he said, "I don't know what to do."

"There's nothing you can do."

"I don't want my own brother to hate me."

"He'll get over it eventually. He's never really seen us together, so let him get used to it."

"Do you think I should talk to him again?"

"I don't know… I think space is what he needs."

His eyes were wide open, and his chest slowly rose and fell while his military dog tags moved with his breathing. He couldn't really be happy with me because the guilt tugged him so hard. He was a man who'd lived a selfless life, and then when he really wanted something, he couldn't have it. It was off-limits. "I just wish it didn't have to be this way."

"I know…" I scooted closer to him and rubbed my hand over his chest. "Me neither."

"How am I supposed to be happy when I feel guilty all the time?"

"You just have to trust that it will pass."

"But when will it pass?"

I didn't have a concrete answer. "Eventually."

I TOOK the stairs up to my floor the next morning, makeup gone from my face, and I wore the same clothes as the night before. I headed down the hallway and watched Colton step out of his apartment, a bag of trash in his hand.

He stopped when he saw me. One glance told him I'd spent

the night at Finn's, and that he'd just dropped me off. When Colton recovered from the realization, he walked forward and headed to the trash chute. "Morning."

"Morning."

He dropped the plastic bag in the chute then turned to me.

I understood Colton's feelings perfectly, but I was still disappointed in his behavior. "You really hurt Finn's feelings last night."

He couldn't keep the derision out of his voice. "Oh, I hurt his feelings? Gosh, I'm so sorry." He turned away and headed back to his apartment.

"Finn didn't want to be with me to hurt you. But you told him you hated him because you wanted to hurt him. It's not the same thing at all."

He stopped. "I didn't say that to hurt him. I said it because that's how I feel."

My eyes narrowed. "You don't mean that. I know you don't."

"Ever since he came back to Seattle, he's been making my life miserable."

"Don't be dramatic."

"I'm not. You and Finn are the only people who think what he did was right. And that's because you're fucking all the pain and guilt away. While everyone else understands he crossed a line he can't uncross."

I was starting to worry that this would never be okay, that this would ruin friendships and relationships. "You told me you wanted me to be happy."

"And I meant that." Sincerity was in his eyes, shining like a beacon.

"You aren't doing a good job of showing it."

"They are two separate feelings. I want you to be happy, even if it is with him. But anytime I see him with you, I think about what he did, that he's with the woman I was married to. It's like incest or something."

"It's nothing like that, Colton."

"It's still a betrayal. You expect me to get over that in a month?"

"No. But I expect you to be a little classier. Telling him you hate him is not okay."

"But I mean it."

"No, you don't, Colton," I snapped. "You're the most loving person I know. I refuse to believe you're capable of feeling something so evil, especially for your own blood. It's perfectly fine to be angry, but don't say cold things like that. I understand Finn's actions were wrong, but he didn't do this out of spite. He did this because he cares about me."

Colton turned away, his eyes filled with anger mixed with resentment. He stopped in front of his front door with his hands on his hips, wearing his sweatpants and t-shirt and carrying his attitude like a cloak.

"Colton."

He still wouldn't look at me.

"You need to tell Finn you didn't mean it."

Silence.

"Colt."

He finally turned back to me, his jaw tight.

"You don't hate him. I know you don't. Make sure he knows that too. He was really down last night."

He watched me, his blue eyes slowly filling with remorse.

"I'm going to be honest with you, Colton. When I first saw you with Aaron, it was hard for me."

His eyes slowly dropped as he listened to what I said. He pivoted closer to me, his attention piqued.

"I wasn't necessarily jealous. I wasn't necessarily heartbroken. It was just...difficult. We used to do everything together, used to come home to each other, and seeing you move on with someone else made me realize we would really never be what we used to be. You'd been mine for so long that it was hard to let you go. Kinda like a parent who watches their kid go to kindergarten the first time. But I knew I had to let it go and be happy for you. That's what I chose to do...and then it became easier."

Colton crossed his arms over his chest. "I get what you're saying, but it's not the same thing. It was difficult for me to accept Jax in the beginning too."

"But I've gone out of my way to make Tom feel welcome. I see the way he makes you happy, so I would still treat him well even if I didn't like him. You started a new life and made such a drastic change, but I've been nothing but supportive. Even when you broke my heart and told me you were gay...I was there for you."

His eyes slowly filled with tears, a thin film of moisture that reflected the light from the ceiling. "I know you were."

"And I'll always support you, no matter what you want, even if you decide you're an alien from another planet. Because love is selfless and infinite. I just wish...you would try harder to be okay with this. I know it's complicated because of Finn, but he makes me feel... I can't even explain it. We should be in the honeymoon phase right now, but the stress of you has killed that momentum. I don't want this relationship to end before it can even start. I just wish—"

"I'll try harder, Pepper."

Finally, I'd broken through his spiteful exterior and reached the compassionate man underneath.

"I know I've made this whole thing about me...which is wrong."

"I really love him, Colton. It may never go anywhere, but I want to be with him nonetheless."

He gave a slight nod. "Then I'll be better." He blinked his

eyes quickly and his tears dissipated. "I'm sorry I've been so diffi-cult. I just get lost in my feelings and forget about the big picture. I need to keep my feelings for Finn separate from your relationship with him."

"Thanks...and I hope you can find it in your heart to forgive him. He never meant to hurt you. And he cares about you more than you realize. He would die for you."

"I've never gotten that impression from him..." Instead of turning angry and spiteful, Colton was still calm and quiet, speaking from the heart rather than from rage.

"Well, he would. I know he would."

He stared at me for a while, his gaze dropping toward the floor.

I stared at the man who used to be my husband and saw all the reasons I fell in love with him in the first place. He was beau-tiful and soft like a rose, but sometimes, his stem was embedded with painful thorns. "I should get going. I've got a business to run."

"Yeah...me too."

I smiled and squeezed his arm. "Good talk."

"Yeah." He wrapped his arm around my shoulders and pulled me to his chest, his lips landing on my forehead. "Love you."

I closed my eyes and sighed against his chest, immediately forgiving him for his behavior the night before. "I love you too."

FINN WALKED INSIDE, in his workout clothes after hitting the gym. Sweat had soaked into his shirt around his neck and under his arms, and I'd never seen sweat stains look so sexy. But this man could pull off anything.

Soldier was close to my side as we watched TV together. He didn't even get up to greet Finn because he was so comfortable.

"How was your workout?"

Finn took a long drink of his water as he walked into the kitchen. "Hard." He eyed Soldier on the couch. "Traitor."

Soldier rested his chin on my thigh.

"He's just comfy." I scratched him behind the ears.

Finn set his bottle in the sink then walked toward me. "Doesn't look like you guys missed me at all."

"Because we didn't."

He narrowed his eyes, but his lips were slightly raised in a smile. "If that dog had to save one of us, he would pick you."

"Only because you would want him to."

His smile faded, and affection entered his eyes. "True."

"So I talked to Colton yesterday..."

"Oh, this should be good."

"He doesn't hate you. He's just emotional right now, and he got carried away."

He stood with his hands on his hips, seeming indifferent, but his eyes showed his true feelings. "I doubt that means things will get better."

"Give it time."

He eyed both of us before his eyes settled on me. "Are you going to get up and give me a kiss?"

I looked at Soldier on my lap, where he was clearly comfortable snuggling into my side, and then looked up at Finn again. "I don't want to disturb him."

He rolled his eyes and chuckled at the same time. "My woman prefers a dog to me."

"Well, he is the better snuggler..."

He headed to the stairs. "I'm going to shower. I have this thing at work tonight. Do you want to come along?"

"Work? You already worked the morning shift."

"It's a dinner party type of thing. The emergency department rents out a room at a restaurant, and we get together...as if we don't already spend enough time together. We give out awards and shit like that."

"You make it sound like fun..."

"Just giving you the rundown. You want to come or not?"

"When is it?"

He glanced at the time on the clock. "In about an hour."

"What?" I asked incredulously. "That's all the time you're giving me to get ready?"

"Aren't you ready now?"

"I'm just wearing your t-shirt."

He shrugged. "Wear that. You'll be the best-looking person at the party."

I rolled my eyes. "Only to you."

"I disagree." He stopped at the top of the stairs. "Wear lingerie underneath whatever you wear."

"Why?"

"Because this party is going to be dull. Gives me something to think about."

THANKFULLY, I had a dress in his closet to wear. It had three-quarter sleeves, a sash around the waist, and it flared out around the hem. It was casual but also a little dressy, perfect to match with a pair of heels.

And it was perfect to hide a one-piece bodysuit underneath.

Finn eyed me up and down when I came down the stairs. "This party definitely won't be dull now." His hand moved into my hair as he leaned in and kissed me, giving me that possessive embrace that made me numb all the way to my toes. His fingers dug into the back of my neck, and he squeezed my lower back.

Soldier sat on the floor near us, and he let out a growl.

Finn pulled away and looked down at him. "Did you just growl at me?"

It was a really good kiss that made me think about what we would do when we got home, but the second the dog growled at him like that, I could barely stop myself from laughing.

Soldier started to wag his tail again once Finn stopped kissing me.

Finn turned back to me, wearing a V-neck gray t-shirt with a black blazer on top. "Looks like you have another admirer."

"We've gotten pretty close."

"I'll say." He leaned in to kiss me again.

Soldier growled once more.

Finn looked down at him. "You're kidding me, right?"

"Maybe he's jealous of me, not you."

He rolled his eyes. "We both know you're the one he's obsessed with." He grabbed his wallet and keys off the counter and placed them in his pocket. "Let's get going." He walked out to the garage.

This time, Soldier followed him.

"I don't think so, man." He looked down at the dog and shook his head. "You can't have it both ways."

Soldier whined as Finn left.

I leaned down and gave him a kiss on the nose. "We'll be back in a couple of hours. I'll bring you some leftovers if I have any."

His tail started to wag again.

I followed Finn out, and we left in his truck.

He drove into the city, a silver watch on his wrist and his cologne filling the truck.

I noticed the scent because he hardly ever wore cologne. "So what are your colleagues like?"

He shrugged. "The boring, intellectual types."

"You don't consider yourself to be the same?"

"God, no," he said with a laugh. "I'm the dumbest one there."

"Why do I doubt that?"

"These guys had formal educations, went to the big schools for undergrad, and stuff like that. I'm the only one in the department who went a different route, so I'm pretty different from the rest of them."

"I don't see why that matters. A lot of astronauts are military pilots. They don't have the same formal training as the others, but they do just fine."

"Well, I'm not a badass astronaut, but thanks for the comparison."

We parked in the parking lot then stepped inside the restaurant. It was a large place near the shore, a restaurant that had a private room in the back with a separate patio and space heaters. White lights illuminated the area, and there was a buffet full of an array of food. Everyone mingled together with drinks in their hands or seated at tables with their dinners.

"Wow, you work with a lot of people."

"And not even all of them are here."

"Where are the rest?"

He gave me a teasing smile. "Working at the ER."

"Oh...that makes sense."

He chuckled then kissed me on the hairline. "Let's get a drink, and I'll introduce you to some people." His arm moved around my waist, and he held me like his woman, like I wasn't just some random girl he'd brought to an event. He made me feel far more special than that.

He introduced me to a few of the doctors he worked with and some of his favorite nurses. Much of the small talk was about working in the ER, and I couldn't follow along with most of it, but it was exciting to be part of his world. He rarely shared anything about himself, and as I'd expected, he was Mr. Popular. Everyone seemed to adore him.

No surprise there.

We helped ourselves to the buffet then took a seat at one of the vacant tables.

That's when I spotted Layla.

Ugh. I was hoping she'd be working.

Gorgeous in a backless red dress, she showed off her incredible body and her ink. Her eyes settled on Finn, and the longing was so obvious that everyone would notice if they looked.

I wanted to punch her in the face. Knowing she'd tried to sleep with him when he gave her a ride home made me despise her. I doubt she was even drunk. It was probably just a pathetic ploy.

"How's your prime rib?" Finn's question distracted me from the declaration of war I'd just made.

"Good. Everything is good."

Since this was a work function, he drank wine, something he hardly ever did. When he wasn't eating, he placed his hand on my thigh under the table, showing his affection rather than restraining it.

"Everyone seems really nice."

"Yeah, for the most part. But that's probably because of all the free food and booze...and they aren't at work. When shit gets rough in the ER, people aren't in such a good mood. It's all down to business."

"I can't even imagine. All I ever have to worry about is having enough lingerie in the right sizes."

"Hey, your job is important." He leaned toward me. "Very important. It's literally the most important thing in the world to me."

I laughed at his perverseness. "I think your job is a little more important."

He weighed between his two hands. "Sex or medicine... I think we know who the winner is."

Layla left her chair then approached us, shaking her hips like she was on a runway. Her choice of dress was a bit scandalous for a work function, and it seemed obvious that the dress was just for Finn.

How would I smile and be polite when I wanted to knock her teeth in?

"Hey, Finn." She stopped in front of us. "How's the prime rib?"

"Since mine is all gone, I'd say it's pretty good." Charming as always, he was irresistible at all times. "How was your dinner?"

"Great. I think I'm going to have a second go."

Where the hell did she put it?

"You're a trooper," Finn said. "Good for you."

Finn had already introduced me at the bar before, but I wasn't certain if she remembered me or not. She probably thought I was just another woman on his arm...one of many. I wasn't important, and I wouldn't be around forever, which was exactly why she wasn't deterred.

"You remember Pepper, right?" Finn asked. "I introduced you guys at the bar."

"Oh yeah..." She nodded her head slowly, going along with it even though she had no idea who I was. "Nice to see you again."

"Yeah...you too." It made me sick to my stomach to think she was making moves on him anytime they ran into each other. But I couldn't expect anything less when I was dating a man so drop-dead gorgeous. Of course women would sink their claws into him any chance they got. It didn't matter if he was seeing anyone. And as far as she knew, I could just be his friend or something.

"I thought it was time to introduce my girlfriend to everyone," Finn said. "I can't keep her all to myself all the time."

It was the first time Finn had called me his girlfriend, and the bolt of joy that spread through my limbs counteracted the poison Layla administered. I felt so warm, so high, that I was soaring above the sky. Whether Finn did it on purpose to keep Layla away, or it just rolled off the tongue naturally, it meant the world to me.

Layla couldn't hide her falling expression. "Yeah...time to get some fresh air. Well, you two have fun. I've got to make a few stops." When she walked away, her hips didn't shake like they had before. Her determination had evaporated once she'd struck out.

The smile on my face felt permanent.

Finn drank his wine then looked around the room, watching his colleagues drink and dine.

"Your girlfriend, huh?"

He turned to me, an innocent expression on his face. "Is that okay? Or are you Soldier's girlfriend now?"

My arm linked through his, and I moved my face to his shoulder. "I just didn't know that's what I was to you."

He faced forward again. "You're the woman in my bed every night. What else would you be?"

"I don't know. I just know you've never had a girlfriend before."

He shrugged. "First time for everything, right?"

I rubbed his arm and rested my face on his shoulder, not caring if anyone else saw. My heart beat at a special rate for this man. The second he came into my life, he made me feel things I'd only read about in books. He was Prince Charming with a hint of badness. "I like being your girlfriend."

"Are you sure? Sometimes I wonder if you'll leave me for my dog."

"I can't love both of you?" I asked playfully.

"Yes. But it's weird that you sleep with both of us."

"Are you really jealous of a dog?"

"No. I'm just jealous that you turned him against me."

"I did not," I said with a laugh.

"Well, you got him to fall in love with you."

"Maybe you should buy him a toy once in a while."

"Nope. I'm not gonna make him soft." His fingers rubbed gently against my bare thigh.

Now I wished we were home, naked in his bed and moving slowly together. "I'm not sure if I can wait until we get home. That back seat of the truck looks big enough…"

He slowly turned to me, his eyes filled with that intensity he only showed me. "That's why you're my girlfriend."

"Really? Because any woman here would say the exact same thing."

"Alright, you're my girlfriend for a few other reasons too."

"And those reasons are?" I never asked him about his feelings or the future because it seemed like a topic that would spook him. But he freely called me his girlfriend and claimed me to a woman who obviously wanted his balls. He could have her whenever he wanted her, but he kept his dick in his pants for me.

"You're my girlfriend because you're the only woman I want to be with. I think that explains it pretty well."

"And why am I the only woman you want to be with?"

"That's a question that doesn't have an answer," he said quietly. "But I think it's good I don't have an answer…because my feelings don't need to be justified or explained."

Just when I thought he was incapable of expressing himself, he said the most romantic thing. This man was so loving without even trying. He made me feel like the only woman who mattered because he proved it. He never looked at another woman in my presence, and he let the world know he was a one-woman kind of man when it mattered. He didn't claim me out of jealousy. He claimed himself because he wanted the world to know he was mine.

My fingers went to his chin, and I turned his face toward mine. My eyes looked into his before I leaned in and gave him a soft kiss on the mouth, a kiss that lingered for several seconds before I had the strength to pull away. "I want you to make love to me when we get home."

He rubbed his nose against mine before he kissed the corner of my mouth. "Yes, baby."

WHEN MY DRESS was on the floor, my black bodysuit was revealed, the crotch unclasped so he could get inside me easily. My heels stayed on my feet, and I dug the stilettos into his back as he ground into me on his bed. My hair was everywhere and my breathing was going haywire. My nails clawed at him as the moans escaped his mouth, deep and sexy.

One of his hands was tangled in my hair, while his face was pressed into my neck. He breathed deep and heavy as he thrust in me, his dick harder than it'd ever been before. It pulsed inside me like a stick of dynamite that would explode at any instant. "You look so fucking sexy in lingerie."

My arms hugged his muscular back, and I felt every inch slam inside me with his thrusts. My chin was tilted to the ceiling, and I existed on a plane of emotion, just feeling and not thinking. Lost in the lust and the love, I was out of my rational mind. All I could do was feel this man deep inside me, feel the connection between our souls. I already knew I didn't want another man for the rest of my life. I wanted Finn every single day, to feel his dog tags drag against my tits every time we made love. He completed me in a way Colton never could. There had always been something missing, but I hadn't known we were missing anything until I found it.

Finn pulled his face out of my neck and looked me in the eye, his sculpted body rocking into mine as his muscles flexed and tightened. His warm breath fell on my face, smelling like red wine.

I was more soaked than usual because I liked knowing that he was there with me, that Layla didn't have a chance because I was the only woman he wanted. Even when he hadn't had me, he still didn't let anyone else have him. He could be anywhere that night, but he was in bed with me, making love to me, skin-on-skin. I got off knowing Layla was disappointed, furious that she'd constantly struck out with Finn.

I was the victor.

"Baby, you're so wet." His hand tightened in my hair, and he gently rocked inside me, moving through my tight slickness until he ran out of room.

"You make me wet."

He cradled his face to mine and kissed me, his lips moving with purpose while his hips never lost their pace. He flexed his hips and pushed himself deep inside me, taking me in a way he'd never taken a woman before. I was special to him for millions of reasons. I was his first in many ways. I was the first woman he actually cared about, the first one who'd turned him monogamous.

As my lips trembled against his, I came. My body produced another wave of moisture between my legs, and I covered him with my slickness. "Finn..." My nails clawed deep into his back, and my thighs squeezed his hips so tightly. This man gave me the best orgasms of my life, the kind that caused cramps in my toes. He put my body through so much pleasure, it actually hurt the next day. This was how love was supposed to be, when you couldn't get enough of your partner no matter how many times you were together. I'd never had this with Colton. I'd never had this all-consuming desire to have him as much as I could.

Finn always made the same movements when he was about to release. His pace slowed down and his thrusts turned deeper, like he was trying to bury himself as far inside me as possible before he exploded. His breathing turned irregular, and he always gave a shudder when the moment arrived.

I grabbed his ass and yanked him deep inside me, wanting his come to fill me as much as possible. When Jax had wanted to skip the condoms, I hadn't been thrilled by the idea of him coming inside me, but with Finn, it was an extra turn-on. I wanted him to fill me with his seed, to let his arousal burrow inside me.

He moaned loudly as he finished, his eyes closing for a brief moment. All the muscles in his body tightened as he released, even his ass muscles underneath my fingertips. The weight came a second later as his come filled my pussy. Slowly, he began to soften, still moaning quietly because every part of the event was sensational. "This pussy..." His face moved into my neck, and he kissed the sweat off my throat, worshiping me like I'd done all the pleasing, when I'd only lain there and been pleasured by him.

My fingers moved into his hair, and I closed my eyes as I enjoyed him, enjoyed the way he kissed me everywhere. This man was obsessed with me, and I'd never felt more desirable in my life.

When he was completely finished and the moment passed, he pulled out of me then lay beside me, his tattooed frame sexy with streaks of sweat. Instead of giving me space to cool off, he wrapped his arms around me and cuddled me from behind, his dick pressed against my ass.

I felt the metal from his tags right against my back, reassuring me he was always there. With every breath, they pressed deeper into me, reminding me of his service and his history.

Soldier whined at the door, smart enough to understand that the fucking was over.

Finn sighed against the back of my neck. "I hate sharing you."

"He hates sharing you too."

"No. He hates sharing *you*." He got out of bed and opened the door so Soldier could get comfortable in his usual spot. Finn came back to the bed and cuddled with me once more, the heat of his body welcome even though I was already warm.

"He loves both of us equally."

He chuckled against my ear. "There's no way you really believe that."

"I do."

His arm tightened across my stomach, and he sighed as he got comfortable.

"Finn?"

"Yes, baby?"

I knew I'd fallen in love with his man a long time ago. But I would never tell him how I felt because he wouldn't say it back. It was far too early for that, so I didn't test the waters. But since Finn was so intelligent, he might have figured it out on his own. "You said you didn't see yourself ever getting married or having a family. Do you still feel that way?" I stared at the wall of his bedroom, seeing the dresser against it.

He was quiet for a long time.

Maybe I shouldn't have asked the question. He'd called me his girlfriend, but somehow, I heard wedding bells. I'd been living in the moment with him, unsure if it would ever go anywhere, but after tonight, we really had a chance.

"I don't know. I don't think about the future much."

That was the best answer I could have hoped for. It wasn't a flat-out no, which was an improvement for him. "I was just curious..."

"As a principle, I don't make plans. For the last ten years, I've always known I could die at any moment. The future has always been an unpredictable illusion I could never trust. So I don't think about it too much. Once you do, it creates pressure and distress. Whatever happens, happens. I have no expectations."

"Not a bad way to live."

"I thought you were looking for a different answer."

"No. The worst thing you could say is no, that you refuse that outcome at any point in time. It's a terrible answer because you're denying yourself a possibility you might want someday. Saying that the future is unpredictable is an acceptable answer. It's a good answer."

He was quiet as he lay behind me, his affection still prevalent. He didn't pull away or twitch uncomfortably. "The second I met you, I was screwed. I've been screwed from the beginning... to meet a woman like you and do nothing about it. I've been all over the world, and I've never met a woman more beautiful, more pragmatic, more understanding. It makes me understand Colton's jealousy—because that's exactly what he is...jealous. He wishes he could keep you, wishes he could be straight. But he can't...so he has to let you go."

FINN WORKED EARLY the next morning, so I woke up alone in the large bed with Soldier right beside me. The second Finn was gone, the dog took the vacated spot and pressed his back directly against mine.

My eyes opened, and I felt a weight in my left hand. My arm was stretched out on the bed beside me, my palm facing the ceiling. My thumbs stroked across the metal in my hand, feeling the distinct grooves carved into the surface. When I brought it close to my face and let my eyes adjust, I saw the metal of his dog tags.

His name was engraved on the surface along with the rest of his information.

It took me a second to understand what I was looking at, that the chain he never removed was sitting in my open palm.

I sat up and stared at it harder, imagining how bare his chest must feel without this necklace plunging far down between his pectoral muscles. He wore it in the shower, to work, and to bed. When he was on top of me, I could feel the smooth metal graze against my skin over and over.

Now it was mine.

I grabbed my phone on the nightstand and opened our messages so I could text him. But he'd already texted me.

I want you to have it.

There was no other explanation.

I picked up the necklace and placed it around my throat, feeling the weight from the chain as well as the tags at the bottom. The metal was cold to the touch, but it was filled with Finn's warm presence. Once it was against my skin, I felt like he was there with me. I felt like the only woman who mattered, the only woman who'd earned such a gift from him.

He said the future was unpredictable, that there was no hoping for tomorrow.

But today, he felt something for me, something he couldn't articulate. It was the sweetest gesture he could have made, to part with something that meant the world to him. But he gave it to me...because I also meant the world to him.

6

___

PEPPER

I WENT HOME AFTER WORK AND SHOWERED SINCE I HADN'T GOTTEN a chance that morning. I looked at myself in the mirror as I stood there naked, seeing the tags hanging around my throat. I was a much smaller person than he was, so they hung much farther down my chest, resting below the valley between my tits.

I couldn't picture myself ever taking them off.

Not even to protect Colton's feelings.

I'd just opened a bottle of wine when Finn texted me. *Can I take you to dinner?*

Finn and I had never done anything outside of the house besides his work party. We chose to have dinner in the privacy of his home so we could do it on the couch or any other piece of furniture that could hold our weight. *Yes.*

I'll pick you up in 15.

I should consider Colton across the hallway, but I was too happy to care. I wished Colton would be more accepting of this relationship, but his disapproval couldn't interfere with my happiness. And I was so happy.

Finn arrived at the door and immediately looked at the chain that was visible around my neck, peeking up from underneath the collar of my blouse. He stared at it for a moment before his eyes lifted to mine, his expression masked by stoicism but his eyes filled with a hint of emotion.

I rose on my tiptoes and kissed him as we stood on the threshold. "Hey."

His arm wrapped around my waist, and he squeezed my lower back. "Hey."

My palms planted against his chest as I used him for balance. "Thank you for the necklace. I love it." That didn't seem like an adequate response to the gift he'd imparted to me. It was such an incredible gesture that I felt like I should say more, but there were no words to explain how much it meant to me.

He lowered his forehead and rested it against mine. His eyes closed, and he held me on the doorstep, his hands gripping my top as it bunched around my waist.

I cherished the moment with him, the special connection we could both feel. I wanted to blurt out my deepest feelings, that I was so in love with him that I would marry him today if he asked me. But I kept my mouth shut and let the impulse pass.

He opened his eyes again. "You're my woman. I want the world to know you're mine."

WE WENT to a restaurant neither one of us had been to before.

Finn ordered a bottle of wine even though he probably preferred scotch, but I was touched he tried to do something romantic.

He looked at the menu as he sat in a t-shirt and jeans. His tattooed arm stretched the fabric of the shirt, and his classically handsome features made him so beautiful under the dim lighting. I didn't even care about the other women who stared at him because I couldn't blame them.

Their interest didn't matter anyway. He was mine.

His eyes scanned left and right across the page until he found something he wanted. He dropped the menu to the table and looked at me.

"So is this our first official date?"

He shrugged. "Depends on what counts as a date. I think sex counts."

"Then this definitely wouldn't be our first date."

The corner of his mouth rose in a smile. "Not even close."

I drank my glass of wine and wanted to pinch myself. Going through my divorce was the hardest thing I'd ever had to endure, and my best friend couldn't help me with it—because he was the one I was divorcing. But I landed back on my feet, and wonderful things happened to me...like this amazing man. "Do you ever take women out for a meal?"

"You really want to talk about other women?" he asked in surprise.

"It's not like I'm jealous. Nothing to be jealous about."

His eyes lingered on my face for several seconds before he answered. "No. I think it's only happened a handful of times, and usually by mistake. I meet them at a bar, and we go straight back to my place. Taking a woman out would subject me to an evening of mediocre conversation with someone I couldn't care less about."

When he was blunt, he could be cold, but his honesty made him admirable. "You like talking to me?"

He gave a slight nod. "You're my favorite person to talk to."

"Because I sell lingerie for a living?"

"That is fascinating. But it's mainly because you wear lingerie so well. If it wouldn't get you arrested, I would suggest you walk around in lingerie all the time."

"In Seattle?" I asked incredulously. "I'd freeze."

He glanced at my chest. "Even better."

"So you'd want your girlfriend parading her junk around like that?"

"No, not my girlfriend," he said. "Only private shows. But if I weren't around, that would be the way to go."

"People would assume I was a prostitute."

"And you could charge a fortune."

I rolled my eyes. "I'd rather do it for free with you."

He smiled. "Good answer, baby." His hand reached across the table and gently touched my fingertips before he pulled away again.

"So...how was work?"

He shrugged. "Same old bullshit. UTIs, chest pain caused by anxiety, and people needing to see a doctor because they don't have health insurance and going to the ER is the only way they can get treatment."

"Does that annoy you?"

"No. I think everyone has the right to health care. What annoys me is that people found a loophole in the system and take advantage of the ER, when our purpose is to treat emergency situations. But we get stuff done fast, like scans and procedures. Even if you do have insurance, it's such a long process to get approval for stuff that it'll take you two months to find relief when you can get it done in hours at the ER. But it causes more grief for the doctors because we have way more patients than we can possibly see. It's a complicated situation..." He drank from his glass.

It never surprised me how intelligent Finn was. He could always eloquently explain complicated situations so simply and so pragmatically. Since he'd been in truly stressful positions, everything else made him unnaturally calm. "You think that will ever change?"

He shrugged. "I don't know about that. But I think emergency medicine will need to expand at some point."

"Health insurance is so expensive. I pay five hundred bucks a month, which is frustrating because I never use it."

"You will someday, and you'll be glad you have it. So how was work for you?"

"It was okay. I was distracted most of the time."

"Why?"

I touched the chain around my neck. "Kept thinking about this necklace..." He didn't leave a note or give an explanation for his actions. Whatever led him to decide to hand it over was impulsive...and romantic.

His fingers gripped the stem of his glass on the table.

"What made you decide to give it to me?"

He swished the wine in his glass, his eyes staying on me. "I just wanted to."

"But you haven't taken it off in ten years."

He shrugged. "I don't know. I guess I wanted to give you a piece of me. I wanted to see that necklace around your neck while I fuck you in my bed. I guess the idea of you being mine turns me on in ways I can't explain."

I understood that feeling all too well.

After a long stretch of silence, he released his glass. "I'm gonna wash up." He pushed his chair in then left the table and disappeared to the back of the restaurant.

My eyes focused on nothing in particular as I fantasized about everything he'd said. My fingers felt the chain at my collarbone, and I pictured his heavy body on top of mine as his tags sat between my tits. I pictured how hard he became when he saw the way he claimed me, the way he made me his for all the world to see.

I was so enthralled by my thoughts that I didn't notice the man who came to the table.

With dark hair, green eyes, and a slight smile on his face, he looked down at me like he was happy to see me, not annoyed like the last time we spoke. At over six feet, he was just as trim as I remember, his arms thick and muscular. "Pepper?"

I stared into Jax's face, unable to believe he was standing right in front of me while I fantasized about Finn. "Hey...long time, no see." The last time we saw each other was on his doorstep in the pouring rain. He gave me an ultimatum—him and or Colton. I chose my gay ex-husband. "How are you?"

"Good. Just had dinner with a friend. You look beautiful... not that I'm surprised."

I thought he would be annoyed to see me. He could have easily walked past my table and pretended not to have noticed me. I wouldn't have noticed him. "You look good too. The real estate business going well?"

"The real estate business is always going well. People always need a place to live."

"How's your sister?"

"Living with her husband here in the city."

"Then you must be enjoying your bachelor pad."

He shrugged. "Can't complain. How's the lingerie shop?"

"Good. People are always having sex, so that works out for me."

He chuckled. "Your business is recession-proof."

"Yeah, I think so." Now that the small talk was out of the way, I expected him to walk away. It would be ideal if he left before Finn returned from the bathroom. Having my new boyfriend and ex-boyfriend in the same space together probably wouldn't be good. Finn wasn't a jealous guy, but I doubted he would be happy about this.

"You know, I'm actually glad I ran into you. I think the way I handled things when we broke up was...a little dramatic."

"It's fine. Don't worry about it," I said quickly, wanting to get rid of him. "It was a long time ago."

"It was like five months ago..."

Felt like an eternity. I'd been with Finn for a short time, but it felt so right that it seemed to last forever.

"I just liked you so much that I came off a little strong. I was overly jealous and controlling...and I'm sorry about that."

"It's fine, Jax. No hard feelings." I spotted Finn rounding the corner and heading this way. Shit.

"I feel like I did a lot of things wrong when I should have just slowed down."

Since he was in such a chatty mood, there was no way I was going to get rid of him before Finn arrived.

Then Finn did arrive, his guard noticeable in his eyes. He approached his chair and looked at Jax, clearly expecting him to be some random guy hitting on me. It took Finn a second to process his familiarity.

Jax looked at him with the same astonishment. "Finn...how's it going?"

This was awkward.

Finn didn't say anything.

Now it became even more awkward.

Jax turned back to me. "Well, I'll let you guys get back to your evening. Just wanted to stop by and say hello."

"I didn't realize you were friends." Finn didn't take his seat. "Friends don't give each other ultimatums, but you did."

Instead of being jealous, Finn was actually angry that Jax had forced me to choose between himself and Colton. Finn was being protective of me rather than upset about the circumstances. Either way, the situation was only getting more tense.

Jax stood rooted to the spot, caught off guard by the intense way Finn came into the conversation. "I just apologized for that."

"No apology necessary," he said coldly. "You're too late. Now leave."

Jax lingered a moment longer, but then he had the wisdom

to abandon the scene and walk out. He was a strong guy, but he was no match for a military man. He turned around and left the restaurant.

Finn finally took his seat. "I leave you alone for two seconds..."

"He just stopped by to say hi."

"And that was all?" he asked incredulously. "Don't expect me to buy that bullshit. There's no way a man could be with you and let you go without regretting it. He stopped by because he knows he made a mistake. He's picked up other women since you and realized they all suck in comparison. He had something great, and he should have toughed it out instead of giving up so easily."

He hit the nail right on the head, but I didn't confirm his suspicions. "He's gone now, so it doesn't matter."

"You're right, it doesn't matter," he said. "He doesn't matter." He picked up his glass and took a drink. "Did you tell him about me?"

"I never had a chance, but I don't think it matters. It's probably pretty obvious that we're on a date."

He shook his head slightly. "What's obvious to you isn't obvious to everyone else. Sometimes you need to make it perfectly clear—like I did with Layla."

The mention of her made me feel guilty, since he'd made it abundantly clear he was off the market in order to chase her away. I should have done the same with Jax, but there really hadn't been an opportunity. "We'll never see him again anyway, so it doesn't matter."

"But if we do, you better tell him."

I enjoyed this side of Finn. He wasn't necessarily jealous; he just wanted to be accurately represented. "I will. I promise."

7

COLTON

I WENT ACROSS THE HALL AND FORCED MYSELF TO KNOCK BEFORE I barged inside. Now that Pepper was serious with my brother for a while, I didn't want to burst inside while they were doing it on the couch. They seemed to stay at his place most of the time, so at least their relationship wouldn't be right in my face.

Pepper opened the door, dressed in her pajama bottoms and a t-shirt without a bra. She clearly had no plans tonight. "Hey, what's up?"

"Can I borrow some salt? I'm fresh out."

"Yeah, sure." She turned away and entered her kitchen. After searching in her pantry, she found a large box of kosher salt. "It might be a little old, but does salt expire?" She walked back toward me, the metal beads of her necklace visible around her neck. It was noticeable because it wasn't the kind of jewelry she would normally wear. It was very masculine and plain since it wasn't silver or gold.

"I'm sure it's fine. I need it for pasta."

"Then that should work. And you don't need to bring it back. I'll never use it."

"Thanks." I glanced at her neck. "What's that?" I pointed at my own neckline. "Looks like a dog tag necklace or something." I noticed everything about Pepper, not just because I was gay, but because I knew her so well that any slight change in appearance was obvious to me.

"Ohh..." Her hand reached for the metal beads around her neck as she suddenly looked self-conscious. "That's because it is..." She reached inside her shirt and pulled out the tags that were engraved with Finn's name and information. "Finn gave it to me."

I stared at the rectangular tag at the end of the necklace, remembering him wearing it every single time I saw him. He never took it off, and even when he had on a t-shirt, the necklace was visible around his neck. He wouldn't hand that over to someone lightly, only to someone who was really special. "Ohh..."

She tucked it back inside her shirt. "Sorry. I know that must make you feel weird."

"No. I'm just surprised, I guess. He hasn't taken off that necklace in a decade."

"I know..." A slight smile stretched her lips, and her eyes filled with affection as her fingers played with the chain. "I woke up one morning and found it in my hand. It was really sweet."

Pepper had told me she'd fallen in love with my brother, and now I had to face the truth. My brother had fallen in love with her too. My brother, the biggest player I'd ever met, had fallen in love with a woman for the first time.

My ex-wife.

"It looks better on you," I said, forcing a teasing sound to my voice. In reality, I was overwhelmed by the truth. This wasn't just some relationship that would end in heartbreak and bitterness. This really might last forever.

"I don't agree with that...but thank you."

"Well...I'd better get cooking. I'll see you later." I crossed the hallway and headed back to my apartment.

"Yeah, I'll see you tomorrow."

I sat on the couch and watched TV, starting to wind down before bed with a beer in my hand. Tom had spent the evening with his friends, and I'd made dinner for one. The apartment seemed too big for one person now. I'd been living with Finn for so long that I was used to having company all the time.

A knock sounded at the door.

It was eight in the evening, so it could only be Pepper.

I opened the door, expecting to see her beautiful brown hair and green eyes as she rocked her pajamas with her hair in a bun.

But I came face-to-face with my brother.

In a dark hoodie and sweatpants, he seemed to have made an impulsive decision leading to his visit, like he sat in his living room and partially watched TV until he couldn't stop thinking about me. Then he decided to drop by and confront me. We hadn't spoken in weeks, not since that horrible double date.

I stepped aside and let him in, not wanting Pepper to overhear our conversation in the hallway.

He walked in and took a look around. "It looks exactly the same. Like nothing's changed."

"It doesn't feel the same. I'm used to having a roommate. Now it feels weird to live alone."

"Yeah, I know what you mean." He stepped farther into the room with his hands in his pockets.

I glanced at the back of his neck, expecting to see the chain from his necklace even though I knew it was long gone.

After he surveyed the living room and kitchen, he turned around to face me. His arms slowly folded in front of his chest, and he stared at me like he expected me to say something first, even though he was the one who'd dropped by without warning.

"I don't hate you. I'm sorry for saying it." Despite how angry I was, I knew that was a low moment for me. My emotions dictated my behavior, and I'd said terrible things I didn't mean. "I'm still angry, but I don't hate you."

His eyes softened, like my apology was important to him. "Thanks...that means a lot to me."

"I've just been struggling with this relationship for a long time. It's hard for me to see you with her. It's awkward and gross in a lot of ways. But I need to let the past go and be more mature about it. I'm hurt by your betrayal, but I need to be supportive of Pepper...especially when she was so supportive of me."

"I'm glad you feel that way. She's been through a lot and deserves to be happy."

"Yeah...I know."

He stepped closer to me, his head tilting toward the floor. "Pepper and I are great together. I won't go into the details, but I'll say that we make each other happy. She makes me feel... alive. But you're my family, my brother. As much as I want to be with her, she's not worth it if I have to lose you. So, if you want me to end things, I will."

His statement made me speechless. "You're serious?"

"Yes." He lifted his gaze and looked me in the eye. "It's difficult being in a relationship with someone when your brother hates you for it."

"I said I don't hate you—"

"But you know what I mean. It's a big deterrent for us. And as much as I want her, I don't want to lose my brother just to keep her. It'll make me sick to my stomach, but I'll do it. I'll have to be honest with her and not protect you when I break it off, but I'll do it. I don't want you to think you don't mean as much to me, because that's not true. I love you, Colton. I'm sorry if I didn't do a better job of showing it. You know I'm not an affectionate or emotional man. It's hard for me to describe the way I feel. Sometimes I just assume my feelings are obvious, but now I realize how presumptuous that is. Anyway...if that's what it takes to make this right, I'll do it. Is that what you want?"

If he'd asked me this weeks ago, I would have said yes instantly. I wanted these two people far away from each other. But now, that was the last thing I wanted—and not just for Pepper's sake. "No...I don't want that."

"Are you sure? Because if it is, you need to tell me now. I can't get any deeper into this relationship. If I do, I'll never be able to walk away."

"No. I really don't want that." As the words left my lips, I felt the relief stretch across my body. All my anger and rage disappeared. The betrayal from Finn seemed to turn numb. "You and Pepper are happy together...and I'm happy for you."

His eyes softened slightly, even though there was still a guarded expression on his face. "Really?"

I nodded. "She showed me your necklace."

His expression didn't change. With a wide-eyed stare, he looked at me for several seconds without even taking a breath.

"I know you wouldn't have given that to her unless she meant the world to you."

He finally released the air he'd been keeping captive in his lungs. "Because she does. If someone told me a woman would make an honest man out of me, turn me into a monogamous and pussy-whipped son of a bitch, I wouldn't have believed them. And I wouldn't have believed I was happy either. But here I am...giving away the most valuable thing I own." His head tilted to the floor again, his eyes turning glossy with unspoken memories.

"I really don't have a problem with it, Finn. At least, not anymore."

He lifted his gaze and looked at me, the relief obvious. "I was worried you would never be okay with this."

"I was worried too. But seeing the way you feel about each other...makes me realize my thoughts on it don't matter. If this relationship is special, then I need to put aside my feelings and be supportive. I'm not happy with the way things happened... but I forgive you."

"That's such a weight off my shoulders, man."

"Yeah..." Holding on to anger was a lot more work than it was worth. It poisoned my blood with every beat of my heart. It turned me into a bitter person, someone I didn't want to be. Maybe I was right for feeling betrayed, but I didn't feel right being the reason they couldn't truly be happy. "When Pepper told me she was in love with you, it immediately killed my anger. All I could focus on was what she said. She doesn't say stuff like that. She doesn't feel stuff like that. With Jax, she could barely tolerate a relationship, but then she stood out in the rain sobbing her heart out, telling me she was so head over heels in love with you, she didn't know what to do with herself. I couldn't be angry at her, not when she was baring her heart like that."

Finn stared at me with wider eyes, his chest rising and falling with the deep breaths he took. They slowly sped up even though he didn't blink once. "She said that to you?"

"Yeah." She hadn't said it to him? When he gave her his necklace, I just assumed that meant he was just as in love with her. I wouldn't come between two people madly in love. My feelings were irrelevant.

His hands moved to his hips, and he turned his head away, his mind working behind his eyes.

"When she told me that, I couldn't be upset with her. Pepper is so pragmatic that falling in love isn't easy. She's picky. She's patient. But with you, she dove in headfirst. Seeing you walk out with some other woman made her hysterical. And if that's how she feels about you, I refuse to stand in your way. And knowing you feel the same way...just makes me realize that this relationship is bigger than the three of us. I have to let it go...and move on."

He continued to stare at the wall, still breathing hard. He didn't seem to hear anything I'd just said.

"Finn, you alright?"

He finally turned back to me, his arms lowering to his sides. "Yeah...just thinking."

I moved to the couch and sat down. "You want to take a seat?"

He lowered himself into the armchair, the place where he used to read when he lived there. His eyes were still wide and empty, like my news caught him off guard. He finally cleared his throat and looked at me. "I'm glad that we can move on from this... It really bothered me. I couldn't live with you hating me. I never thought I would be the kind of man to be disloyal in that way...but I couldn't stay away from her. It wasn't about sex or attraction. It was about something much deeper."

"Yeah, I can see that now. I insulted you when I said you would just use her then toss her aside. I should have taken your feelings seriously. I'm sorry I didn't. I was cold and unfair...and I apologize for that."

My brother stared at me, his hands on the armrests. "It's okay, Colton. I get it."

"Now that I see you together, I realize this is the real deal. And if that's the case, I should be happy. This way, Pepper will always be part of my family. I'll always see her for the holidays. Her kids will be my nieces and nephews. If you think about it that way, this is the best-case scenario for me." I got to keep Pepper as close as possible. Her last name would always be my last name. And we really would be family. Her children would have my DNA. Instead of being upset by Finn's betrayal, I should see all the good in it. Wasn't it better for her to end up with my brother instead of a guy like Jax, who had a problem with our closeness?

"I think you're getting pretty far ahead, man. There's no need to talk about marriage and kids. We are nowhere near that right now. We're just spending time together."

"But if you love each other, then that's where this is going."

He turned his head and stared at the blank TV.

"And I'm glad that's where it's going. That's what I'm trying to say. I really think I'm okay with this now. When it was just you two hooking up, it made me uncomfortable. You risked our relationship for something you could have with any other woman. But knowing you guys are in love is a totally different story. It's a good story."

He rubbed his fingers along his jaw, his eyes still on the TV.

I watched my brother, unsure what to make of his mood. "You're awfully quiet."

He slowly turned his head back to me. "I just...don't know what to say."

"I don't think there is anything to say. We've buried the hatchet. We can move on now."

"Yeah...and that's great news." He gripped the armrests and nodded his head slowly. "But there's something that concerns me."

"What?"

"If I don't marry her, aren't you just going to be angry with me again?"

"No, I didn't say that."

"That's how it sounded."

"No. I'm just relieved you aren't using her. This is a real relationship with a future. You guys have real feelings for each other. I basically feel like a father who wants you to have good intentions toward her. Now that I know you do, I'm happy. That's what I'm trying to say."

He nodded his head slowly. "Got it."

Now that the conversation was over and the whole thing was really behind us, I felt better. "Zach and I are going to a Mariners game tomorrow. You want to come along?" I hadn't spent any time with my brother in a long time. I'd ignored him or screamed at him whenever we were in the same room together.

He relaxed at the change of subject. "Sure. That sounds like a good time."

"You could bring Pepper if you want. She likes baseball."

"Nah. It's been a while since we've done anything together... just the two of us."

8

PEPPER

I STEPPED INSIDE MEGA SHAKE AND FOUND COLTON SITTING AT our usual table. He had two orders of food in front of him and two root beers.

"I love it when you get here before me." I sat down in the plastic swivel chair and grabbed my burger with both hands.

Dressed in a black suit and tie, he looked like the powerful lawyer he was. "Because I pay for the food?"

"Yep. And I don't have to wait." I took a bite and felt the juiciness between my teeth. The buns were toasted to perfection, with just enough oil to add to the flavor. The condiments were in perfect proportions to the meat-to-bun ratio.

"I need to be late more often, then."

"Hey, I let you borrow that salt."

He rolled his eyes. "Salt that's three years old."

"Whatever. Still worked, right?"

"My spaghetti didn't taste funny, if that's what you're asking."

I grabbed a handful of fries and shoved them into my mouth, losing my manners because this man was used to all my flaws. "How was work?"

"Nothing worth talking about. But I do have something else worth discussing."

"Tom?"

"No. Better than that."

"You got a gift certificate for Mega Shake?"

"No, not that either. Finn stopped by my apartment last night."

"He did?" Finn had been right across the hall from me, but he didn't stop by before he went home? Or he didn't he call me and tell me about this conversation?

"Yeah. We had a long talk. I apologized for the mean things I said to him."

"That's good. I'm sure that meant a lot to him."

"Yeah, he said it did. We talked for a long time and buried the hatchet."

"Really?" I asked, finding that too good to be true.

"Yeah. When I realized how serious you guys were, I decided I needed to drop the whole thing. He said he would end things with you if that's what it took to make me happy, but I said that was the last thing I wanted."

"That's good to hear."

"So, we finally made amends and agreed to move on. We're seeing the Mariners this afternoon."

"Wow...it's nice that you guys are spending time together again. I never thought this day would come."

"I just needed to get over it. Instead of focusing on how much his betrayal hurt, I needed to focus on the good things. With the two of you being serious, that means a lot of good things for me."

"Like?"

"If you guys ever got married, we would actually be related. Our kids would be cousins. We would still spend all the holidays together and never have to worry about a guy keeping us apart. You would be my sister-in-law. That's pretty cool."

I smiled when I heard the sincerity in his voice. "Yes, that would be amazing. I would love that."

"I would too. So, I've decided to focus on that."

"It's a pretty picture."

He grabbed his burger and took a few bites. "You guys don't have to worry about me anymore. Now you can be whatever you want to be, no strings attached."

"That'd be nice. I'd love to have game night or do something else fun. It seems like all of us don't hang out anymore because everything is so complicated. It's such a relief that it doesn't need to be that way anymore."

"Yeah, it is."

"More importantly, I'm glad the two of you are brothers again. He really loves you."

"Yeah...I know he does."

I sipped my soda and felt the weight disappear from my shoulders. Now I didn't have to tiptoe around Colton anymore. I could spill my heart out to him and tell him how much I loved Finn, how happy I was every single day. "Finn and I went to this dinner party that his work hosted—"

"He took you to a work function?" he asked in surprise.

"He gave me his necklace, but you find that surprising?"

"Good point." He kept eating. "What happened there?"

"That stupid skank Layla happened."

"Ooh...that bitch."

"She was wearing the most inappropriate dress for a work event, an obvious hook, line, and sinker for Finn. She strutted up to him, did the whole thing where she flipped her hair and batted her eyelashes, making a move on him right in front of me."

"Please tell me you slapped her." Colton grabbed a handful

of fries. "She needs to lay off Finn. She's been trying to get his dick since he moved here."

"I didn't need to. Finn said I was his girlfriend, and that chased her off."

"Wow, another thing I didn't expect Finn to do."

"Neither did I. But that's what he said...and I melted right on the spot. We'd never really talked about the future up to that point. I didn't want to scare him off because I knew he was weird about commitment. He's been drifting around his whole life. I knew if I let him warm up to the idea on his own, he would get there. And he did."

"I can't believe this guy is my brother. He's a whole new man."

"I know."

"And I like this version a lot more than the old one." He kept eating, seeming truly relaxed, as if discussing Finn really didn't make him uncomfortable.

"Me too. Then we were at dinner the other night, and we ran into Jax."

"Ooh...that must have been awkward."

"Finn was in the bathroom at the time. Jax said he was sorry for the way he ended our relationship, not that I care because I haven't thought about him much since we broke up. Then Finn came back, and shit got really awkward."

"I bet," he said with a chuckle. "Finn isn't a man you want to piss off."

"No, he's not. Jax left, and Finn was irritated I didn't mention Finn and I were dating. But I didn't have a chance. The whole interaction took place in two minutes."

"Finn had a chance to tell Layla..."

"But he works with her all the time. Hopefully, I'll never see Jax again."

"Good point."

I picked up my burger again and ate half of it before I washed it down with my root beer. It was such a relief to feel like friends again, the kind that could talk about anything, especially the people we were sleeping with.

"I wonder when he'll tell my parents."

"I don't know. We haven't talked about it."

"I think my parents would be really thrilled about it. They love you, and they'll love finding a way to keep you in the family."

"I hope so. I was worried they might just think it's weird..."

He shrugged. "When they see you together, they won't think it's weird. My mom has always been afraid that Finn would never settle down. She'll be able to realize that he's found someone, especially someone she likes."

"Yeah, I guess that's true. I'll let him decide when he's ready. The key with Finn is not to push him into anything—let him get there on his own."

"I think he's already ready," Colton said. "That necklace meant a lot to him, and he didn't hesitate to give it to you. That could only mean one thing."

My fingers absentmindedly came into contact with the necklace, thinking about the morning when I woke up with it clutched in my hand. Finn gave it to me freely, for no reason at all. He didn't wear his heart on his sleeve, but I could see it in his eyes. Even if he didn't tell me he loved me or even felt that way yet, he obviously felt something special for me. In his eyes, I was one in a million. I was his. And he wouldn't give away his necklace unless he thought he would still see it every day.

I didn't need to hear his pledge of love to know how he felt.

Not when he declared it in his own way.

WHEN I GOT HOME from work, I called him.

"Hey, baby." He answered the phone in his typical deep voice, a sound that left most women paralyzed.

Including me. "I had lunch with Colton today. He told me about the long talk you had."

The sound of keys and footsteps filled the background, along with Soldier barking. "Yeah, it went well. Now I'm leaving the house to pick him up. We're going to the Mariners game."

"Yeah, he mentioned that. I'm so happy you guys made up."

"Me too. I should get going. I'm already running late."

"Of course. You want to sleep over when you drop him off?" I didn't get to see Finn last night, and if I didn't see him tonight, that would be two nights in a row. For most relationships in the beginning stages, that was fine, but now that I was having the best sex of my life, just one night without it was too much for me.

"I got stuck with the morning shift again, so since I'm gonna be out late, I think I'm just gonna go home."

"Alright…" I tried to mask my disappointment but failed miserably.

"But I'm off the following day. How about you come over then?"

At least that gave me something to look forward to. "Okay. I guess I can wait that long."

"Miss me already?"

The teasing tone in his voice turned me into a puddle on the floor. All I wanted to do was tell him that I was so deeply in love with him, it scared me. I wasn't one of those women who were obsessed with getting married. After my divorce, the idea of getting remarried terrified me, but now I wanted to rush into it at a sprint. I wanted to come home to him every day, see him leave for work every morning. "I always miss you…"

He was quiet over the line, letting the emotional statement

echo in both of our minds. "I miss you too. I'll see you soon." Then he abruptly hung up.

"How was the game?"

Colton had stopped by on his lunch break, splitting his sandwich with me at the counter. "Good. We all ate hot dogs and chugged down as much beer as we could. The game went into extra innings, so we were there pretty late. I've been so tired at work, but it was totally worth it." He held the sandwich to his mouth and took a bite.

"I'm glad you guys had fun. Was it awkward in the beginning?"

"A little, I guess. He was kinda quiet. But Finn is always kinda quiet."

"Yeah, I guess that's true."

"We got a lot of free beers while we were there. Women kept buying us rounds—"

"You mean, buying Finn rounds?" I rolled my eyes because it was impossible for that man to go anywhere without getting free shit.

He shrugged. "I was trying to be sensitive."

"I know I need to get used to it, but I never do."

"That would get old after a while. I would hate to watch men hit on Tom everywhere we went. But if it makes you feel any better, Finn keeps his eyes to himself."

"I know he does." He was a loyal and faithful man. He would never fool around on me, even if he could get away with it. That was the kind of man he was. If he committed to something, he was completely invested.

"He dropped me off pretty late then went home."

"I asked him to sleep over, but he said he had to work pretty early this morning."

"He did?" Colton asked. "He told me he had to work at eleven."

"You must have heard him wrong." Finn wouldn't lie to me, and if he had been wrong about his schedule, he would have told me.

"Maybe." He finished his half of the sandwich then looked at the time. "I should head back to work. I was thinking we could have a game night at my place this weekend. You down?"

"Of course. But how are we going to do the teams? You and I always dominate."

"I figured it would be couple teams. You and Finn, me and Tom, and Zach and Stella."

"What about Tatum? She's not seeing anyone right now. Don't want to make her feel left out."

He shrugged. "I'll tell her to bring someone. If she can't, whatever. We'll play anyway." He leaned over the counter and kissed me on the cheek. "See you later, babe."

He hadn't called me that in so long that I forgot how good that nickname felt. Full of affection and familial love, it made me feel like we were back to what we used to be, best friends. "Yeah...see you later."

———

WHEN I GOT HOME, I picked out a sexy piece of lingerie and prepared to go to Finn's place. I packed a bag because I intended to stay there a couple of nights and through the weekend. Now I was so used to sleeping with him that my bed felt lumpy and uncomfortable. His deep breathing was a lullaby I needed to hear to get to sleep. Without it, I tossed and turned until exhaustion finally pulled me under.

He called me a few hours later. "Hey, baby."

"Hey. I just finished packing my bag. You want me to bring anything?"

"Actually, can we do a rain check?"

The disappointment was even worse this time than last time. "Everything alright?"

"Yeah, I've had this crazy migraine since last night, and I'm just not in the mood for company."

Did he consider me company? I considered myself to be more than just company. "You want me to get you anything? I have Tylenol."

"I already took a few. Not doing the trick."

"Maybe you should go to the ER."

"No, I'm not that desperate," he said with a chuckle. "I'll feel better tomorrow. The house is a mess anyway. I've got to catch up on laundry."

I didn't want to accuse him of making excuses, but it was starting to feel like that was what he was doing—making excuses. "Finn, I know you wouldn't lie to me, so I'll believe whatever answer you give me...but is there something wrong?"

He was quiet over the line for a long time.

That wasn't a good sign.

He suddenly turned hostile. "I told you I have a headache." His playfulness disappeared, and now he seemed irritated with me. "We spend a lot of time together. I can't have a few days to myself?"

He'd never spoken to me like that before, like I was the most obnoxious person on the planet. "When I have cramps, I don't act like a bitch. Just because you have a headache doesn't give you the right to be an asshole." I loved this man so much it scared me, but I wouldn't put up with bullshit like this. "Judging from your behavior, I can only assume there is something wrong, but you don't have the balls to tell me what it is. So, you hide behind your excuses like a coward. I didn't realize that was the kind of man you were."

"Don't you—"

"Bye." I hung up on him. And since it was my turn to be an asshole, I turned off my phone.

WHEN A FEW DAYS passed and we didn't talk, I knew things were bad.

He was stubborn like Colton, so he refused to reach out to me after I hung up on him.

Well, I was more stubborn, so two could play that game.

I wouldn't cave. I did nothing wrong, and he was the one acting like a jackass. All I wanted was to spend time with him, and since we were together almost all the time, it wasn't wrong of me to assume nothing had changed.

Despite my anger, I was also scared.

Scared that something terrible was about to happen. We'd been so happy lately, and I didn't know what had happened to change his attitude so drastically. It seemed to take place after he spoke to Colton, and it made wonder if something else transpired during that conversation.

Was Finn going to dump me?

That couldn't be possible. He'd just given me his necklace, something that was so valuable to him. That couldn't be it.

Then what was the problem?

After I finished dinner and drank a bottle of wine on my own, a knock sounded on the door. It was almost nine, so it could only be Colton or Finn. Colton usually went to bed around nine, so it was unlikely to be him.

That meant Finn had caved.

Good. Because I sure as hell wasn't going to.

I peeked through the peephole and saw him standing on the other side, a slight beard growing across his jawline. He was in a black sweater, the dark color contrasting against the fair skin of his face. He was looking at the ground.

I opened the door, my guard up high. "Yes?" I kept one hand on the door, making it clear he wasn't welcome to step inside. Until he apologized and made amends for his behavior, he wasn't a welcome guest in my home.

He lifted his chin and looked at me, his blue eyes dull and lifeless.

I held my ground and suffered through the silence. It was Finn's best attack, but I was used to his intimidating stare.

He finally released a breath through his flared nostrils. "Can I come in?"

"No."

His eyes narrowed. "So you want to have this conversation in the hallway?"

"Doesn't make a difference to me. Colton is asleep."

"How do you know that?"

"Because I do." I started to close the door so less of him was revealed. "Unless you're here to apologize, I don't see what else there is to talk about. Because I'm obviously not going to apologize to you—since I did nothing wrong."

His hands slid into the pockets of his jeans. "I want to talk inside."

"I said that's only going to happen if—"

He yanked the door open and helped himself inside, forcing me back with his size. He pushed the door shut and stepped farther into the room, making me move back because there was nowhere else for me to go. "Yes, I was an asshole. I didn't handle that situation well, and I said some stupid stuff. What I want more than anything is just to forget about it and move on."

I crossed my arms over my chest, my hair and makeup done

because I'd been expecting him to drop by unannounced at some point. "You expect me to drop it without an apology or explanation?"

"I am sorry." He looked me in the eye as he said it, like he wasn't just saying what I wanted to hear. "I was a dick to you when I shouldn't have been. I don't have a good justification for acting that way, so I'm not going to bother. But I want a pass. Can we just forget about it and move on? I'm here because I miss you. I'm here because it's been days since I've had you and I want amazing make-up sex. I'm here because I want to sleep beside you and forget this nightmare ever happened."

So, he wasn't going to dump me. That was a relief. "Why don't you want to tell me what's bothering you?"

He broke eye contact. "I don't want to talk about it. It's pretty simple."

"But what could I have done to make you so angry?"

He bowed his head and sighed. "I said I don't want to talk about it. Let's forget about it."

"But what if it makes you upset again?"

He lifted his head, lost for an answer.

"Tell me, Finn. We can't move on from this unless we talk about it. If I'm doing something that's bothering you, you can tell me. I'll stop. Am I overstaying my welcome at your place? Is my hair stuff hogging up your bathroom? Does it really bother you when I buy Soldier treats?"

"No. You aren't doing anything wrong."

"Then what made you flip out like that?" Now I was drawing a blank, having no idea what would make Finn lie to me and push me away. "You told me you had to work early, but Colton told me that was incorrect. Did you lie to me?"

He closed his eyes for a moment, as if he was embarrassed.

"If you feel like you need to lie to me, then there's something wrong."

"I just wanted space."

"Why? We were happy days ago, and now you've pulled this stunt." His necklace was still around my neck because I never took it off. Even when he pissed me off and I hung up on him, I still didn't take it off.

He kept his mouth shut, refusing to give me an answer.

"Finn, you're scaring me. Everything seemed fine to me until recently. If you're unhappy, I want to know about it."

He took a step back and pulled his hands out of his pockets. "Just let this go, baby. Please."

"I can't."

He watched me for a long time, his eyes filled with unease. "Fine."

I waited for the explanation that would explain all of this strange behavior.

"When I talked to Colton, he told me that you said...you were in love with me."

Once the truth was out in the open, I suddenly felt embarrassed. I didn't think Colton would be stupid enough to tell Finn that, and now my cheeks were reddening in shame and there was nowhere for me to hide. We'd only been dating for a couple months, and that was way too soon to drop a bomb like that... especially on someone like him. Now it all made sense. Colton spooked him, and now he was so uncomfortable, he didn't know what to do.

"Is that true?"

He obviously didn't feel the same way, so I wanted to lie and pretend it never happened. I'd told Colton that in confidence, assuming he would take the secret to the grave. Why the hell would he tell Finn that revelation so nonchalantly? "Colton took that out of context."

"He did?" His left eyebrow rose. "Because he seemed pretty confident about it."

"I started crying when you left with Layla. I said a lot of things out there in the rain, and he must have misheard me." I wished I could come up with a better explanation, but since I was put on the spot, I couldn't think straight. My heart was beating too fast at the moment.

"So, you don't feel that way?" he asked, being more direct and cutting Colton out of the conversation entirely.

I looked him in the eye and lied to his face. "No. Not yet, anyway."

He tilted his head slightly, thinking about what I said. "When Colton told me that...it freaked me out. He started talking about marriage and us having kids together..."

I'm gonna kill him. Fucking kill him.

"He said our kids would be his nieces and nephews. It just... overwhelmed me. We haven't talked about those sorts of things because I don't know what I want in life. I don't know where I'll be in the next five years. I've been a nomad for my entire adult life. Settling down in one spot forever...terrifies me. I'm not scared of anything except that. The mundane, the ordinary." He cupped his face and dragged his palms toward his neck. "It freaked me out. I just needed some space from you."

"Now it makes sense. Thanks for telling me." I kept a diplomatic attitude, but inside, I was a bit heartbroken. I knew Finn didn't want any of those things, at least not right now, but hearing him respond to my love so negatively hurt anyway. "Colton might have the wrong idea about our relationship. He saw me wearing your necklace, and I think he assumed that meant you loved me." That was a reasonable explanation, so I clung to it like a life preserver.

Finn watched me for a long time, his blue eyes filled with a universe of emotions. "I do love you..."

I heard the words so clearly, but I struggled to put stock in their credibility. He was so distressed by the thought of my love that it chased him away, so how could he possibly say those words to me? I stared at him for several heartbeats, examining the heartfelt expression in his eyes for validation. "What...?"

"That's why I'm confused. Everything has happened so fast, and I'm not ready for it. I was fine when it was just us living in the moment, but picturing our future kids and shit just made me angry. I know that's what love leads to. And now that I'm in love...I'm scared that my future is set in stone. I don't want those things, but I also don't want to lose you either."

Everything else seemed irrelevant in comparison to those three little words. Maybe he didn't believe my lie about not being in love with him, or maybe it didn't matter to him if I loved him or not. "I'm sorry Colton upset you with that conversation. I'm not looking for a proposal or a family right now. I've barely been divorced for a year. We have all the time in the world to live in the moment. We can worry about that stuff later."

His shoulders relaxed slightly. "I'm just not sure if I'm ever going to want those things. I can't picture myself being a father. And I know you need to have a family..."

"I do want a family, Finn. I'm not going to lie about what I want in life. I want to go to sleep with the same man for the rest of my life. I want to have children with him, have grandchildren. I want to be in love even when I'm seventy. But we don't need to talk about that stuff right now. I'm sorry Colton provoked you into this conversation you weren't ready to have."

His hands moved to his hips. "I'm sorry I acted like an asshole."

"It's okay. Next time, just talk to me. I'm pretty understanding."

"Yeah...I realize that now." He rested his forehead against mine and closed his eyes. "Any time love is mentioned, it's always the catalyst for proposals and kids. But could we just be two people who really care about each other? That's it?" He pulled his head back and looked at me, showing a vulnerable side he never let the world see.

Now I wished I'd been honest when he'd asked me about my feelings. I'd lied when I shouldn't have, and now I had to admit my wrongdoing. "I lied before...I do love you." My eyes lowered and broke contact because I was ashamed of my embarrassment. I should have just told the truth without caring about the repercussions.

His fingers moved under my chin, and he lifted my face. "You do?"

I looked into his blue eyes and felt weak everywhere. "Yes..."

"Why didn't you tell me that before?"

"I assumed you didn't feel the same way."

"You should never assume with me. You think I would have given you the most valuable thing in my possession if I weren't an idiot in love? You think I would have risked my relationship with my brother to be with you if you weren't the woman of my dreams? You think I'd be monogamous with a woman I wasn't even sleeping with if my heart didn't belong to her? Baby, I've loved you since the moment I kissed you. And I've only loved you more since."

My body turned rigid with the unexpected declaration. He said the most romantic thing, something a rugged man like him had been incapable of feeling. Cold and detached, he was the last man I expected to say such heartfelt things. It was a dream come true, to have this perfect man love me. It made all my past heartache worth it. I suffered so much, but I was now rewarded a million times over. "I love you too..." The air left my lungs in the form of relief, feeling so comfortable getting that secret off my chest. My eyes coated with a thin layer of film because the tears were uncontrollable. I loved him with all my heart, and it felt so good to say it out loud. "When I watched you leave with Layla, it broke my heart. I ran into the rain because I didn't know where else to go. When Colton came after me, I told him I was so in love with you. I told him I was so shattered by you with Layla that I didn't care about anything anymore, even telling him the truth. That was why he wasn't angry with me for being with you...because he saw how hard I'd fallen."

Finn stared at me for a long time, his blue eyes combing over the emotional expressions I was making with my eyes and mouth. "You need to forget about Layla. She's got nothing on you. Yes, she's beautiful and covered in ink, the kind of woman people assume I would want, but I don't want her. There's only one woman who's ever made me feel something—and she's standing right in front of me." His hand cupped my cheek, and his thumb brushed along the curve of my bottom lip. "There's no other woman who could make me faithful without sex. Once Jax was gone, I had my eyes set on you, and I wasn't going to stop until I had you. I could have kept sleeping around, but I just didn't want to. All my interest evaporated like water in a dry riverbed. That lifestyle suddenly felt mundane and exhausting. It was the same bullshit over and over again." His hands moved to my top, and he pulled it over my head, revealing my bare skin underneath. He tugged off his shirt next, displaying the rock-hard, sculpted physique that made all the women go crazy. "Can we just be two people who love each other? With no tomorrow and no yesterday?"

I could fight for the future I wanted, but Finn had already given me plenty to work with. I was still young, so I had years to waste on a man, even if it didn't go anywhere. And if it was going to go somewhere, he had ample time to come to that decision on his own. "Yes..."

We got the rest of our clothes off then made our way into my bedroom. I lay back on the sheets, and Finn moved on top of me, his thighs separating mine as he prepared to take me. He hadn't even kissed me yet, saving it until he was ready. His eyes lingered over the necklace around my neck, the chain that rested in between my tits. "Looks a lot better on you than it ever did on me."

"I don't agree with that." I loved feeling that metal drag against my skin as he moved on top of me, the steel making my skin prickle because of the history it contained. My fingers started at his chiseled stomach then slowly moved up the grooves until I reached his hard chest. My fingers felt the warmth of his skin, brushed against the artwork all over his body.

He studied my expression as his dick slowly pressed inside me. He squeezed between my lips and forced me wide apart as he made his slow entrance. His crown came into contact with my moisture, and he groaned quietly from deep in the back of his throat. Slowly, he sank farther inside, moving through the slickness as he laid siege to the land he already conquered so many times.

My hands held on to his biceps as I felt him enter me so deeply. I released a shaky breath, feeling my body obey his command to stretch as far as I could. As if it were the first time we were together, we took our time and savored every second.

When he was deep inside me, he lowered his mouth to mine and kissed me.

I drew in a harsh breath when I felt his lips. Showered with love, I felt like the only woman who mattered. I was the only one to have him this intimately, skin-on-skin. I was the only woman he ever loved, the only woman who made him so committed. It made me feel like the most beautiful woman in the world, a woman Layla could never possibly compete with.

He moved inside me as he kept kissing me, making love to me with slow thrusts. He cared more about the movements of our lips than the thrust of our bodies. Every time he moved inside me, he pushed himself as deep as he could go. "I love you, baby."

My arms wrapped around his neck, and I pulled him tightly against me, feeling myself slip away even further. Just when I thought I couldn't love him more, I did. He blanketed me with his beautiful affection, made my toes curl for a whole new reason. "I love you too."

9

COLTON

Pepper burst into my apartment the following morning without knocking. "I've got a bone to pick with you." She shut it hard behind herself then marched to the dining table where I was sitting and enjoying breakfast.

I was about to drink my coffee, but I slowly lowered it back to the surface instead. "What did I do now?"

She strode to the table and looked down at me, two conflicting emotions on her face. She smiled like she was the happiest person in the world, but her eyes were also narrowed like she wanted to slap me upside the head. "You told Finn that I was in love with him? What the hell were you thinking?"

"Uh...I thought he already knew."

"You can't just make assumptions like that. I told you that in confidence."

"Everything you say to me is in confidence, you know that. But I just assumed you guys were at that level already. You know I wouldn't betray your trust on purpose."

"I know. I'm kinda stuck in the middle between being mad at you and being happy with you."

I raised an eyebrow. "Okay, now I'm lost."

"When you told Finn all that stuff, it freaked him out a little, so he ignored me for a few days. When he finally confronted me, he told me what you said and said he wasn't ready for something serious. Marriage and kids freak him out. But he also told me he loved me...and that wouldn't have happened if you hadn't scared him. So I'm happy with you but also pissed at you."

"In that case...I'm sorry and you're welcome."

She poured herself a mug of coffee then sat down. "Thank you and I forgive you." She added sugar into the black coffee and took a drink.

"So, are we good, then?"

She shrugged. "I guess." When the conversation was finished, her smile emerged, like the sun breaking through the clouds. "I understand Finn is nomadic and settling down forever scares him, but I'm just happy we made it to this point in our relationship. I honestly thought he would never love me."

"I think it's obvious that he does. What else would that necklace mean?" I knew I was really over the situation with my brother when I could have this conversation without feeling my blood pressure spike. There was no anger or resentment on my part. Now it seemed like she was talking about any guy.

"I just wasn't expecting him to be so blunt about it. I thought he might feel something for me, but I never expected him to admit it."

"He's an honest guy."

"I guess so." She drank her coffee again, smiling as she looked into the blackness.

This was exactly what I wanted, to see Pepper happy and in love. I wanted her to have everything she deserved, a good man who treated her right. Finn was the last person I'd expected to fill that role, but he filled it well. "I'm happy for you."

She lifted her gaze and met mine. "Really?"

I nodded. "Looks like Finn stepped up. I couldn't be happier for you." I'd feared he would break her heart and kick her to the curb, but he ended up being the romantic guy she dreamed about.

Her eyes softened. "Thank you, Colton. I don't think I've ever been so happy." When she realized what she said, she tried to correct it. "I just mean—"

"I understand, Pepper. We were really happy, but there was always something missing. I feel that missing link when I'm with Tom. You obviously feel it with Finn. That's a good thing. We can still have each other in our lives, but we also have what we really want. I think this is the best thing that ever happened to us."

"That's a good way to put it."

"So, you're okay with Finn saying he doesn't want to settle down?"

"He didn't really say it was off the table. He's just not in that place right now, which is fine. We've only been together a couple months. I'm young, so I have time to waste. Maybe in a few years, he'll feel differently. Just the fact that he's in this relationship and saying he loves me is a big step for him. I'm sure he can take that next step in the future...when he's warmed up to the idea."

"Yeah, you're probably right. He just needed to find the right woman to get his shit together."

She smiled. "And I guess I'm that woman."

———

FINN and I got a drink after work. He'd worked the morning shift, so he was off at the same time I was. We went to the same bar we always went to, grabbing a booth with a nice view of the TVs.

The tension had disappeared now that I'd forgiven him, but

there was still a hint of awkwardness that would take longer to evaporate. But at least we were talking again, not yelling at each other.

Finn ordered a beer.

I raised an eyebrow. "No scotch?"

He shook his head. "Pepper says I drink too much hard liquor."

"I've told you the same thing."

"Yeah, but she's the boss in the relationship."

"She is?" I asked in surprise, shocked a man like Finn would say that.

He shrugged. "I let her think she is. Gets me better sex."

Finn just mentioned fucking my ex-wife, and I was surprised it didn't make me throw up in my mouth a little. I knew they were sleeping together almost every night, so maybe I'd become desensitized to the whole thing.

"Sorry," he said. "When I have a drink in my hand, I can't control what I say."

"It's alright. I'm the same way."

Layla emerged from the direction of the bar, in denim jeans with a tube top that showed her ink along her arms and chest. She came up from behind Finn, holding a short glass with amber liquid inside. It seemed like she was bringing Finn his favorite drink. "Heads up. Layla is on her way."

Finn bowed his head and sighed, his frustration palpable.

She reached the table and set the glass down. "What is that? Beer?" With one hand on her hip, she posed like a model on the runway, hoping Finn would admire her curves in the skintight clothing.

I was tempted to throw my beer on her clothes, in defense of Pepper.

Finn looked up at her, not pasting a fake smile on his lips. He felt annoyed so he looked annoyed. "I'm good with the beer.

Now I'll get back to my conversation. My brother and I are talking about something pretty serious."

"Ooh...drama." She continued to do her best to flirt with Finn, even though he clearly wasn't interested. "That's what you need a scotch for—or several. And I could always give you a ride home."

Was that her master plan? To get Finn drunk and take advantage of him? If I were a woman, I'd yank her hair out of her scalp.

Finn wasn't a patient man, and judging from the hostility in his eyes, he didn't have a drop of patience left inside him. "Layla, you know I have a girlfriend."

Her eyes fell as her perkiness evaporated.

"And even if I didn't have a girlfriend, I don't get involved with coworkers. So you need to drop this act. I'm not interested, and I'll never be interested. Stop sending me drinks, stop flirting with me, and just give me space. You're a beautiful woman who should have more self-respect. Don't throw yourself at a man who clearly doesn't want you. It's desperate and pathetic."

My eyes looked down into my drink because I suddenly felt awkward, wishing I weren't there to witness the biggest insult in the world. Finn didn't put her down gently. He publicly humiliated her and would probably send her to the bathroom where she could cry in the bathroom stall. I clenched my jaw tightly and tried to fade into the background.

Layla stayed at the table, her eyes burning with hatred at Finn's dismissal. "Your girlfriend isn't even that pretty. I don't know what you see in her."

My head slowly turned back to her, like I was gasoline and she was the match. She immediately set me on fire with rage, talking about the woman I loved with so much disrespect. "Bitch, what did you just say?"

Layla turned to me, seeming to remember I was there.

"Pepper is the hottest bitch in this place, and you're nothing but a trashy-ass skank." I slammed my beer down and caused the contents to spill over the rim. "And any woman who has the audacity to insult another woman like that is nothing but a whore. So get the fuck out of my face before I pour this shit all over you."

Layla obviously felt outnumbered because she turned around and walked off.

I yelled after her. "Don't come back here. Pepper's girls will shove your head in the toilet and drown your ass." I grabbed my beer and took a long drink, wishing she were a dude that I could drag outside and throw in a dumpster. "Dumb bitch…"

Finn couldn't restrain the smile that slowly crept over his face. He looked at me with a mix of admiration and humor. "I've never heard you talk shit like that."

"Neither have I. But she pissed me off."

"I'll say…" He chuckled.

"Who the hell does she think she is?"

"A hot piece of ass who's used to getting whatever she wants." He pushed the glass of scotch to the side because he obviously had no intention of drinking it. "She probably doesn't even want me that much. She just hates the fact that she can't have me."

"I doubt it. She seems pretty determined."

He shrugged. "That little stunt just made me hate her more."

"That sucks you have to work with her."

"I don't care. I just do my job and go home." He drank from his beer and returned to being relaxed, like a fight hadn't almost just broken out. "I like the way you defended Pepper. That was sweet."

"I'm not letting some ho talk about her like that. *Not that pretty*?" I rolled my eyes. "Pepper doesn't need a bunch of tattoos and makeup to be pretty. She could roll out of bed and still turn heads."

"I couldn't agree more. I thought Layla would forget about me when she realized I had a girlfriend. Guess not."

"Well, she better forget about you now. Because Stella is gonna break her nose. She works out like every single day, so she's strong. She'll beat her unconscious then shave her head."

"I have a feeling Pepper wouldn't want that."

I rolled my eyes. "She's too classy for revenge."

"And she already has me. What's better than that?"

"In this case, I don't think that's enough."

We watched TV for a while as the tension slowly dissipated. I was still angry about the whole thing, and until Layla had a black eye, I wouldn't be satisfied. But as we drank more beer and talked, we slowly started to forget about the ordeal. "So...Pepper told me about that big conversation you had."

"I guess I should assume that she'll tell you everything that happens between us?"

"Yep."

"That's not weird at all..."

"Well, she doesn't share every single detail. The personal stuff stays personal...and I wouldn't want to know those details anyway."

"That's a relief."

"I'm sorry I freaked you out with everything I said about marriage and kids. I assumed that's where you guys were. Giving her your military dog tags is a pretty big deal...I just assumed."

"You should have assumed I loved her, because I do."

It was the first time I'd heard him say that, and I wished I'd caught it on camera because I'd assumed Finn would never feel that way about a woman as long as he lived. But the confession rolled off his tongue so easily, like he wasn't ashamed in the least.

"But marriage..." He shook his head. "I'm not interested in that right now."

"It's only been a few months."

"I have a different philosophy about life. It's unconventional, so most people don't agree with it. Marriage seems to be an age-old practice for a man to control a woman, so she can give him children and carry on his legacy. Nowadays, marriage seems important for raising a family. But if there're no children in the mix, then there's no reason to be married. Can't you just be with someone you love and have that be enough?"

I drank my beer as I considered what he said. "Pepper and I didn't have children, and we loved being married. Those years were some of the happiest of my life. Marriage isn't about having a family or owning a woman. It's when two people love each other and want that to be recognized by the world. It's different from just living with someone or being in a relationship with someone. It's a lot more special. You've only been in a relationship for a few months, so maybe in a few years you'll start to broaden your understanding of the different levels of love and commitment."

"I don't know... I like knowing I could still do anything I want in my life. I could return to the army. I could work with Doctors Without Borders. I could literally do anything."

"Why couldn't you do that while being married?"

He held his beer as he stared at me.

"Why can't you have both?" I pressed. "People do it all the time."

He shrugged. "Pepper is rooted here because of you and her business."

"But she would give it up in a heartbeat if you wanted to relocate."

He shook his head slightly. "I don't believe that."

"I do. She would prefer to be close to me, but we both have

our own lives. I'll be married someday with my own family. We can't always be best friends who live across the hall from each other."

He drank his beer then returned the empty bottle to the coaster. "I told her I'm not ready for that kind of commitment so we should stop talking about it." Once he reached his threshold of thinking about the future, he shut off.

I didn't push it. He'd just told Layla off, so it was clear he was committed to Pepper as much as he could be in that moment. "Are you going to tell Mom and Dad?"

"Tell them what?"

"About Pepper."

His eyes moved to the TV in the corner, and he watched the recap of the Mariners game as he thought about his answer. "I don't know. If I tell Mom, she'll have the exact same reaction as you...talking about babies and shit. But if I don't tell her, she'll find out some other way and slap me silly."

"There's another option. She might be weird about the whole situation."

"I doubt it. She loves Pepper. If there's a way to keep her in the family, Mom'll be thrilled about it."

Yeah, probably. "You know, I never imagined you would be a one-woman kind of guy. But here you are...turning down sexy women without batting an eye."

My brother shook his head a few times before he answered. "I didn't think this would happen either. But there's something about Pepper that makes me different. The moment I met her, there was something there. Everything she said fascinated me. When she dated that loser guy, I kept thinking she could do better. Every time I would see her first thing in the morning, I thought she was so beautiful. Whenever I would go out to the bars and pick up a woman, I wished Pepper were the person I was taking home." He stared at his empty glass when he finished his speech.

"When did you fall in love with her?" Hearing my brother have real feelings for someone made me happy. I didn't want him to be alone his entire life. I wanted him to have someone who would love him for his good qualities as well as his flaws. If Pepper was that woman, so be it.

It didn't take him long to come up with an answer. "The first time I kissed her. I know that because I've never felt so much adrenaline in my chest from kissing someone. I felt like a teenager."

"When was this?"

"A long time ago now. She was kinda seeing Jax at the time. It was just the two of us on the couch, and she asked if I felt the chemistry between us. Any time we were in a room together, I could feel this charge in the air. There was more sexual tension in that moment than in all my lays combined. I told her yes then kissed her. I knew it was wrong, but I couldn't stop myself. I kissed her, and it felt so damn right." He didn't look at me as he spoke. "We talked about it later and agreed it couldn't happen again. I wanted her so much, but I valued my relationship with you more. So did she. But as the weeks passed...it just became more and more difficult. When Jax was gone, I couldn't restrain myself anymore. I've never wanted anything so much in my life."

Now I felt bad for giving him such a hard time about it. "Why didn't you tell me you loved her? If you had, I would have been a lot more understanding."

"I wasn't ready to admit how I felt. I wasn't even sure how I felt. Could I really love a woman that quickly? I'm a pessimistic person with a constant level of skepticism. Maybe what I felt was lust. Maybe it was something else. But love...I didn't think I was capable of it."

"Everyone is capable of love, Finn."

"I don't know if I believe that. I think I was only capable of love because she's a special person. If I'd never met her, maybe I never would have known love at all."

I WALKED across the hall and let myself into her apartment. "It's me."

"Do you knock?" She stepped out of the bedroom, straightening her top and fixing her hair.

"I figured Finn wasn't here."

"So? I don't burst in to your apartment."

I raised an eyebrow. "You do every morning."

"But the morning is different. You and Tom won't be on the couch having sex at seven in the morning."

"Hey, it could happen. We both wake up early on the weekends."

"Well, I've got a super-hot boyfriend, so you should definitely knock from now on."

"Message received." I saluted her. "I wanted to tell you about my run-in with Layla."

Pepper walked to the kitchen and grabbed a bottle of wine from her cabinet. Without asking me if I wanted any, she grabbed two glasses and filled them both. "That bitch..." She carried the glasses to the couch and sat beside me. "She reminds me of a gnat. She's an insect that just won't go away, no matter how hard you throw your hand around." She took a drink and smeared her purple lipstick against the glass.

"I was out with Finn when she made another pass at him."

She rolled her eyes so hard as she took another drink. "I actually feel bad for the girl. She's making herself look like an idiot."

She was taking this better than I thought she would.

"Let me guess, she bought him another scotch."

"Yep."

"I bet she spiked it with the date-rape drug."

"Wouldn't surprise me."

"What else happened?"

"Finn told her off. That was fun to watch."

"He did?" She held her glass at her side and grinned. "Sounds about right."

"Told her to get some self-respect and stop acting desperate."

She slapped her knee and laughed so hard. "Oh my god. I can't believe he said that."

"Finn has always been blunt..."

"But still. He works with this woman."

"I don't think he cares. Then she said she didn't think you were very pretty...so I lost my shit. I went into full-blown bitch mode. If she were a dude, I would have punched her so hard her nose would have been permanently broken."

"That's very sweet of you, Colt. You always have my back."

"Hell yeah, I do."

"But her insult is meaningless. She's just pissed that I'm the one fucking Finn and she's not. I almost can't blame her. I can't blame any woman for hating me. He's a real man, and there's so few of those in the world now. He's so straightforward, and it's refreshing. He doesn't get jealous or controlling. He's just...perfect."

"I don't know about the perfect part, but he's definitely macho."

"He's not macho either. I can't explain it."

A knock sounded on the door. "Are you expecting anyone?"

"No. But it must be Finn." She set down her glass. "Come in."

The door opened, and Finn stepped inside, wearing a gray zip-up jacket with black jeans. The hood was over his head, probably because it was raining outside. He pulled it back and revealed his face, his clean jawline and his ocean-blue eyes. "Girls' night?"

I flipped him off.

He chuckled as he watched Pepper rise from the couch and walk toward him. "You look beautiful."

"In a sweater and jeans?" she asked, mildly surprised.

"In anything."

She rose onto her tiptoes, wrapped her arms around his neck, and kissed him right in front of me.

His large hands circled her petite body, and he pulled her hard into his chest as he continued the kiss.

I looked away and took a long drink of my wine, uncomfortable with their affection. It had nothing to do with the fact that he was my brother. It was just awkward to watch anyone make out unless it was in a porno.

Pepper was the first one to pull away. "What brings you by?"

"Do I need a reason?" He squeezed her ass cheek then let her go.

"No, of course not. You want some wine?"

He made a face. "I don't have the palate for it."

I rose to my feet, knowing I should leave because they probably wanted to be alone. "I should get going. I'll put on some dinner then do paperwork."

"Nonsense." Pepper grabbed my hand and pushed me back down onto the couch. "There's no reason why the three of us can't hang out."

"Good point." Finn moved into the kitchen and raided her fridge for a beer.

I lowered my voice so only Pepper could hear. "It's really fine if you guys want to be alone—"

"We can be alone later. How about we order a pizza and watch a movie?"

I appreciated the fact that she made me feel included even if

I was crashing their privacy. She wanted us to all be close, to still have the same friendships we used to have. "Alright...if you're sure it's okay."

"It's definitely okay. This has been my dream for a long time."

"What?"

She smiled. "This...the three of us together."

10

PEPPER

I woke up that morning with my head on Finn's chest. It was a cold and rainy day outside, but I was so warm with this personalized heater beside me. His chest rose and fell slowly, rocking my head like I was a baby. I could hear Soldier snoring lightly from the edge of the bed.

Rain or shine, every day was a beautiful day when I woke up beside this man. There was always a smile on my face and a fullness in my soul. I could do this every day for the rest of my life if he asked me to.

Hopefully, he would ask someday.

I opened my eyes and looked down his body, seeing the top half of his big dick peeking out from underneath the sheets bunched at his waist. His morning wood was always impressive, especially when it was pointed right at me like it had a mind of its own.

I propped myself up on my elbow and looked at his handsome face. Every morning there was a slight shadow on his chin because his hair grew in overnight. He was so strict about his appearance that he shaved the hair away as soon as he brushed his teeth. It was a nice look on him, but then again, he looked beautiful no matter what his appearance was.

I shifted my body closer to his waist and opened my mouth wide to take in his perfect cock. He was impressively thick instead of just long. He had a nice girth, beautiful ridges, and his crown actually deserved a real crown on top. He kept his balls perfectly maintained, and his length had only a very slight curve that pointed to the right. A large vein ran along his shaft, more noticeable the harder he became. I pressed a kiss to his head then parted my lips to take him, getting off on the fact that he was mine to taste and no one else's. I flattened my tongue and moved down, bringing him into the warmth of my throat.

He moaned quietly, his body slightly shifting as he became aware of the warm mouth around his length.

I moved him to the back of my throat then out again, going at a gentle pace that would feel good without waking him up. I could taste the come from the night before along his crown, and I gobbled that up like I hadn't already had enough.

He slowly woke up to the feeling of my mouth around his length. Quiet moans filled the bedroom, and his muscled legs tightened in pleasure. His breathing picked up, and his hand slowly glided to my hair. "Good morning to you too, baby." His hand moved to the back of my neck, and he guided me up and down, showing me the easy pace he liked.

I pushed him until I was inches away from his balls then pulled back again. I wanted to take all of him, but since it would make me gag, I stayed conservative. I kept my tongue flat as a cushion and moved him in then out again.

He lay back with his head on the pillow, his eyes closed as he enjoyed it. His breathing grew deeper and louder as the pleasure continued. His fingers rested against my neck, but he didn't guide me anymore. Now, he just enjoyed it.

I pulled him out of my mouth then straddled his hips,

wanting to get off because his big dick in my mouth had turned me on so much. I leaned forward and arched my back as I grabbed his base and slowly lowered myself onto his length. Inch by inch, I took him, my saliva providing the perfect lubrication for him to sink with no friction.

He moaned louder that time.

I leaned forward and gripped his forearms for balance, restraining him at the same time so he couldn't touch me. I slowly sank down and arched my back, getting him deep before I rose again. Having his dick in my mouth had made me so wet, so I moaned as I treasured his long length inside me, worshiping his dick because it was god's gift to women. And for now, god's gift to me.

He watched me with an intense expression, that sexy look he gave without even trying. He showed it to me even when we weren't fucking, like when he liked the dress I wore or when he wanted me from across the room. He fought against me as he tried to grab my hips.

I pushed him back down and kept rocking. "No."

He released an irritated breath, his cock throbbing inside me.

Like he was just a man I was using for sex, I fucked his dick and rubbed my clit against his hard body, bringing myself to a climax that made me coat him in a flood of wetness. My pussy clenched him like an iron fist, and I came, my nipples so hard, they could slice through concrete.

He thickened inside me more, groaning as he watched me come around his dick.

I rocked into him hard as I finished, working my back muscles as I pounded him until I was finished. I slowed down once I was done, using him to my satisfaction. My fingers stopped digging into his muscular forearms, and I returned to a slower, more seductive pace.

Finn got a hold of my arm then yanked me toward him, forcing my back to curve further as I came close to him. He propped himself up on his elbows then dug his hand into my hair, bringing us close together for a kiss.

It was so good, I almost stopped moving.

With his gentle breaths filling my mouth, he kissed me slowly, his lips feeling mine with masculine purpose. He loved my upper and lower lip equally, taking his time with each one before he supplemented the embrace with his tongue.

God...this man.

He lowered his hand and supported himself as he continued the kiss, as his cock throbbed with desperation between my legs. He breathed into me with quiet moans, so visibly turned on by me that I felt stunning.

I wanted this every day for the rest of my life. I wanted him to be the only man inside me until the day I died. If he felt the same way, I would run down to the courthouse and become his wife. I'd never felt so certain about anything in my life. Even with Colton, there wasn't this degree of belief.

It was different with Finn.

"Damn, baby." He spoke into my mouth between kisses. "I love you..."

My kiss stopped so I could inhale a deep breath. He turned me on all over again, made me want to ride his dick until I had another climax. My fingers felt numb, and my breath felt shaky. Hearing him confess his feelings so easily was so sexy. He'd never said those words to another woman before. I was his one and only in so many ways. It made me feel special, made me question my love for the other men in my life. "I love you too."

He bent his head down and kissed my tits, his tongue swiping over the nipples. His warm breath fell across my skin and made bumps appear everywhere. His cock thickened inside me, and his body tightened as he prepared to come.

"No." I sat on his dick.

His blue eyes narrowed.

"I want to come again." I rose directly up and down, riding his dick from tip to base. I gripped my ass cheeks and spread them as I pushed his length through my pussy lips.

He closed his eyes and moaned. "Fuck..."

"You can come when I say so. Not a moment sooner."

He pressed his lips tightly together and groaned. "Yes, baby."

FINN DRIBBLED the ball in his driveway, shirtless and in his workout shorts. His torso was covered with blank ink, and his muscles shifted under his skin with every move he made. The prominent V of his hips was distracting, and the tightness of his back made him look like a sculpture rather than a human.

Zach stood next to the hoop, shirtless and muscular, but not possessing that layer of ink. "Make your shot, asshole."

Finn smirked and kept dribbling.

Colton was the only one with a shirt on. "You're just going to make him take more time."

"You're really that stubborn?" Zach asked incredulously.

Just to make his point, Finn kept dribbling.

I sat on the grass with Soldier in front of me, rubbing him behind the neck and digging my fingers into his fur. My fingertips had turned black from the dirt in his hair, but that never stopped me from giving him affection.

Stella was beside me, rubbing his head.

Tom was on the other side, rubbing his back. "Man, this dog has it made."

"I wish I were a dog," Stella said. "People think you're cute all the time and give you massages and treats...and they never really gain any weight."

"You aren't going to play?" I asked Tom.

"No," he said with a laugh. "I don't even know how to drible. I'm not a sports kinda guy. I'm more of a couch-potato kinda guy."

Colton walked toward us with his hands on his hips. "You know, it would be nice if we had a fourth player. We could make teams."

Tom stared at him blankly. "I hope that statement wasn't directed at me. I have no coordination...unless it's in the bedroom."

Colton grinned as his cheeks tinted slightly. "What about you? Stella, you're fit."

"So?" she countered. "Why would I want to play basketball when I could hang out with Soldier? He's the best-looking guy I've ever seen."

"Hey," Zach said in offense.

"Sorry," Stella said with a shrug. "It's true."

Finn finally made the shot and let the ball fall through the net. "Baby, get your ass up and play with us."

I cocked an eyebrow. "You better not be talking to me with that tone."

He walked toward me, his hard chest glistening with a beautiful sheen of sweat. "You bet I am. We need another player, so you're up."

"I don't play basketball," I argued.

"But you watch basketball. You know the game better than any of us."

"So?" I countered, copping an attitude.

"Get up, or I'll make you." He turned back to the hoop.

"Ooh..." Stella turned to me. "Let him make you. That sounds pretty hot."

I got to my feet and brushed the grass off my butt. "This is payback, isn't it?" I rode him for a long time yesterday, pleasing myself and making him wait until I was completely satisfied. It was torture for him.

He grabbed the ball and passed it to me. "Something like that."

"You wanna be on my team?" Colton asked.

"Sure." I dribbled the ball and passed it to him.

We got the game started, and I had a hard time running around in my tight jeans and shoes. Thankfully, Finn's driveway wasn't the size of a full court because I would really be in trouble.

Colton passed me the ball, and I prepared to make a shot from the back corner.

Finn stormed me, towering over me with his height so I couldn't possibly throw the ball without him stealing it. He even put his hands on my hips and gripped me while he wore an evil grin.

I slapped his hand away. "That's a foul."

"What are you gonna do about it?" He wrapped his arms around my waist and kissed me, making me lose my grip on the ball.

"What the hell?" Colton snapped. "One, that's gross. And two, you're a damn cheater."

"Thanks, baby." He took the ball and dribbled to the hoop. Then he sank a two-pointer.

Colton turned to me, furious, with his hands on his hips. "You just let that happen?"

"It happened really fast, okay?" I countered.

He rolled his eyes and got the ball from Zach. "Keep it in your pants."

At that moment, a couple of girls walking their small dog passed the house on the sidewalk. They stared at the guys without their shirts, while they wore tight little shorts and tops even though it wasn't that warm of a day.

Stella glared at them.

I could tell they were mainly looking at Finn, but I'd stopped caring about the attention he constantly received. When a man was that pretty, it was inevitable. I could throw a tantrum every time or just let it be.

Zach stole the ball from Colton and then quickly passed it to Finn.

Finn was close to me, but he made the shot before I could even do anything.

I put my hands on my hips and glared at Colton. "What the hell was that?"

He dropped his head in defeat.

Finn grabbed me again, his large hands pressing on the small of my back as he pulled me into his chest. He gave me another kiss, angling his neck down so he could give me a passionate embrace right on the court. "You suck at basketball. But at least you're good at sex." He smacked my ass before he turned away to get the ball again.

I turned back to the end of the driveway and saw that the girls had moved on. I wasn't sure if Finn saw them and wanted them to know he wasn't available by being affectionate with me. Or he didn't notice they were there at all…and wanted to kiss me for no reason whatsoever. I wasn't sure which was better.

———

I WALKED across the hall and knocked before I barged inside. "It's me."

"Come in." Colton's voice sounded from the couch.

I walked inside and found Colton and Tom sitting on the couch, leaning forward as they watched the news. "You guys are watching the news?" In my three years of being married to Colton, he'd never watched the news. Not once.

"You haven't heard about this crazy storm?" Colton looked over his shoulder and faced me over the couch. "Florida is about to be hit by two hurricanes. The winds are already over a hundred miles an hour."

"Oh wow…" I moved to the back of the couch and rested my hands along the top. "No, I didn't hear about that."

"It's called the storm of the century," Tom said. "A lot of people are going to lose their homes."

"Scary," Colton said. "I know it rains here all the time, but at least we never get hurricanes."

"Not yet, anyway…" I whispered under my breath.

Colton turned down the volume and rose to his feet. "So, what brings you here?"

"I need a reason?"

He crossed his arms over his chest. "You're hungry, aren't you?"

I shrugged. "No…but if you guys had extra, I would help you out."

He rolled his eyes. "You never change, do you?" He walked to the kitchen and started pulling out the ingredients from the fridge and cabinets.

"Nope."

"Is Finn working tonight?"

"Unfortunately. He prefers nights, but I like it when he works in the morning. We're off at the same time."

He filled a pot with boiling water then set it on the stove. "He probably likes working nights so he doesn't have to see you— and cook for you."

"He loves cooking for me."

He pulled the pasta out of the plastic bag. "No…it's not the cooking he enjoys."

I chuckled. "Yeah, probably not."

"He cooks for you so he can get dessert later."

Everything finally felt normal, like Colton was really okay with me being with Finn. It was so relaxing, it practically felt like a vacation. "Need any help?"

"No. You'll just wreck it."

"Come on, give me more credit than that. Who's the one who had salt in their apartment?"

He broke the pasta noodles in half and dropped them into the pot. "You had a bottle of three-year-old salt, and you think you're a chef?"

"I'm just saying, who doesn't have salt in their house?"

"Someone who uses it all the time and runs out, maybe."

Tom spoke from his seat on the couch. "Are you guys still married? Because it sounds like it."

I chuckled. "It does sound like it, huh?"

Colton shrugged. "Some things never change, right?"

"Yep. Sounds right."

I DIDN'T HEAR from Finn the next day. He had to work late, but he usually texted me whenever he woke up the next afternoon.

But my phone was silent.

The boutique was slow because no one needed any sexy lingerie that afternoon. It seemed like when I was busy, I was super busy. And when I was slow, I was dead. It was one extreme or the other.

By the time I got off work, I still hadn't heard from him. I didn't want to be one of those girls who wanted to be with their boyfriend all the time...but when Finn was your boyfriend, that was impossible.

I went to the bar and met Stella and Tatum.

"He doesn't text you in twelve hours, and you freak out?" Stella asked incredulously. "You remind me of Zach. If I don't text him back right away, he thinks I skipped town with some other guy."

"Well, I don't think he's run off with anyone. I just miss him." My beer was untouched in front of me, and I wished I were at his house with Soldier next to me on the couch. If Finn ever asked me to move in, I would give up my apartment in a heartbeat. Not just because his house was nice, but because he came with the place.

"I think it's sweet," Tatum said. "She's in love and wants to be with him all the time."

"I'm beyond in love..." I wiped my finger around the rim of the bottle.

"Wedding bells?" Tatum asked. "Like, ever?"

I shrugged. "He's not thrilled by the idea of commitment, but he's not completely opposed to it."

"It seems like the more handsome a man is, the less likely he is to settle down," Tatum said. "Only when he's humbled by aging does he start to think about settling with one woman."

"Well, I'm not waiting until Finn is forty," I said with a laugh. "Not gonna happen. He's older than me, so that might work in my favor."

"How much older?" Stella asked.

"Four years."

"If you're willing to wait until you're thirty, that could work. He would be thirty-five," Tatum said.

I cringed. "I don't want to get married when I'm thirty. I kinda want to be married by the time I turn twenty-eight, then pop out a kid at thirty."

"Hopefully, he changes his tune by then." Stella drank her cosmo until the glass was empty.

My phone was sitting on the table, and it started to ring. Finn's name appeared on the screen.

"There he is," Tatum said.

"Now she's going to ditch us." Stella rolled her eyes.

I answered, feeling that same thrill shoot down my spine every time I was about to talk to him. "Hey."

"Hey." His deep voice was oddly serious. "What are you doing right now?"

"Drinking with the girls at the bar."

Instead of making a joke or teasing me about something, he stayed serious. "When you're finished, come by the house. I want to talk to you about something." He was unusually abrupt, talking to me like I was a random person rather than his girlfriend. Last time we were together, everything seemed fine. We had sex in the shower, right up against the wall as the water ran down our bodies. But now he spoke like that was the last time we'd ever be together.

"Alright...see you soon." I hung up.

Stella and Tatum obviously overheard his end of the conversation because they both had raised eyebrows and open mouths. "Oh my god," Stella said. "Is he dumping you? Talk about a two-faced asshole."

"It did sound bad," Tatum said. "No one says they need to talk unless it's bad..."

I feared the worst, but my logic also came into play. "He's not going to dump me. We're happy. There's no reason to break it off."

"Unless he's starting to feel smothered," Stella said. "Maybe it's starting to hit him. Guys are weird like that."

"Yeah," Tatum said. "They are."

"Aren't you supposed to be supportive?" I questioned. "Talk me off the ledge?"

"Uh, no," Stella said. "We're supposed to toughen you up and prepare you for the worst. If the guy is gonna dump you, you've got to be prepared to seem indifferent, to show him what he's missing. There's a science to it."

"You really think he's going to dump me?" I asked, starting to worry.

Tatum shrugged. "Well, I don't think he's going to say anything good…"

"Yeah," Stella said. "Whatever it is, it's bad. That's the only thing we know for sure."

I took an Uber to his place and let myself into the house.

Soldier immediately ran up to me and pawed my chest.

I gave him a shorter rub-down than I normally would because my mind was elsewhere. All I could think about was the haunting way Finn had ordered me over here to have an ominous conversation.

I moved into the living room and found him on the couch. The news was on, showing the progress of the crazy storm that was slamming into Florida. The first hurricane had already caused irreparable damage and loss of life. The second one hadn't even struck land yet.

He turned off the TV then rose to meet me. Still brooding and tense, he looked at me like he wasn't the least bit happy I was there. He stopped in front of me and sighed quietly, his jaw clenched tightly and his nostrils slightly flared.

"You're scaring me…" Soldier sat at my side, pushing the top of his head into my palm. It was the only time I ignored the dog because he didn't seem important in this moment. My life was about to change forever.

And Finn had all the power. "I had to go back into work today because of the situation in Florida."

I didn't expect him to address the storm everyone was watching on the news. It was at the opposite end of the country, almost a whole other planet away. What did that have to do with us? "I don't follow."

"The Red Cross is looking for volunteers. There're a lot of people who need medical attention in the streets and in the stadiums. Living conditions will turn fatal once the power is out everywhere, the sewers aren't working properly, and flooding is spreading bacteria all over."

When I'd walked in the door, this was *not* the conversation I expected to have.

"So, I volunteered." His blue eyes were almost apologetic. He stared at me like he'd done something wrong, like he expected a fight to ensue.

I'd been expecting to get dumped, so this came as a relief. "Oh...that's not what I expected you to say."

"What were you expecting me to say?"

I shrugged. "Something much worse than that..."

He rubbed the back of his head and glanced at the blank TV screen. "I thought you would be upset with me."

"Why would I be?" He was offering to drop everything in his life to go help people in need. How could I be upset about that? He wouldn't even get paid, and he didn't care. It was noble.

"Because I'll be gone for a month."

There was the slap in the face, the sting of pain. An entire month would feel like an eternity, especially when I couldn't last a day without him. "Wow...that's a long time."

"There will be a lot of casualties. Even when the storms end, the damage continues."

"But will you be safe?" The weather conditions were bad, but there would also be chaos. I didn't want him to be killed trying to save someone else.

"I've lived through much worse. Don't worry about me."

"I'll always worry about you. It's my job." The man I loved

would be risking his life helping other people. I would count down the days until he was home.

"I expected you to fight me on this."

Impulsively, I wanted to. I wanted to tell him he wasn't leaving, but that would be selfish. I understood Finn's need to travel wherever the wind carried him. He wouldn't be happy staying in one spot forever, so letting him leave for a month at a time was a good compromise. "I would never stop you from doing what you're passionate about."

His eyes slowly softened.

"We'll still be together even when we're apart."

He stepped closer to me, his hands moving to mine. "I'll miss you."

"I know. I'll miss you too."

He lowered his head and rested his forehead against mine. "I knew you were the woman for me when we met. But now I'm even more convinced you're the only woman for me." He moved his lips to my forehead and pressed a kiss to my hairline. "Thank you."

I would hate every single day for the next thirty days. I would wait desperately for the month to pass, until this man was back in my arms once more. It was so heartbreaking that I considered changing my mind and demanding for him to stay. But I kept my mouth shut, knowing a relationship with this man wouldn't be easy. He would always need his space, always need to explore. I would just have to accept that if I wanted to keep him. "No need to thank me. I'm proud of you."

"You are?" he whispered.

"Yes...very proud." My hands snaked up his arms, and I felt his strong biceps, hoping I would get him back in the same condition as when he left. "When do you leave?"

He released a quiet sigh. "The day after tomorrow."

11

_____

COLTON

I GRABBED ANOTHER BEER FROM THE FRIDGE AND TWISTED OFF THE cap. "What did Mom say?"

He stood at the counter with a bottle in his grasp. "She was a little disappointed, but also proud. Since I'm only going to be gone for a month, she isn't that upset. That's nothing compared to the years when I couldn't leave base at all."

"True. Did you tell her about Pepper?"

He drank his beer while he kept his eyes locked with mine. "I did, actually."

I hadn't sure if my brother would ever admit the truth. He'd seemed on the fence about it for a long time. "Her reaction?"

"She was thrilled. She asked how you felt about it, and when I told her you gave us your blessing, she was really happy about it. Says there's no better woman for me."

"Well...that's a relief."

"Yeah. One less weight on my shoulders."

"Does Pepper know?"

He shook his head. "I haven't told her yet."

"She'll be happy to know my parents approve."

"Yeah, I know."

I pulled leftovers from last night out of the fridge. "You wanna stay for dinner? I made spaghetti."

"Sure."

I scooped it onto two plates and popped the first one into the microwave. "So, Pepper was supportive about the whole thing?"

"She didn't blink an eye over it."

That didn't sound like her. She seemed far too clingy with Finn to let him go that easily. "She probably understands how important this is to you."

"Yeah, she does," he said with a nod. "She's one hell of a woman, Colton. I never would have fallen in love with anyone else but her."

I knew Pepper was an absolute catch. Sometimes I wished I were straight and still married to her. Tom was great, but I suspected I would never have the same kind of close relationship with him that I had with Pepper.

"If I marry anyone…it'll be her." He stared at the bottle as his words echoed in our minds.

The microwave started to beep, but I didn't open the door and pull out the food. "Then why don't you marry her?"

He shrugged. "I've got a lot of life to live."

"You can live that life with her." I opened the door and pulled out the food and placed the next one inside. I hit the timer, and the food started to spin around.

"If it happens, it'll happen."

"Just keep in mind that you can't wait forever. Pepper is one in a million. If you don't want her, someone else will take her."

"I'm not stupid, Colt." He set his beer down. "But this is way down the road. She knows I'm not looking to settle down right now…even though I love her so much that it scares me. All the other women in my life have just been toys…stuff to do. But with her…she's the first woman that I actually respect, that I actually admire. She's like my best friend."

"Yeah...I know what you mean." I pulled the food out of the microwave when it beeped and set it on the counter. Instead of taking a seat at the dining table, we both stood in the kitchen and ate standing at the counter. "What about Soldier?"

"Pepper is going to stay at my place. She'll be able to keep an eye on him and use my truck."

"So you let her use your truck but not me?"

"She's got a license now."

"Still..."

"And she'll need to pick up groceries and grab dog food."

I spun my fork in my noodles and grabbed a large helping of pasta before placing it in my mouth. "Well, I'm going to miss you. It'll be weird not having you around for a month."

"Yeah?"

"Yeah. And I'll be stuck with Pepper all the time."

He chuckled. "Don't act like you aren't looking forward to that."

"Whenever you're at work, she raids my fridge."

"That's your fault for moving across the hall from her —again."

I guess that was true. "Where will you be staying?"

He shrugged. "Sometimes a tent. Sometimes a hotel. It just depends on where they put me. But I'm there to work, and since I'm free labor, they're going to squeeze every last drop out of me."

"You won't have a paycheck for the entire month?"

"No. My food and expenses will be covered, though."

"What about your mortgage?"

"That's what a savings account is for."

I had some money stashed, but not enough that I could quit working for a month without stressing. "And the hospital is fine with it?"

"They were the ones that told me about it."

"That's pretty cool. Any other doctors going with you?"

He stabbed his pasta with his fork and spun it around to get a good bite. But he kept staring at his plate without bringing it toward his mouth. "Yeah. One other doctor."

"Someone you know?"

He sighed. "Layla."

I lowered my fork, annoyed that bitch wouldn't give it a rest. "Geez, she needs to back off."

He shrugged. "I'm not sure if she knew I was going when she volunteered. Could have been a coincidence."

I narrowed my eyes.

"But it probably wasn't..."

"Pepper must have been pissed."

"I haven't told her yet."

She would lose her shit once she found out. "She's not going to be happy."

"I know. I'm dreading the conversation."

"I thought you weren't scared of anything?"

He lifted his chin to meet my gaze. "Pepper is an exception."

12

PEPPER

HE GRIPPED BOTH OF MY WRISTS AGAINST THE SMALL OF MY BACK as he pounded into me. His large dick hit me deep and hard every time, and he kept one hand pressed against the back of my neck as he buried himself inside me.

I breathed against the sheets and felt him dominate me, filling me with come over and over again. He used my body as much as he could to satisfy his needs since it would be so long before he had me again. Sometimes he made love to me, and sometimes he fucked me like I meant nothing to him.

Since I enjoyed both, I had no preference.

He rocked his hips hard as he thrust into me, making my body shake with his momentum. His powerful arms kept me in place as he consumed me, as he treated my pussy like he hadn't been destroying it all night.

Then he shuddered with his release, filling me with another load that would barely fit. He groaned as his fingers tightened on my slender wrists. His grip deepened against the back of my neck, reminding me that he owned me.

He finished with a satisfied sigh then pulled out of me.

I couldn't believe I'd have to survive a whole month without this.

He lay on the bed, his long body stretching out on the king-size mattress. His hand rested on his chest, and he breathed hard as his body returned to a comfortable state.

I stayed on my hands and knees then slowly slid down into a prone position. My knees bent, and my toes pointed toward the sky.

He stared at my ass then rested his arm in the deep curve in my back. "Be careful, baby."

"What?" I asked playfully.

"You know what." He pulled his eyes away from my ass to look at me. "I'll pound you into this bed until you can't walk again."

"I've never been fond of walking anyway."

His fingers grazed my skin lightly, feeling the curve from my ass all the way to my shoulder blades.

He was leaving in the morning. I had to drop him off at the airport and feel my heart break when he walked away. I would still have his t-shirts, his bed, and his dog, but I would miss him so much. Being supportive was a lot harder than it seemed.

He continued to watch me, his fingers following the path his fingers took. "I have good news."

"The storm stopped and didn't cause that much damage, so you don't have to leave?" That would fix all my problems, allow me to stay with him every single night.

"Not that good." He smiled slightly. "I told my mom I was leaving."

"She must have thrown a hissy fit."

"No. A month is a piece of cake to her."

If that was good news, he didn't understand what good news really was. Good news was saying he picked me up a cake from the bakery and I could eat all of it without gaining a pound. That was my definition of good news. "That was your good news?"

"Not entirely. I told her about us…"

I hadn't known if Finn would tell his parents about our relationship. No reason to get them excited when it might not be that serious. But if he told them, then he obviously thought this would last a long time.

And that was good news. "What did she say?"

"She was happy…as I expected her to be."

"Good."

His fingers stopped at the top of my ass. "She said it makes perfect sense, and there's no better woman for me."

That was nice of her to say. Hopefully, she would always be my mother-in-law. "I'm glad we won't have any problems there. I was afraid she would think it was too weird or something."

"No. She loves you too much." His fingers started to move again, to touch my skin as he enjoyed the sight of my curves. Minutes ticked by as he enjoyed the sight of my bare skin. Then his eyes returned to mine as he stared into my soul, as he gazed at me so openly. "I have something else to tell you…"

"Your tone implies it's bad."

"Well, you aren't going to like it."

"Alright…" Every time I feared the worst was about to happen, I was wrong. So instead of being afraid of what he might say, I stayed calm. "You always make everything ominous, but it's never that bad."

"We'll see you if you feel differently about this one…" He pulled his hand away and rested it on his chest.

"What is it?"

He faced the ceiling and broke eye contact. "There's one other doctor who volunteered with me."

He didn't even need to give me a name. It only took me a nanosecond to figure out who the culprit was. Only one bitch would be desperate enough to follow a man across the country in the hope of cornering him. "That skank needs to give it a rest."

"I'm not sure if she volunteered because of me. She's done stuff for the Peace Corps in the past."

"Oh, whatever." I rolled my eyes. "We both know she's taking advantage of this opportunity to get your dick."

He didn't deny it.

I was annoyed this woman wouldn't quit, but it also didn't change anything. He was already committed to going, and I knew he wouldn't cheat on me. She could try to get him into her room at night, but nothing would happen. Unless she full-blown raped him, nothing would happen. And even then, I doubted he could get hard.

"Do you want me not to go?"

"Don't be ridiculous."

"I'm not. It's just going to be the two of us, and unfortunately, we'll be spending a lot of time together. Like, every day."

I didn't want to think about her checking him out every single day, but I couldn't control what she did. I couldn't stop all the women in the world from wanting him. That wasn't possible. Even when he was in his fifties, it wouldn't be possible. "Whatever. Doesn't change anything."

"You're serious." His eyes narrowed on my face, genuinely surprised that I wasn't calling this whole thing off.

"Of course, I'm serious. She can want you all she wants, but she can't have you. I know you would never betray me."

Slowly, his hard features softened, and he looked at me like I'd touched his heart in a new way. His eyes fell slowly as his hand moved up my back, his breathing picking up slightly. He breathed a deep sigh before he moved closer to me. "You trust me."

"Of course I trust you." This man told me he loved me almost every day. He didn't say it when we got off the phone like most couples, but he said it during lovemaking or across the table at dinnertime. That made it more special.

He rolled me onto my back and placed his heavy body on top of mine. His hand slid into my hair, and he locked his eyes on mine. "But you really trust me." His legs separated mine, and he pressed his rock-hard dick against my clit. He'd taken me so many times throughout the day that it didn't seem like he could get so excited again, but there he was, harder than he'd ever been.

"You love me..."

He pointed his dick at my entrance then slowly slid inside. "Yes. I fucking love you." His hand returned to my hair, and he moved inside until he was completely sheathed. "You're my woman, and I don't want anyone else. This is the only pussy I want." He gave me a soft kiss on the lips. "This is the only mouth I want." He rocked into me. "You're the only woman I'll ever love. So yes, you should trust me. Because I'm desperately, pathetically, in love with you."

I DROVE his truck to the airport and parked in the loading zone at the curb.

Ugh, I really hated this.

Putting the truck in park was almost too difficult for me. I wanted to start crying because this was so difficult. He would only be gone for a month, but I felt like I was losing him for a lifetime.

I could barely look at him.

"Baby, it'll only be a month."

I kept my voice strong even though I felt so weak. "I know." I raised my chin and met his gaze, forcing myself to smile and pretend everything was alright.

"I know you're about to cry." He moved his hand into my hair and pulled it from my face. "I know you better than you give me credit for."

My lips turned into his palm, and I kissed it as a tear slipped free and streamed down my cheek.

He wiped it away with his thumb. "I'll miss you."

"I'll miss you too."

He brought his lips to my forehead and kissed me. "It'll be over before you know it."

"Yeah…" Maybe for him but not for me.

He got out of the truck and pulled his bag from the bed.

I got out so I could hug him goodbye. I didn't care if anyone noticed my red eyes and puffy cheeks. I was tempted to handcuff his wrist to mine so he could never leave.

He set the bag on the ground. "I'll call when I can. Send me some dirty videos, okay? I need something to get me through this month."

"No internet down there to watch porn?"

The corner of his mouth rose in a smile. "I'd rather fantasize about you." He moved in close to me and cupped my cheeks with his palms. "Especially when you're in my bed wearing my t-shirt. That'd be hot."

I knew he was trying to make me feel better, but nothing could erase the pain throbbing behind my eyes and in my chest. "I'll see what I can do." My eyes felt someone staring at us, so I glanced to the left and found Layla standing there. She'd just stepped out of the cab, and she wasn't dressed for a long flight. She was in a tight t-shirt and skinny jeans, pumps on her feet. She looked over at us, but she seemed to only notice Finn.

This was going to be a long-ass month.

Finn didn't take his eyes off my face, indifferent to the people surrounding us. "I love you." His thumbs swiped across my cheeks before he leaned in and kissed me on the mouth. It was a soft kiss, one filled with love and devotion, not desire and lust. He kissed me like he loved me, just like the men did in the movies. He made me feel as secure as any woman could be when a drop-dead gorgeous rival was prepared to do everything she could to take him away from me.

He ended the kiss and rested his forehead against mine, his thick arms around my waist. He pulled me close to him and closed his eyes, enjoying the last few minutes we had together. The truck couldn't stay in the spot much longer, but he didn't seem to care.

"I love you too," I whispered. "So much that it scares me. I've never loved anyone the way I love you...not even Colton."

"Because we're supposed to be together." He rubbed his nose against mine. "And we'll be together when I get back. I want my drawers to be stuffed with new lingerie by the time I get back. I'll make sure I have a few days off so we can make up for all the time we lost."

"That sounds nice."

He pulled away and grabbed his bag. "Take care of Soldier for me."

"I will." This was the moment where I had to say goodbye, to let him leave me for an entire month. I had to let him go and let Layla do whatever she wanted.

"And Colton," he teased.

"Of course."

He hooked the bag over his shoulder. "Bye, baby."

"Bye..."

He gave me one final look of longing before he turned around and walked off. He didn't notice Layla standing off to the side waiting for him. He walked inside without giving her a second glance.

I wasn't heartbroken that this woman would try to take him away from me. I was devastated that I had to live without him for so long. I didn't even make it back inside the truck before the tears hit my cheeks.

13

COLTON

Tom sat across the dining table from me, eating the tacos I'd made for dinner. "Have you talked to her?"

"No..." It'd been five days since Finn left, and Pepper had disappeared off the map. She didn't respond to my text messages, so it seemed like she wanted to be alone. She took his absence even harder than I expected her to.

"Maybe you should go over there."

"If she wanted company, she would respond to my messages."

"But maybe you need to force her. Get her out of her funk."

"Yeah...maybe." The situation reminded me of our divorce. She took it really hard and vanished for a long time. We didn't interact at all, and it broke my heart that I couldn't comfort her... because I was the person responsible for her heartache. This time, I wasn't.

"What if we wrap up some tacos and drop them off? I'll give you a ride."

"Really?" I asked. "It's supposed to be our night."

"Who cares," he said. "We have plenty of time for date nights later. Be there for your friend. She's a good girl going through a hard time. I admire Finn for what he's doing, but I also feel bad for Pepper. I would never be able to leave you."

"And I would never let you leave." I felt guilty for being so happy when Pepper was so miserable. I had a great guy with a deepening relationship. We only seemed to get closer, become more compatible. If he had to leave for a month, I'd be in tears too.

He set his napkin on the table. "Let's box this up and get going."

"Thanks, Tom. I appreciate it."

He shrugged. "She's family. Family comes first, right?"

I KNOCKED on the door a few times before she finally answered. In Finn's t-shirt and sweatpants, she was wearing clothes a million sizes too big for her. She didn't flash me a smile, not even when she noticed the food in my hands. Her face wasn't stained with tears, but her eyelids were heavy with exhaustion, like she couldn't sleep.

"You want some tacos?" I held up the container. "They're fresh."

"That's nice of you, but I'm not hungry." She kept her hand on the door and didn't invite me inside. Soldier was stuck to her side, being her guard dog.

"You gonna invite me inside?" I asked, stepping into the house without waiting for her answer.

"Oh, sorry." She stepped aside then shut the door behind me.

Soldier seemed to have absorbed her melancholy because he didn't paw at me with excitement. He seemed just as sad by Finn's absence.

I walked inside and carried the container to the kitchen. "You want me to heat some up for you."

She crinkled her nose. "No thanks. I'm not hungry."

"Maybe you should eat anyway." I suspected she hadn't been eating much since Finn left.

"I'll eat later." She moved to the couch and took a seat, Soldier squeezing into her side and laying his snout on her thigh. Her hand automatically moved to his head and pet him gently, used to having him right beside her.

I got comfortable on the same couch and looked at the TV. She was watching the news, seeing the coverage of the storm and the destruction it was causing. People were still missing, and the causalities were piling up. People were taking shelter in stadiums and churches. I turned to Pepper and watched her stare at the screen blankly. "Have you talked to him?"

She shook her head. "He hasn't called. He's probably been working since he got there."

"And he might not have cell service in those conditions."

"Yeah…" She continued to pet Soldier.

"Did he mention Layla?" I assumed my brother wouldn't lie to her about it. He wasn't a coward.

She nodded.

"You know nothing is gonna happen, right?" After my brother confided his deep love for Pepper, I knew there was no chance he would ever betray her. He was head over heels for Pepper. Layla didn't hold a candle to her.

"I'm not worried about her."

"You aren't?" Layla seemed pretty adamant about getting in Finn's pants.

"That's not why I'm sad. I just miss him. I hate that he's not here. I thought I would get over it in a day or two, but I'm lost without him." She shrugged. "I'm surprised I'm like this. It's not like he's not coming back."

"It's already been five days," I said. "So only twenty-five more to go."

"Every day is a lifetime for me..."

"I'm glad you aren't worried about Layla because you have no reason to be."

"She's a major pain in the ass, but whatever. Finn would never hurt me."

It was crazy to think I'd been against this relationship for so long. Now they were two of the most committed people I'd ever known. My brother, the biggest playboy ever, said he would marry her if he ever settled down. That was a big statement from someone like him. And the fact he loved her so openly was surprising too. "I'm here if you need anything."

"I know, Colt." She forced a light smile. "Thank you."

"You want me to stay with you until he gets back?"

"No, of course not," she said. "I've got Soldier, so I'm okay. He snuggles better than Finn, but he certainly doesn't feel like Finn."

I chuckled. "He's a good dog. He'll take care of you."

"Yes, he's my baby." She leaned down and kissed him on the head. "I'll probably make him a soft lap dog by the time Finn returns."

"Probably?" I asked incredulously. "I think you already did."

She shrugged. "Oh, well. If he gets mad, I'll tell him it's his fault. He's the one who left."

14

PEPPER

A WEEK HAD PASSED, AND WHILE I WAS EATING NORMALLY AGAIN, I was still in a terrible mood. His bed wasn't comfortable without him in it, and I worried about him constantly. Were they working him like a rented mule? Was he eating enough? Resting enough? When would he call me?

I was grateful to have Soldier for company. He was the best support I could have asked for. He understood something was wrong, so he comforted me all the time. The second I was home, he blanketed me in his affection. He quickly took Finn's spot on the bed, cuddling right beside me like he was an actual human.

I was lying in bed, unable to sleep even though I was exhausted. I considered calling Finn, but I assumed if he could talk, he would call. It was unusually warm that evening, so Soldier was at the foot of the bed.

Then the phone rang.

It was Finn.

I grabbed the phone so quickly, I knocked it onto the floor. "Shit." When I picked it up, I realized I had hung up on him somehow. "Dammit." I lay back down and called him back, hoping I could get through.

He answered. "Hanging up on me, baby?"

Just the sound of his voice, so deep and playful, was enough to bring tears to my eyes. "I miss you so much..." I couldn't respond with the same casual banter because the emotion was too strong. I wanted to be supportive, but it was so difficult. I wanted him to come home and never leave. There was no way I could go through this again.

He was quiet over the line, absorbing my sadness. "I miss you too, baby."

"It's been a week, but it feels like a month."

"It's definitely been the longest week of my life."

I was complaining, but I was the one enjoying the comfort of a beautiful house and amenities. He was working in dangerous conditions with little sleep. "How are you?"

"Tired."

"What was your week like?"

"I was in the field the entire time, treating patients in the area. I was in one of the stadiums most of the time. I slept in a sleeping bag on the floor and didn't shower. Didn't even get to brush my teeth. No way to charge my phone. I would have called sooner if I could."

"That sounds terrible..." But if those were the conditions, then Layla had no chance of seducing him.

"It wasn't so bad. It's not forever."

"Where are you now?"

"They took us a few hours out of the zone so we could stay at a hotel. I took a shower and ordered some terrible room service, but it was also the best thing I've eaten in a week."

So that bitch was nearby. She'd probably come to his door in her underwear. "I'm glad they are giving you a break."

"Yeah. I have the day off tomorrow. Then I'm back in the field for another week."

"I hate that they are overworking you."

"Don't. I signed up for this. I don't mind helping people." Finn was too strong to complain. He was too selfless.

It made me love him more. "I'll make you something good when you get home."

He chuckled. "I'll order a pizza instead."

"Hey, I'm not that bad."

"You burned the stew that time. How does that happen?"

"Come on, that only happened one time."

"But how?" he countered. "How do you burn a soup? Only you could accomplish that."

I pulled the sheets to my chest and turned on my side, feeling better now that we'd been talking for a while. "Soldier misses you."

"Change the subject..."

"He does."

"I bet he's happy I'm gone. Gets you all to himself."

"No. He's definitely the happiest when he has both of us."

He sighed over the line, like he was getting comfortable in bed. "This is the most comfortable thing I've slept on in a week... The only thing missing is you."

"And Soldier."

"No. I just want you right now." He turned quiet and let his final words float in the silence between us.

It'd been a week filled with soul-crushing pain, so sex was the last thing on my mind. If he were here, that would be a different story.

"Can I have you, baby?"

Knowing Layla was just a few doors away made me want to be whatever he wanted. I should feel grateful that I was the one who got all of his attention. I needed to put aside my sadness and be what he needed. "I've never done that before."

"Just pretend I'm there. I put a vibrator in the drawer."

"You what?" I blurted.

"You heard me. He'll have to do while I'm not there."

"So you want me to get off with a vibrator?"

"I want my lady satisfied while I'm not there. And I prefer a toy to another man. So put the camera on and let me see you. I could open my laptop and watch something dirty, but I would much rather watch you. Come on, baby."

My cheeks blushed when I listened to his request. It was romantic, to hear him beg to see me because he preferred it to porn, preferred me to the women with perfect figures and big tits. "Alright."

"There's my girl." A smile was in his voice. "I want you in blank panties. Nothing else. I love those tits."

"I'm not wearing any makeup."

"You don't need any makeup. I always want to fuck you harder in the morning than at night."

"Well, I want you wearing nothing at all."

"Consider it done. I'll call you back in a second." He hung up.

I did as he asked and pulled on a black thong. I fluffed my hair and lay on the bed, my tits feeling the cold air once my t-shirt was gone. I found the vibrator in his nightstand where he said it would be. It was still in the package, like he wanted me to know he'd really bought it for this occasion and it hadn't been previously used.

He called back using his camera.

I took the call and held the phone above me.

He sat up against the headboard, naked with his throbbing dick against his stomach. His tattoos and muscles were visible because his bedside lamp was on. He had a bottle of lube next to him, and he'd already squirted the liquid all over his length.

It looked even bigger on screen.

He took in the sight of me as he released a deep breath. "Fuck...that's exactly what I wanted to see." His hand wrapped around his length, and he started to jerk himself hard, like he was so aroused his head was about to explode. "Just like that, baby…"

CONNECTING with him comforted me in his absence. It made missing him a little easier, like we were in a long-distance relationship but the separation wouldn't last long. I would only get to talk to him once a week until he came back, but I could live with that.

I worked for the next few days, putting in longer hours since I had nothing else to do. The only thing waiting at home for me was a dog. I organized the storage unit in the back of the store, did a deep clean of the front, and reorganized everything. Thankfully, I'd booked a few bridal parties over the weekend, so I had something to keep me busy.

It seemed like I'd stepped back in time when the bell above the door rang. Just like on that sunny afternoon, a handsome man walked inside, someone who didn't belong in my store. With a smile brighter than the desert sun, he looked at me with his kind eyes as he approached the counter.

Now I was over six months in the past.

I could hardly believe what my eyes were seeing. "What are you doing here?" It was rude and abrupt, but I hadn't expected him to stop by the store ever again. With the exception of that late night at dinner, I didn't think we would ever cross paths.

"Just picking up something for myself."

He was there to buy lingerie for his new woman? That was awkward. "Oh…"

"You don't realize I'm kidding…" He gave a self-conscious smile, a dimple visible in each cheek. His eyes were green with vibrancy, and his handsome features overshadowed his good soul. He seemed too kind for a man so attractive. "I'm definitely kidding."

"Oh, okay," I said with an awkward laugh. "That would have been weird."

"Yes, it would have." He rested one hand against the edge of the counter and stared at me.

I waited for an explanation of his appearance.

It never came.

"What brings you here, Jax?" I'd spent my entire morning thinking about the dirty thing I'd done with Finn a few nights ago. I'd never been so adventurous like that, but with Finn, it felt easy. And he seemed to enjoy it, which made me enjoy it more. It was also a big fuck-you to Layla. Hopefully, she could hear him moan through the wall.

"Well...I kinda haven't stopped thinking about you."

Oh shit. That wasn't good.

He tapped his fingers against the counter, wearing a t-shirt and jeans. He probably wore a suit when he showed houses in nice areas, so he must be off today. He came to my shop to talk to me, but he could spend his time picking up any woman he wanted. It was hard to believe he was here, still interested in me. "I made a mistake with the whole Colton fiasco. I was just so into you that I got jealous easily, even insecure. That's not like me at all. I'm over thirty, and I've never had a real relationship with anyone because I've never been invested. But with you...I didn't see it coming. Here I am, months later, still thinking about one woman. So, I'd really like it if we could get a cup of coffee or something. Bring Colton if you want, I don't care." He obviously had no idea Finn and I were together. He must have assumed we were two friends getting dinner. It wasn't that crazy since Finn and Colton were brothers. Would I really date my ex-husband's brother?

In my case, yes. If Finn knew this was happening, he

wouldn't like it one bit. He wasn't the jealous type, but he wouldn't appreciate my ex hitting on me. It seemed important to Finn that Jax knew we were together, and now I regretted not mentioning that to Jax sooner. "Jax, I'm seeing Finn." I hated to crush his spirit and humiliate him, but there was no better response. That was the truth.

He didn't react at first. It seemed to take him time to transfer the information into his brain. When it finally hit him, his eyes slowly fell in disappointment. "Oh...I didn't realize. I just thought you two were just friends."

"We aren't. We've been together for a few months now." I didn't want to hurt Jax because he was a good guy, but I knew Finn was up front about his relationship status with me when women hit on him. I needed to be just as loyal.

"So you started dating him when we broke up?"

"Basically."

He nodded slowly. "Colton didn't have a problem with that?"

"He did at first. But then he got over it."

"So, it must be pretty serious, then. I can't imagine a guy screwing over his brother like that unless he had good reason."

It might not end in marriage, but it was serious to me. "I love him." That was a hurtful thing to say, but I couldn't sugarcoat my feelings. I didn't want Jax to waste any hope on me. "And he loves me."

Jax bowed his head and looked at the floor as his hand tightened on the counter. An angry laugh escaped his lips. "Damn. I should have just let the Colton thing go..." He sighed then faced me again. "I'm not sure why it bothered me so much at the time. Colton was never my competition. Apparently, Finn was. Was he the guy you kissed?"

When Jax and I were together, we'd both had moments with other people. At the time, Jax never asked who it was, so I never had to tell him. "Yes."

His eyes filled with disappointment again. "So you wanted him the entire time?"

"It wasn't like that, Jax. I liked you. I just didn't want to move as fast as you wanted. It was a lot of pressure. When you dumped me, I was sad about it."

"You say we went too fast, but you just told me you're in love with him."

"Yeah…" I couldn't come up with a good response to that. It made me look like a liar. "It just happened… I don't know. I didn't tell him I loved him until a few weeks ago. It's not like it happened overnight or the day you and I broke up."

"I'm sorry," he said. "I'm interrogating you when you don't owe me anything." He slid his hands into his pockets. "I've never been in a relationship before, so I'm not very good at them, apparently. I wish I'd done things differently."

"Me too."

He took a step back. "I'm glad I came here anyway. I guess I can get some closure."

"Yeah…"

He turned around and prepared to walk out.

I felt bad about the direction of the conversation, but there was nothing I could do. It was better to let him be hurt than to give him hope.

He stopped and turned back around. "If it doesn't work out, give me a call."

"I think it is going to work out."

He gave a slight nod. "You're a special woman to make guys like us commit. He's a lucky guy. Hope he doesn't make the same mistakes I did." He left the store and disappeared from the windows.

"Yeah…me too."

15

PEPPER

FINN CALLED ME A WEEK LATER.

"How's it going?" I lay in bed with Soldier dead asleep at the foot of the bed. It'd been almost two weeks since we last spoke, and I'd started to worry again.

"It's been hectic. I didn't get a day off last week because of all the work I had to do. There're too many patients and not enough doctors. The critical cases take a lot of my time, and I have to stabilize them before we get to the hospital. And I've had to donate a lot of blood, so I've been more tired than usual."

"Why are you donating blood?"

"We're low, and I'm a universal donor."

This man literally gave all of himself for other people. I couldn't believe a man so cold on the surface could be so kind underneath. "Don't overdo it. You can't help anyone if you're passed out."

"Don't worry about me, baby. I'm made of steel."

"Stronger than steel."

He stayed quiet on the phone.

"So, you're at the hotel now?"

"Yeah. We arrived late last night. I was in the shower for like thirty minutes, then I passed out on the bed. Didn't wake up until three in the afternoon."

"Because you're exhausted."

"Tell me about it..."

"But everything else has been good?" I wanted to ask about Layla, but my pride inhibited me. I refused to give life to her presence in a conversation. Any time spent talking about her only gave her more power.

"Yeah...for the most part."

I caught the shake in confidence at the end of that sentence. "What is it?"

"I'm not sure if I should tell you. I had an incident with Layla."

"Of course you did..."

"I don't think it's worth talking about, but I feel weird not mentioning it. Makes me feel like I'm hiding something."

"What did she do?"

"Came to my room last night wearing almost nothing."

I was gonna bust her teeth out the next time I saw her. "She came into your room?"

"No. She tried to."

"So she just stood at your hotel door naked?"

"Pretty much."

That bitch... "What happened?"

"What do you mean, what happened? I shut the door and bolted the lock."

I knew he wouldn't take the bait, but it was disgusting that she kept trying. "Why does she want a man who would cheat on his girlfriend anyway? He would just do the same to her."

"Pretty sound logic. Maybe she hasn't thought it all the way through."

"I know hate is a strong word...but I hate that bitch."

He chuckled. "I'm not her biggest fan either. Nowadays,

people take sexual harassment very seriously, but I feel like that's exactly what's happening to me. She's persistent at getting me to see her naked, but since I'm a man, it's no big deal. Double standard."

"It's true."

"And I can't just beat her up like a man. That's how I usually solve my problems, but that won't work."

It could work for me.

"So I guess I'll just wait until she loses interest."

"If she hasn't lost interest by now, she never will."

"Fuck, I hope that's not true." He sighed before the sound of movement came over the line. "How's my baby?"

"Good. Soldier and I are just lounging around."

"Good. I hope the place smells like you when I get back."

"It'll definitely smell like dog, I can tell you that much."

He chuckled. "Then it'll need a deep clean."

"I'm not the maid, so don't ask me."

"You can't cook and you can't clean...at least you can fuck."

I laughed. "I'm glad it gets me out of chores."

"That's how good you are."

We turned quiet when the conversation died out. Even though we hadn't seen each other in weeks, we didn't have much to say. We spent most of our time making love when we were together. When we couldn't do that, we ran out of things to discuss.

"Anything else new with you?"

I thought about Jax. He'd stopped by the shop just a few days ago. Since Finn had told me about Layla, I should probably mention it. "Actually...Jax stopped by my shop a few days ago."

"Oh?"

"Yeah. We talked for a bit, and I mentioned we were dating."

"And what did he stop by for?" His tone darkened noticeably, like he was provoked the second I mentioned Jax's name. For not being jealous, he was certainly territorial. He didn't play it cool, not like he usually did.

"Just to talk."

"He came by a lingerie shop just to talk? Baby, I was straight with you about Layla. You better be straight with me."

"I didn't want to make you mad."

"Do I sound mad?"

Was that a trick question? "A bit…"

"I'll ask again. What did he want?"

This time, I didn't hold back. "He asked me out. Said he made a mistake and hasn't stopped thinking about me…"

"He did make a mistake. He's a fucking idiot."

"I told him we were serious, so he backed off."

"Good. Now I don't have to break his pretty face. It'd be hard to sell houses with a broken nose and a black eye."

"I thought real men didn't get jealous?" Finn had told me he was too confident to be threatened by another man, but his blown temper suggested otherwise.

"Never said I was jealous."

"You sound it."

"I just don't appreciate it when an asshole hits on my woman."

"In his defense, he didn't know I was your woman."

"Because you didn't tell him." His tone darkened further. "You should have told him sooner."

"Sooner? It's not like I'm friends with the guy. I didn't know I was going to run into him."

"Look, I'm up front about my commitment to you. I get ass offered to me all the time, but I don't dance around the fact that I'm unavailable. I spit it out and get to the point."

"Whoa, you get ass offered to you all the time? What about that whole being honest thing?" We hardly got to talk to each other, and in our limited time, we were yelling at each other.

The idea of him being hit on all the time pissed me off, in addition to the accusation in his voice. And he had smoke coming out of his ears.

"If I told you about every little thing, we wouldn't have time to talk about anything else."

"Wow...that's a dick thing to say."

"Well, I'm a dick. Go figure." He was fuming over the line, showing me the dark side of him that he'd only shown once before.

"I don't hide my commitment to you, Finn. It just happened that way—"

"It shouldn't have happened at all. You should have told that asshole you were with me. But you kept your mouth shut."

I missed this man so much, but now I wanted nothing to do with him. "I told him I was in love with you."

Silence.

"He told me to call him if it doesn't work out. You know what I said? It *is* gonna work out." Fed up with this bitter version of Finn, I hung up the phone and dropped it onto the sheets beside me. Fighting when we were in the same city was different because he always felt so close. If I ignored his calls, he could come to my door and face me like a man. But he was on the other side of the country, and if I didn't talk to him now, I'd have to wait another week.

So when he called back, I answered. "What?" I was pissed that he was being hit on constantly, so often that there wasn't even time to tell me about all of them. I was pissed that he treated me like a criminal when he had a naked woman showing up at his door. I was pissed that he wasn't in bed with me, that we were having this fight over the phone because we couldn't be together.

His voice came out quiet when he spoke, his rage gone and his serenity full. "I love you."

Just like that, the fight was over.

"I love you," he repeated. "And I'm sorry."

I would never get tired of hearing those three little words. "I love you too."

"I don't know why I got so angry. I guess..."

"You're jealous."

He sighed into the phone.

"It's okay, Finn. I'm jealous too. I'm jealous of that gorgeous woman who wants you so much that she flashed her perfect body at you, and she probably looks much better naked than I do. It's okay to be jealous. A little jealousy is good in a relationship."

"I'm jealous," he finally admitted. "And I didn't even look at her body because I was looking at her face. You're the sexiest woman I've ever been with, and your appeal has nothing to do with looks. Your beauty comes from deep within. So, don't feel threatened by someone so ugly. It doesn't matter if they're supermodels or porn stars. No one can compete with you—at least not to me."

16

COLTON

I sat across from Pepper and Stella at the bar, a beer sitting in front of me. "You better knock that bitch out the next time you see her."

"I'll do it for you," Stella said. "What kind of person does that? It would be hot if he were a single guy, but if she actually saw you say goodbye at the airport, tears streaming down your face, that's just cold."

"He could probably press charges," I said. "That's harassment. She keeps doing it and won't stop."

"Finn isn't the kind of guy to call the cops—for any reason," Pepper said.

"Yeah, you're probably right." I drank my beer and was relieved to see that Pepper was in a good place, despite the ordeal with Layla. She'd taken Finn's departure really hard, but she managed to bounce back. "At least he'll be home soon."

"One more week," she said, sighing at the same time. "This month has been torture. I only get to talk to him once a week, so that just makes it worse."

"And you aren't getting laid." Stella stirred her martini with the olive spear and took a drink. "That's gotta be the worst part."

"No, the worst part is him not being here," Pepper said. "I miss him. I miss sleeping with him, talking to him, just being with him…"

"I thought you were sleeping with Soldier," I noted.

She rolled her eyes. "Not the same thing."

"At least it's almost over," Stella said. "He already served ten years in the military and he did his humanitarian work, so hopefully he just sits still for a very long time now."

"I don't know." I knew Finn in a way neither one of them did. Growing up, he always played with toy soldiers and tanks, wanting to be in the army when he grew up. When we got older, he only became more anxious to serve. Then when he turned eighteen, he was out the door so fast. "He's always been that way. He doesn't like to be in one spot for too long. Even when he was in the military, he didn't come home that often. He would always volunteer for extra missions because he preferred to be overseas than at home. My mom doesn't know that, but he told me. So don't be surprised if he does more stuff like this in the future."

Pepper's face turned pale, like that was the last thing she wanted. "I admire his sacrifice and how selfless he is, but I couldn't do another month apart. This has already been hard enough. I couldn't imagine being an army wife. That's just torture."

"At least you know he'll never go back in the military," Stella said. "So you never have to worry about him running off again—at least not for a long period of time."

"And he wouldn't have bought a house unless he intended to settle," Pepper added.

I shrugged. "Buying real estate is a sound investment."

Stella glared at me. "We're trying to make Pepper feel better right now."

"Well, I don't think those reasons are enough to keep him

around," I argued. "But there is one thing that will probably keep him around for a long time."

"What?" Pepper asked, holding her drink.

"You." My brother's personality and behavior had changed since he'd met her. He was loving, affectionate, and monogamous. He experienced feelings he'd never felt before. She completely changed his life, made him into a new man. "After being gone for a month, he'll probably never want to leave you again. So I think that's the one thing that should give you comfort."

I WAS HOME ALONE one night when the phone rang.

It was my brother. "Whoa, didn't expect to hear from you."

"I thought I should check in. I just talked to Mom, and she almost cried on the phone."

"Why?"

He sighed. "I don't know. She worries about me too much."

I rolled my eyes even though he couldn't see me. "She's just emotional."

"I've survived worse, so she shouldn't be worried." He sounded the same, a little distant and slightly bored. "Pepper doing alright?"

"Why don't you call her?"

"I'll call her when I'm done with you. I save the best for last."

"So, I'm not the best?" I teased.

"Not even close. So, how's she doing?"

"She was pretty upset when you left. She didn't talk to anyone for a few days."

He was quiet.

"It took her about two weeks to really accept the fact you were gone. But she still tells me how much she misses you and can't wait until you get home. She's not happy about Layla either."

He released a heavy sigh, expressing all his anger and rage in that simple act. "She's a pain in the ass, man. That woman doesn't understand rejection. She obviously doesn't understand desperation either."

"Stella is gonna kick her ass."

"Good. Hopefully, she can't come into work anymore."

"So, how is it over there? Pepper said it sounded gruesome."

"Oh, it definitely is. I'm excited to come home—and not just because I miss my woman."

I put my feet on the coffee table and turned down the volume on the TV. "I'm excited to have you back. I don't like seeing Pepper so bummed out. I didn't grasp how happy you made her until you were gone."

"I'm glad you feel that way, man. Being without her has been hard. I don't think I could do it again."

Maybe Finn really was ready to settle down. That was not something he would normally say. Maybe he didn't even realize what he'd said. "She feels the same way."

"Especially with Jax snooping around…"

"I wouldn't worry about him. Seemed like an honest mistake."

"Whatever. He had her and blew it. The guy needs to move on."

He blew it because of me. At first, I felt bad for being the reason they broke up, but after seeing Pepper with Finn, maybe that was the best thing that could have happened. "I'm sure he will. If he comes around again, I'll take care of it."

"Thanks, man. Only a week to go, and I'll be home. Mom wants to have a barbecue."

"That would be nice. You can bring your new girlfriend."

He chuckled. "Yeah...I guess I could. I have a feeling they'll like her."

"No," I said. "They'll *love* her."

"Well, I'll let you go. Just wanted to check in."

I knew our relationship was different now because he'd never called me before. Throughout his entire in the military, he never made an effort to have a relationship with me. I barely got a text from him on my wedding day. But now, it seemed like we were friends, not just brothers. "Thanks. I'll talk to you later."

"Thanks for keeping an eye on Pepper. I feel better knowing she always has you."

"Yes...she'll always have me." For better or worse, in sickness and in health, Pepper would always have me to look after her, take care of her, and love her. I wasn't married to her anymore, but I still honored my vows. Because our love didn't die when she stopped being my wife. That love continued on like nothing had happened at all.

17

PEPPER

THE FOUR WEEKS HAD COME AND GONE—AND FINN WAS FINALLY coming home.

Thank fucking god.

He called me late at night, waking me up at midnight. It was three a.m. his time, so I didn't know why he was calling me so late.

I spoke into the phone, mumbling incoherently. "Mm?"

Soldier released a quiet growl, like he was annoyed I was keeping him awake.

"Sorry to wake you, baby. I just wanted you to know I finally got a flight. We had to drive a few hours to the next big airport."

"Oh, good..." That meant he would be home tomorrow. This hell was finally over.

"My plane lands at two in the afternoon."

"We'll be there."

"We?"

"Me and Soldier. He misses you."

"Alright...I guess I miss him too."

My eyes cracked open, and I saw the time, realizing he would be home in a little over twelve hours. And I would get to sleep through most of the wait. "I'm excited you're coming home."

"Me too. Miss my woman."

"She misses you too...we both do."

"We?" he asked again.

"You know exactly what I'm talking about."

He chuckled. "*He* misses you guys too. I'll see you when I land."

"Alright. Love you." I couldn't wait to say that phrase to his face, to see him smile at me with joy.

"Love you too."

I WAITED at the terminal with Soldier on a leash. There were crowds of people coming and going, but he sat still and didn't get distracted by the stimuli. He was calm and quiet, acting like a police dog that had never retired.

"He should be here soon..." I was used to talking to Soldier like he was a real person.

He whined quietly, as if he understood exactly what was going on.

A few minutes later, Finn emerged from the crowd, his black duffel bag over his shoulder. In a t-shirt and jeans, he looked exactly the same. The only exception was the shadow of hair the sprinkled his jawline. He was usually meticulous about shaving, but since he didn't have the same luxuries he used to possess, he probably didn't have the opportunity.

When his eyes found mine, a look of pure longing burned from deep within. His lips spread slightly in a smile, and he headed toward me like nothing in the world would stop him.

Soldier tugged on his leash and whimpered when he recognized Finn. Then he broke off at a dead run and bolted right for him. He released a bark just because he collided into Finn and jumped up his body, his paws dragging over Finn's frame. Soldier whined with emotion, like he'd been missing Finn as much as I had.

"Hey, boy." Finn smiled at his dog then leaned down to rub him.

Soldier went crazy and wagged his tail vigorously, still whining.

Finn wrapped his arms around his dog and pulled him for a hug, even letting him lick his face. "Wow, you really did miss me."

I smiled as I watched them interact, not jealous that Soldier got to kiss him before I did. "I think he might have missed you more than I did."

Finn scratched him behind the ears as he looked up at me. "I doubt that." He dropped his bag then rose to his feet, his handsome smile just for me. His arms circled around my waist, and he pulled me into his chest, hugging me like he never wanted to let go.

I almost cried because it felt so good. He was really back, really there with me. Hopefully, I would never have to drop him off at the airport ever again.

He rested his chin on my head as he held me in the terminal, oblivious to all the people walking by and preparing to leave the terminal. All he cared about was me. His hands snaked up my back, and he pressed a kiss to my forehead. "You're even more beautiful than I remember."

"Wait until we get home..."

That brought a smile to his face. "I'm not sure if I can." He rested his forehead against mine and continued to hold me, Soldier pawing at his leg because he wanted more attention. He gripped my lower back then rubbed his nose against mine. "You ready to go?"

"Yes."

He picked up his bag and pulled it over his shoulder. "Come on, boy." He grabbed my hand, and we walked out together, Soldier following at our side trailing his leash behind him.

When we stepped outside, I spotted Layla standing at the curb waiting for an Uber. Her black luggage sat beside her, and she was in black leggings that left little to the imagination and a t-shirt that showed her belly along with her tattoos. It was hard to believe this woman was a doctor because she always looked like a whore.

Finn tightened his grip on my hand. "She's not worth it. Leave it alone."

I was normally too classy to say anything to someone so low, but I was tired of taking the high road. This woman was a nasty pest that just wouldn't go away, even when you chopped off her head. "Nope." I pulled out of his grasp and walked up to her, my heart pounding with rage.

She turned to look at me, her eyes dilating in fear when she realized she was the target on my radar. Her entire body tensed, and she flinched when I walked right up to her.

"You don't have a lot of girlfriends, do you?"

She blinked several times, like she couldn't believe that was the first thing that came out of my mouth.

"Let me teach you something about women. We don't steal men from each other or talk shit about one another. We don't say a woman isn't pretty enough for her man. We hold one another up because we want the same respect in return. So take a look at yourself and think about who you want to be. Do you want to be the kind of woman that's so selfish she doesn't care about hurting someone else? Because one day, you're going to fall in love with a man, and when you see someone younger, more beautiful, and more successful trying to take him away from you, you're going to be scared...very scared." I turned around and walked back to Finn, unsure if those words would ever sink in. What I really wanted to do was punch her in the face and make it bruised for weeks, but words were more powerful than violence. I returned to Finn and took his hand again.

"What did you say to her?" We crossed the road and heading to the parking lot where the truck was waiting.

I shrugged. "Just some girl talk."

HE WAS ALREADY naked when I came out of the bedroom. Sitting against the headboard with his rock-hard dick on his stomach, he stared at me like I was the sexiest thing he'd ever seen. The curves of my small love handles aroused him rather than deterred him. The way my thighs jiggled a little when I moved didn't lower his opinion of me at all.

I wore a black baby doll dress without any panties underneath. I knew they wouldn't stay on long anyway. The push-up bra made my tits enormous, and the see-through material had little sparkles in the fabric. It was one of my new items in inventory, and even though it was expensive, I'd bought it myself.

I was happy I had someone to buy lingerie for.

His eyes watched me move closer to the bed, his dick getting harder and darker the longer he waited. His hands rested by his sides, but he seemed restrained. When he swallowed, the muscles in his neck shifted. His lips pressed tightly together, like he was so turned on, it actually hurt.

I crawled onto the bed and made my way up to him.

His hands gripped my hips, and he pulled me into his lap, setting my slit right against his shaft. He squeezed my body as he brought me in close for a kiss, a soft kiss that was delicate and slow.

Our mouths moved together, opening and closing as we enjoyed the affection of the kiss. Our breaths mixed together before they became heated and passionate, our tongues getting into the mix.

His hand moved into my hair, and he rocked against me, rubbing his fat length against my clit.

My arms circled his neck, and I held on tightly as I enjoyed him, so happy to be back in his arms. The moment was so perfect, it was hard to believe it was real. My hands flattened against his chest, and I ground against him harder, so excited to feel him stretch me so good.

He directed my hips forward and backward, making me smear my slickness against his length. He started to shine when there was so much of it. My body defied the laws of nature and produced copious amounts.

He pulled me harder and dragged me against him, kissing me at the same time.

I was already about to come. I was on the threshold the second I saw him in the airport. I'd missed him so much, missed his mind, body, and soul. "Easy..." I fought against his direction. "I'm about to come."

"I want you to come." He dragged me harder again. "Come on." He rocked his hips with me, grinding into me until he pushed me into a euphoric state.

It was much better than the evenings with my vibrator, the fantasies I acted out with Finn through a screen. Smelling his scent and feeling his kiss heightened the sensations until I was a shaking mess on his lap—and he wasn't even inside me. "God..." My nails clawed at his chest, and I moaned right in his face.

He moaned as he watched me, like he was getting off on my orgasm.

When I finished, I stopped rocking against him and stared into his eyes, seeing the way he looked at me. He looked at me like I was special, like I wasn't just some good lay. He looked at me like he loved me more than I loved him.

His arm wrapped around my waist, and he rolled me to my back, getting between my thighs and sliding inside me with moves that were so orchestrated, it seemed like he'd practiced in his mind. He sank inside me, moving inch by inch until he was completely sheathed.

I breathed against his mouth and squeezed his thighs with my hips. My heart beat like a drum, so loud, I swore we could both hear it. His month of absence only made me appreciate him more, made me cherish this moment more profoundly.

"Baby, I'm not gonna last long." His hand moved into my hair, and he closed his eyes as his dick treasured the inside of me, the slickness that my body produced just for him. His lips moved to my neck, and he kissed me before he even began.

"It's okay. We have all night."

He only thrust a few times before he hit his threshold. He came with a groan and filled me, losing his load like a teenager having sex for the first time. He tugged on my hair and growled like a bear, filling my pussy with so much come, it felt like several loads.

His performance would be disappointing to someone else, but to me, it was sexy. Seeing this man lose himself in me so easily made me feel more beautiful, more desirable. He'd been celibate the entire time he was gone, and now all he wanted was to release deep inside my pussy, the place his dick called home.

It turned me on all over again, made me so wet that I didn't need his come for lubrication.

He rested his face in my neck as he recovered, feeling the last waves of pleasure spread through his body. He lifted himself once again, his softening cock quickly changing directions and getting hard again.

"I love watching you come." I loved watching this man turn

into a pile of hormones when he was inside me. He could have any woman he wanted, could have slept with Layla and I never would have known about it, but he stayed faithful to me because he loved me. The second he slid between my legs, he could barely keep himself together—because he never fooled around on me.

He started to rock inside me again, his cock getting harder with every thrust. "Fuck, I missed this pussy." He moved into me harder, like he couldn't control himself and go at a slow pace. His hips bucked hard like he couldn't get his dick inside me quick enough. Stripped down to a man with only his basest instincts, all he could do was fuck me—and fuck me hard.

That was fine with me.

I squeezed his hips with my thighs and gripped his ass with my hands, tugging him deep inside me. "Give it to me, Finn..."

"Fuck." His face moved into my neck, and he fucked me until he hit his limit again, coming with a deep groan. He bucked his hips hard and exploded inside me, filling me with another load of come. "I've never been this horny in my life." His cock softened, but he didn't pull out of me, as if he expected to get hard again in just minutes.

"Me neither."

He kissed me again, slowly rocking with me even though his dick hadn't swelled just yet. He breathed into my mouth and played with my hair, his lips making love to me when his body didn't. In minutes, he was back to full-mast, stretching my channel in every direction once more. Now that he'd been satisfied with two climaxes, he slowed his thrusts down and made love to me the way he used to, having control over his urges. He kissed me and rocked into me, being there for me rather than just himself.

Feeling his come drip from my opening while he moved deep inside me made the sensations that much better. I liked feeling my man give in to his desires by pumping deep inside me. It was the best foreplay I could have asked for.

Now it was my turn to come all over him.

"I love you." He looked me in the eye with his dick fully inside me, his lips lightly caressing mine. He expressed that sentiment rarely, only when he really felt it. When we got off the phone or he dropped me off at home, he didn't usually say it. But when he was deep in the moment, he said it without thinking twice.

I felt my body tighten as I prepared to come around him. "I love you too..."

WHEN I WOKE up the next morning, Finn was gone.

I went downstairs and found the house empty.

Soldier was gone too, so I assumed they were on a run together. After I made a pot of coffee, the garage door opened and they both came inside. Soldier bolted for the water bowl, and Finn grabbed his water bottle and took a long drink. His chest and forehead were drenched in sweat, like he'd done eight miles at a sprint.

"You just got back from a month-long trip, and you decide to go on a run?"

He took another drink, his eyes glued to mine. "I wanted to do some bonding with Soldier. He loves our runs."

"But still..." I took Soldier on a walk every day, but he always tugged on the leash because he wanted to go so much faster. He preferred long runs instead of the boring walks I took him on. "That's crazy."

"I didn't exercise the entire time I was there."

"Because you were working."

He shrugged. "Doesn't matter. I can't keep up this muscle tone without working at it."

I was glad he didn't have any expectations for how he wanted my body to look. I was a couch potato—and he had no problem with that. "When do you go back to work?"

"They gave me three days off."

"Three?" I asked incredulously. "That's it?"

"I've got bills to pay. Plus, I have a huge dog to feed."

"I guess…"

He poured himself a cup of coffee then blotted the sweat away from his forehead with a paper towel. "Don't worry, baby. You'll live with me for a few weeks so we can catch up on all the time we lost."

"Really? I haven't been to my apartment in so long…"

"It'll still be there when it's time to go back. But for now, I want you with me every single day—and every single night."

There was nowhere else I'd rather be. "That sounds nice."

He drank from his coffee mug while his eyes stayed glued to my face. He was just in his running shorts, so his skin was tanned from the sun and his muscles bulged more because of the blood pounding in his veins. "My parents want to have us over for dinner tonight."

"They do?" I asked in surprise.

"They want to hear about my trip. And they want to see you too."

"So, they'll see us…together."

He nodded.

"Huh…" I already knew they didn't have a problem with me, but for the last few years, I'd been going to their house as Colton's wife. Now I was going as their ex-daughter-in-law and potentially their new daughter-in-law.

He studied my face. "Baby, it'll be fine."

"I know. It's just…different. Will Colton be there?"

He nodded. "I think he's bringing Tom."

"Wow...that's a lot of change for your parents."

He shrugged. "Whatever. They'll get used to it."

"Maybe I should make something..."

"I thought you wanted them to like you?" he teased.

I glared at him. "Don't be a dick so soon. I like it when you're sweet and affectionate."

"I'm always sweet and affectionate." He came toward me, his chiseled body shifting with his movements. His eyes were set on me like a target. When he reached me, he wrapped his arms around me and brought me close.

I didn't care about his sweaty arms or the way he smelled like the inside of a gym locker. Naturally, I melted like I had a million times before. My hand went to his arms, and I waited for whatever would come next. "You have no idea how much I missed you."

"No...you have no idea how much I missed you." I was the one who broke down in tears the second I dropped him off at the airport. I was the one who snuggled with his dog every night for comfort. I was the one who had to worry about some gorgeous doctor trying to take him away from me.

He stared at my lips as he held me. "I want you in my bed every night from now on. I hated sleeping alone. I hated knowing you were alone, missing me. I want your body all over mine, your hair across my chest, your breath in my ear."

It sounded like he was asking me to move in with him, but I didn't take his invitation literally. He probably just wanted to make up for all the time we'd lost, to get reacquainted with each other. "That sounds nice..."

18

COLTON

Tom pulled up to the two-story house in the quiet neighborhood. "Wow, they have a nice place."

"Yeah. It's the same house I grew up in."

"Doesn't look that old."

"Hey," I said in offense. "I'm not that old."

He pulled out the bottle of wine he'd picked out. "You think they'll like this?"

"My mom drinks anything. I've seen her drink Cristal like Jay-Z and drink that blush wine out of the box. She doesn't have any standards when it comes to booze."

He nodded. "I like her already."

"Yeah, she's pretty cool."

"You think your parents will be okay with this? Or should I go in there with my guard up?"

"No. My parents are fine with it. They took it hard in the beginning because they like Pepper so much, but now that she's dating my brother, I don't think they care. They've always liked her more than me."

"That worked out in our favor." He glanced in the rearview mirror. "I don't see Finn's truck anywhere."

"He's usually punctual, so I don't know what's slowing him down."

"Pepper," he said with a laugh.

We walked inside and greeted my parents. It was the first time they'd met Tom, and they were nice and warm. My mom hugged him hard and accepted the bottle of wine with gratitude, and my dad shook his hand and clapped him on the back like he was one of my friends.

"We've got burgers in the back," Mom said. "Let's go take a seat."

We moved to the picnic table outside under the gazebo while Dad flipped the burgers on the grill. The salad, macaroni, and condiments were on the table with plastic covers, while the plates and utensils were at the end of the table.

Mom poured us both a glass of wine while Dad kept working on the grill.

"Anyone want any pineapple?" he asked.

"I'll take one," I said.

"Me too," Tom said. "Not a bad idea."

"Need any help, Dad?" I asked.

"No," he said with a chuckle. "This is the one thing I'm good at."

"So," Mom said. "Colton tells me you're an accountant."

"Yep," Tom said. "It's a boring job but steady pay. I work normal business hours, and I'm off on weekends. I used to be a server at Applebee's, so I'm just happy to be out of customer service."

"I bet," Mom said. "I used to do that when I was young too. People can be such jerks—and terrible tippers."

Tom chuckled. "Very true."

My parents talked with Tom like everything was normal. They didn't treat him differently or seem uncomfortable by the fact he was my boyfriend. Like he was a girl, my parents didn't seem to care at all.

That was nice.

Mom glanced at the time on her watch. "Finn is really late... that's not like him."

"Well, he has a girlfriend now...which is also not like him," I jabbed.

Mom swished her wine then shook her head. "I can't believe it...Finn and Pepper. When he first told me, I was surprised. But after I thought about it, it all made sense. Pepper is such a lovely girl, it's no wonder Finn fell for her like the rest of us."

"Yeah...she's perfect." I didn't have a single bad thing to say about her.

"And I'm glad you were so supportive about it." Mom looked at me with pride in her eyes, a look I hadn't received in a long time. "Anyone else would have made a fuss about it, but you were so selfless...putting their happiness first."

Tom didn't say anything, even though he knew I'd made a huge ordeal out of the whole thing.

I didn't feel worthy of the praise, so I changed the subject. "Finn is head over heels for her."

"He is?" she asked, her excitement obvious. "I've always worried he would take too long to settle down, when all the good girls were gone. But I guess he just needed to find the right woman... I'm so happy for him."

"Yeah, I am too." It was hard to believe sometimes, but it was the truth. My brother was in love.

"I hope it lasts," she said with a sigh. "I want Finn to have his own family someday. He's always been a lone wolf, but he needs to realize family is the greatest gift life can give you. Hopefully, Pepper makes him see that."

"Maybe," I said. "He tells me that he loves her pretty often."

Her eyes softened. "Really?"

I nodded.

"Did you hear that?" Mom turned to Dad.

"Yep." Dad kept flipping the burgers. "Looks like we'll have lots of grandkids soon enough."

"Oh, I hope so." Mom turned back to us. "They could have a few, and you could have a few...and we'll be so blessed."

It meant a lot to me that my mother pictured us having kids, that she would love my adoptive children as much as she would love Finn's biological ones. "Yeah...that would be exciting." Tom and I hadn't talked about the future to that extent. For now, we were just living in the moment—which was fine with me.

The back door opened, and Finn stepped out, dressed in a black t-shirt and denim jeans. His aviator sunglasses hung around the collar of his V-neck, the ink from his tattoos noticeable. "Something smells good." He stepped out first, and Pepper came a moment later.

She wasn't as casual as she usually was. It was obvious she was uneasy about this whole thing, uncomfortable that she was with my brother when she'd been married to me for so long. "I can smell the pineapple."

Mom rushed to Finn and cupped his face as she kissed him on the cheek. "I'm so glad you're home. It must have been rough down there."

"It wasn't the best time I've ever had," he said with a chuckle. "But we helped a lot of people. So many lost their homes and everything that mattered to them. And a lot of people got seriously hurt."

"Aww..." She patted his chest with her palm. "You have such a big heart."

"I get that from you, Mom."

She hugged him tightly then moved to Pepper. "My girl...I'm so happy to see you." She hugged Pepper tighter than she hugged her own son. "I'm so glad you and Finn found each other. You're meant to stay in this family, one way or another."

Finn greeted Dad. "Need any help, old man?"

"Nope. You would just screw it up." He hugged him hard and patted him on the back. "So, it was rough down there?"

"Yeah. I slept in a sleeping bag on a stadium floor almost every night," Finn said. "But it was worth it. When disaster strikes, we all have to band together and do what we can."

Dad clapped him on the back. "I'm proud of you, son. You never stop helping people. You know, when your mom and I had you, everyone asked if we were going to enroll you guys in private school and make sure you went to the best colleges. But all your mother and I wanted was for you guys to be good people. We succeeded—a million times over."

Finn turned quiet, so touched by what Dad said, he didn't know what to say.

After Pepper finished talking to Mom, she headed over to my dad and made small talk.

Finn shook hands with Tom then greeted me with a pat on the back. "It's nice to see you guys. I missed you."

"You missed me?" I asked in surprise.

"Yep. I can't believe it either." Finn chuckled then sat down. "But it was a long month. A really long month."

"You must have seen a lot of crazy things," Tom said. "That was a strong storm. They still don't have power everywhere down there."

"Yeah," Finn said in agreement. "But I only agreed to a month. It's someone else's turn now."

"I doubt Pepper would let you go anyway," I said. "She was so lost without you."

He pressed his lips tightly together as the emotion touched his eyes. "Yeah...I know. I was lost without her too."

Pepper came to the table and took the seat beside Finn.

He immediately put his arm around her waist and dragged her closer to his side on the bench, showing her the same level of affection as if my parents weren't there. His lips moved to the shell of her ear, and he kissed her before facing me again.

If someone had told me my brother would end up with Pepper, I would have said that wasn't possible. For one, they never would have gotten together in the first place. And secondly, they wouldn't have lasted this long. But I was looking at it right in the face, two people clearly in love.

PEPPER AND TOM volunteered to do the dishes, so the four of us sat together outside. There was a bowl of watermelon in the center of the table, so I snacked on pieces as we enjoyed one another's company.

Mom was over the moon about Pepper, so she couldn't stop talking about her. "You guys are so cute together."

"Yeah, I know," Finn said with a chuckle. "She's great. She turned me into a man I didn't think I was capable of being. But there's something about her. She earned my respect the moment we met. She's selfless like me. She's...perfect." Finn never had deep conversations about anything, let alone women, so both of my parents had looks of shock on their face.

"That's how I felt when I met your mother," Dad said. "Sometimes you just know..."

"Yep," Mom said. "Pepper is so special. She's the woman you want to bring home to your parents. She's got a good heart and an even better mind. That woman is so independent. A strong man needs a strong woman...seems like a perfect match to me."

Finn stared at the picnic table as he drummed his fingers against the surface. Lightly, his fingers tapped against the wood, making a backdrop of noise. When he took a deep breath, he straightened and expanded his chest. "Yeah, it is. That's why I'm asking her to marry me." He said it nonchalantly, like he didn't just drop an atomic bomb on the entire table.

We were all stunned. Mom's jaw dropped like she'd seen a ghost. Dad's immediate reaction was to twist his neck so he could look at Mom.

I didn't know what my reaction was, but I was definitely shocked.

My brother was going to propose to Pepper.

Could this really be happening?

It took nearly a minute for someone to say something.

Mom went first. "Finn, are you being serious?"

"Yep." He pulled his phone out of his pocket and pulled up the picture. "I bought the ring this week."

She yanked it out of his hand and stared at it. "Wow...it's beautiful." She showed it to Dad. "Oh god, I'm gonna start crying. I've got to keep my shit together..." Mom never cussed, so it was comical to hear those words fly out of her mouth.

"Wow, that's very nice, son." Dad looked at the picture then handed it to me.

I almost couldn't look at the picture because I wasn't ready to accept it. Everything had happened so fast. They hadn't even been together that long, less than six months. My brother went from a life of complete solitude to buying an engagement ring for a woman he'd been dating a short time.

I stared at the solitaire ring, the simple design with the large diamond in the center. My hand shook as I looked at the image, imagining Pepper wearing a ring different from the one I had given her. I slowly handed the phone back to him.

Finn watched me, studying my expression since I didn't have the same reaction as our parents. "She doesn't have a family, so I don't have anyone to ask for permission. Since you're the closest thing she has...I want to ask you. Do I have your blessing, Colton?"

I felt his eyes on my face, along with the stares of my parents. He was putting me on the spot, so I didn't have any choice but to be supportive. "You don't think this is a little fast?" Maybe that wasn't the answer he wanted to hear, but I had to ask the question anyway.

"Yeah, it is really fast," Finn said. "But I did a lot of thinking while I was on that trip...and it feels right. It felt right the moment I met her." He hid the photo on his phone then slipped it into his pocket. "You never answered my question, Colt."

Now was the moment of truth. I'd thought I was okay with them being together, but now I realized I was really letting her go. She would marry Finn and no longer be my ex-wife. She would be someone else's wife. Everything was moving so fast, but at the end of the day, it didn't change anything. Pepper was happy...and I wanted her to be happy with Finn for the rest of her life. "Of course, man. Take care of her."

He placed his hand on my back and gave me a gentle pat. "You know I will."

19

PEPPER

Since I was out of clothes, I went by my apartment to pick up a few things. Now I was taking walks with Finn and Soldier on a daily basis, so I needed more workout clothes. Losing weight had never been important to me, so I never bought clothes to wear to the gym. But now, Finn was indirectly forcing me to have a healthy lifestyle.

I looked through my things and tossed everything into a bag.

The front door opened. "Pepper?" Colton raised his voice. "Are you here?"

I stepped out of my old bedroom. "Yeah. What are you doing here?"

"I ran out of toilet paper, so I came to steal yours." He held up his key. "But the door was already unlocked."

"How long have you been taking my shit?"

"Not nearly as long as you've been taking mine."

I rolled my eyes. "I'm just picking up more clothes before I head back to Finn's. I've been doing all these walks with him, so I need more workout clothes."

"Oh, you must hate that."

"It's not so bad, but he likes to walk so far. His goal is to make Soldier tired by bedtime."

"But he's making you tired?" he teased.

"Something like that."

He helped himself to the bathroom and grabbed a couple of rolls. "With you here, I feel like I have a Costco right next door."

I stuck out my tongue at him.

"Payback is a bitch, ain't it?"

"Ain't isn't a word."

"It sure is to me—and I'm a lawyer."

"Put that in your documents, and you'll be a fired lawyer."

He set the toilet paper on the table near the door. "So, what's the plan? Are you living there now?"

"I don't know. He wants me to stay with him for a while, but I'm not officially moving in. So...I'm not really sure."

He crossed his arms over his chest and nodded.

"It's been nice being with him all the time. I missed him so much, and I'm glad he doesn't feel smothered."

"It doesn't seem like he's smothered at all..."

"Yeah. I'll keep crashing there until I get the hint that he wants me to leave."

"Maybe he'll never want you to leave."

I chuckled. "I doubt that. But it would be nice to get rid of this place. I'm paying a fortune in rent for no reason. At least I'm not paying for utilities."

"Yeah, true. I wonder what half of Finn's mortgage is?"

I shrugged. "Even if I moved in with him, he would never let me pay half. He's way too proud."

"True."

I zipped up the bag and held it over my shoulder. "What are you doing tonight?"

"Just chilling at home."

"No Tom?"

He shook his head. "Just me."

"Well, I would ask you to do something, but I don't think I've seen Finn enough. He's been home for a couple weeks, but it only feels like a few days."

"Don't worry about it," he said. "I know you guys missed each other like crazy. Soldier too."

I kissed him on the cheek before I walked out. "Don't take all my stuff, alright?"

"We'll see."

I turned around when I got to the door. "I'll see you later."

"Yeah...I'll see you later." Colton looked at me with emotion in his eyes, as if we were saying goodbye. It was as if I was on the precipice of leaving forever, as if we would never see each other again.

"Everything alright?"

"Yeah." He slid his hands into the pockets of his jeans. "I'm just happy for you..."

"Happy for me?"

"You know...that Finn is home and you guys are doing so well. It went well with my parents. It just seems like everything is working out for you."

"Yeah...I am happy. Things seem to be going well with you and Tom too."

"Yeah...things are good." He grabbed the two rolls of toilet paper and stuffed them under his arm. "It's just crazy how things change sometimes. The four of us had dinner with my parents last night like it was no big deal... Who would have thought that would ever happen?"

"True. I guess it is crazy."

He nodded then walked past me into the hallway. "A year ago, I never would have thought we would be here...but here we are." He crossed the hall back into his apartment then shut the door.

While that felt like a positive conversation, Colton seemed a little off. He appeared equally sad and heartbroken. Maybe the most serious my relationship with Finn became, the more Colton realized that we were both moving on. Sometimes I forgot I was his ex-wife because it seemed like we were just really good friends. But maybe Colton was struggling with that more than I realized... especially after seeing Finn and me together with his parents. Maybe it bothered him, but he didn't want to admit that out loud.

Maybe I should talk to him about it.

Or maybe it was better left unsaid.

"WHAT'S THIS?" Finn came in the door wearing his dark blue scrubs with his stethoscope around his neck. Even in the baggy clothing, he looked like the sexiest piece of man candy in the world.

"Soldier and I made dinner."

He set his keys and wallet on the counter then raised an eyebrow. "You and Soldier?"

"Well, mostly Soldier."

He walked to the stove and looked at the pan of chicken enchiladas. "Wow, those look pretty good."

"Why are you surprised?"

"I guess I shouldn't be...since Soldier made them." He turned to me with that sexy smile then kissed the corner of my mouth. "You don't have to cook, baby. I don't mind doing it."

"I wanted to. When you work all day, I thought it would be nice to come home to a hot meal."

He grabbed a fork from the drawer then took a bite. After slowly chewing and savoring the sample, he gave me a look of approval. "That's pretty damn good. Where did you learn this?"

"YouTube."

"Looks like your bad cooking streak is over." He pulled out a couple of plates and scooped the enchiladas and rice onto his plate. "Unless you were being serious when you said Soldier did all the cooking?"

I shrugged. "He might have helped a bit."

We gathered our food and sat at the dining table together. He drank water instead of scotch, and all his paperwork for dictation was beside him. He cut into his food and ate quickly, like he hadn't eaten anything all day.

"You seem to like it."

"Because it's good. This is a home run."

Soldier sat on the ground next to the table, hoping a scrap of food would fall for him to feast on.

"How was work?" I asked, knowing his day was far more interesting than mine.

"Uneventful, with the exception of one thing." He finished chewing before he kept talking. "I worked with Layla today."

"Oh?"

"She was quiet, left me alone, and she didn't bother me at all. She barely even looked at me. It was nice."

Maybe my words got to her, after all.

"You must have said the right thing to make her change her attitude like that."

I shrugged.

He watched me, approval in his eyes. "Any other woman would have punched her in the face, but you didn't. You have so much power, you don't need violence. You always know what to say for any situation."

"I don't know about that..."

"Well, whatever you did obviously worked. It's made my life a lot easier."

I was glad I'd struck a chord with Layla. Now I wouldn't have to deal with her desperation anymore.

"What about your day?" With his elbow on the table, he sat forward and shoveled the food into his mouth, eating like a hungry bear that couldn't get enough sustenance.

To me, it seemed like we were a married couple, two people sharing their lives together. We talked about our day while we shared a home-cooked meal. It was nice...so nice that I wished we could do this forever. "It was good. But I had a weird conversation with Colton."

Finn stopped eating. He abruptly raised his hand from his plate and looked at me, turning still and quiet as he considered what I'd just said. "What did he say?"

"I went to my apartment to pick up a few things, and he stopped by to get some toilet paper...because he's a thief." I rolled my eyes. "But then we started talking about us, and he said he was happy for me...but he also seemed sad as he said it."

Finn's appetite must have vanished because he set his fork down even though there was still plenty of food on his plate. He sat back against the wood of the chair and stared at me, his mind working furiously behind that pretty face. "And that was it?"

"He didn't say much, but what he didn't say concerns me. I think seeing us together at your parents' house stirred him up a little bit. The two of us used to go there together all the time, for holidays and birthdays. Now, everything is different. Maybe it bothered him, but he doesn't want to admit it."

His eyes drifted away, and he sat in silence. He didn't express his thoughts to me, choosing to let the moment be overshadowed by his sullen mood. His hands rested on the armrests, and his stethoscope shifted slightly around his neck with his movements.

"I might be overthinking it."

"Maybe," he said noncommittally. "I'll talk to him and make sure he's doing alright."

"That's a good idea. If he were unhappy, he probably wouldn't tell me."

"Yeah...you're probably right." He leaned forward again and picked up his fork, but this time, he didn't take a bite. He just stirred his fork around the contents of his plate, his mind elsewhere.

"What's wrong?"

He lifted his chin and looked at me again. "Nothing, baby."

20

COLTON

I'D JUST PUT A LOAD OF LAUNDRY INTO THE WASHER WHEN THERE was a knock on the door. Since it was laundry day, I was in old sweatpants and a t-shirt with holes on it. Tom wouldn't stop by unannounced, so I assumed it was Pepper.

I opened the door and came face-to-face with my brother instead. He was dressed in his scrubs, and it was clear he'd just finished his shift in the ER. "Hey, what brings you here?"

"Can we talk?" He stepped inside without waiting for me to initiate an invite.

"Sure...everything alright?"

"Does it seem like everything is okay?" He turned around and faced me, looking furious with his tight jaw and hostile eyes. His shoulders were tense, and his forearms were lined with veins. He didn't need to convey much to show his irritation, and right now, his distaste was amplified to a decibel-breaking volume.

"I'm not following."

"Pepper told me you guys had a weird conversation the other day. She said you were behaving strangely. She didn't know what to make of it, so she just assumed you have a problem with us.

Seeing the two of us together at Mom and Dad's freaked you out."

I hadn't put much thought into our conversation. I'd assumed she hadn't noticed anything was out of the ordinary.

"If you aren't careful, she'll figure out what's going on."

"Trust me, she has no idea. The last thing she expects you to do is propose."

"You're still messing with her head. I don't want her to say no because she thinks you have a problem."

I laughed because it was absurd. "She won't say no."

"Whatever. So what the hell was that about?"

"What?"

"Your weirdness. Why did you act like that?"

I stepped back, wishing I had a beer to swallow this drama down. "Look, you dropped a bomb on me and Mom and Dad."

"Mom and Dad seem fine with it. In fact, they seem thrilled about it."

"Well, I've proposed to Pepper before, so it's a little weird. I had the exact same conversation with Mom and Dad—at that very table. Sorry if I freaked out a little, but I'm also not sorry."

"You gave me your blessing."

"And you still have it. But it's just weird..."

He still wore the same pissed-off expression. "Are you sure you're okay with this? Because I can't afford to have you acting weird around her and tipping her off. Or worse, getting her to think that being with me is a bad idea."

"Hey, I said nothing like that to her. In fact, I told her I was happy for her."

"But you seemed sad about it."

"I am sad," I blurted.

My brother stared at me, his eyes turning less angry.

"I'm not sad that she's going to end up with you. I'm sad that...I'm losing her. Now, she'll have her own life with you...she won't live across the hall from me. She'll be remarried, so I'm not really her ex-husband anymore. I guess...it's hard to let her go. She won't need me anymore."

Pity entered his gaze. "Isn't that a good thing?"

"It is...but everything is changing. It happened so fast."

He closed the gap between us and came closer to me. "It did happen fast. And change is always hard...but you need to accept it, Colton."

"I do accept it. I am happy for her. It'll just take some time to get used to."

"Colt." He didn't continue speaking until I looked at him.

My eyes shifted back to his face.

"If you aren't ready for this, I won't ask. I'll give it some time. I want this to be a happy moment for everyone. Maybe I was insensitive when I asked, but once you gave me your permission to be with her, I thought that was it."

"But I didn't expect you to propose so quickly. Last time we spoke, you acted like you might never get married..."

"Well...I changed my mind."

"And why did you change it so drastically?"

He rubbed the back of his neck, sighing under his breath. "Being apart from her made me realize how much I love her. It also showed me how supportive she is. She trusted me to do that with Layla trying to get in my pants every night. And she never tried to talk me out of going. She understood it was important to me, and she didn't ask me to stay. I want a woman like that. I want someone who will always be supportive that way, who understands my need to do humanitarian work like that. She's it, man. Why wait?"

"That's romantic, but did you think about other things? What about kids? You know she wants a family."

He shrugged. "I'm not there yet, obviously. But maybe I'll

change my mind about it. She changed my mind about marriage."

"Finn, you can't marry her unless you're willing to give that to her. Don't propose unless you're on board with that. You'll just hurt her when you have the conversation later. I'm telling you, kids are important to her. It's a deal-breaker."

He searched my gaze as he considered what I said. His eyes shifted back and forth as he internalized my statement. After what felt like an eternity of silence, he spoke. "I'll do it. If it's important to her, then we'll have some kids. But she's only twenty-six, so we have plenty of time together before we need to start popping them out. That's a fair compromise."

I couldn't believe he'd agreed so easily. My brother really wanted to marry her.

"The only thing standing in our way is you—frankly. So, are you okay with this or not?"

"Of course I am—"

"Be honest with me, Colton. Because when she says yes, there's no going back. I'm marrying her, even if you don't like it. So, speak your truth now, or forever hold your peace."

I understood my pain came from a deep place in my heart. It was a personal feeling of loss, of losing something I'd had for so long. But I had to remember I'd lost her a year ago. I wasn't losing her now...I already had. It was time to move on, to really let go. "Yes, I'm okay with it. Marry her."

He studied my gaze, looking for sincerity.

"I mean it."

"Good. Now stop acting weird around her."

I rolled my eyes. "I didn't mean to."

"Well, do a better job."

"Geez, alright." I crossed my arms over my chest. "I can't believe my heart-breaking, player brother is getting married."

"I'm not getting married. She's got to say yes first."

"Dude, she's going to say yes."

He shrugged. "You never know. Maybe I'll ask, and she'll realize she can do way better than me."

"Finn, you're stupid. She's head over heels in love with you."

He grinned. "She is, isn't she?"

I rolled my eyes again.

"That woman will be mine for the rest of my life. Pretty exciting." Now that the difficult part of the conversation was over, he finally relaxed and let his threatening demeanor dissipate.

"Yeah...you're a lucky man."

"I know I am." He leaned against the back of the couch, still wearing a slightly boyish grin.

"When are you going to ask her?"

"Not sure. I haven't decided when or how. I want it to be simple, just me asking her to marry me. She doesn't seem like a woman who cares about fancy dinners or dramatic gestures. She seems like someone who prefers whispers, something quiet and from the heart."

My brother might know her better than I did. "That's a good idea."

"I also want her to be surprised. That's important to me."

I chuckled. "She'll definitely be surprised, man. She'll have no idea it's coming..."

"As long as you don't fuck it up."

"I said I would keep my mouth shut, alright? When did you get the ring?"

"A few days before I showed you. I looked online for a bit before I found a store nearby that carried the ring I wanted. I picked it up, and the rest is history."

"It looks expensive."

"You think I'm going to have my wife wear anything that isn't expensive?"

"Pepper doesn't care about that kind of stuff."

"I know. But I want her to look down at that ring every day and love it. And I want every guy who looks at her to know there's a powerful man behind that ring."

"Who knew you could be so romantic..."

He chuckled. "Definitely not me." He straightened then dropped his hands to his sides. "I'm glad we got this straightened out. It's a big deal. A lot is about to change."

Our old wedding photos would have to go into storage, and we would have to move on with our lives. Our marriage might turn into a secret we never spoke of. When they had kids, they probably wouldn't want their kids to know Pepper had ever been married to me. But it was time to move on, to find our new places in this world. "Yeah, it's about to change for the better."

21

PEPPER

"His parents were totally fine with it." My empty glass sat in front of me, needing a refill. "I thought it might be a little weird, but it felt oddly normal...like that's how it should have been from the beginning."

"That's sweet," Tatum said. "Maybe the reason you were with Colton was to find Finn. Maybe that was the big man's master plan all along."

"It's cool that they didn't make a fuss about it." Stella had her hair in a slick ponytail, looking a lot like Ariana Grande with her dark skin and petite frame. "That's not a normal situation, but they kept an open mind. They sound like cool parents. Their son was there with his boyfriend, and their other son is sleeping with their former daughter-in-law. That's quite a barbecue."

"True." I didn't have a family, so I cherished Colton's parents even more. Even though they had a slip-up with Colton, they were good people. They stood by their sons no matter what. And they were always so proud of Finn and all of his sacrifices. Whenever Finn spoke to his mother, he turned into a respectful mama's boy—which I found adorable. She'd obviously earned his respect. "I'm gonna get a refill." I slid out of the booth and walked to the bar. I'd headed over right after work, so I was in my skinny jeans, booties, and a long blouse with a gold necklace. Since I kinda worked in fashion, I had to look nice all the time, but there were definitely days when I wished I could wear scrubs like Finn. "I'll take a cosmo."

"And I'll pay for it." A guy I didn't recognize as a regular appeared at my side. Tall, handsome, and friendly, he kept a respectable distance between us. "A pretty girl like you shouldn't be buying her own drinks."

"That's awfully nice of you." Since the bartender was working on my glass, I stayed at the bar, feeling this man stare at me hard. When I was unattached, I didn't get hot guys chasing after me, but now that I was settled down, they were somehow attracted to me. "But I should tell you, I have a boyfriend."

"Having a boyfriend doesn't make you less pretty."

"That's subjective."

He held his beer in his hand and glanced at the TV. "You watch baseball?"

"I love baseball. Mariners fan."

He smiled. "Are you sure you want to keep your boyfriend?"

Finn was the love of my life, the man I couldn't live without. "Yes."

He scooted closer to me, making the area around us heated when he crossed an invisible line. "Let me tell you something about men." His arm moved around my waist.

Whoa...

"They are all the same. They all want one thing—"

"Yes, I can tell." I pushed his arm down and noticed the heavy smell of booze on his breath. "You know what? I'll get my own drink—"

"Listen to me." His arm moved around my waist again, and he tugged me toward him. "My ex-girlfriend just left me for her boss...some arrogant prick who drives a Jag...and I'm not as trusting as I used to be."

This guy was totally hammered—and it was Tuesday. I wanted to cut him some slack because he was clearly heartbroken, but I didn't appreciate being groped like a doll. "Enough with the touching, alright?" I pushed his arm off. "I know you're going through a hard time so I'll give you a free pass, but do it again and—"

"You'll what?" He grabbed me and yanked me into his side.

The bartender spotted trouble, so he grabbed his bat from behind the counter.

I didn't need his help. "Don't touch me, asshole." I slapped him across the face.

He stepped back with the hit, his eyes burning into a raging storm. He turned back to me, bloodlust in his gaze.

That was my moment to run, but I'd learned never to turn your back on an enemy. I was afraid if I turned away, he would attack me from behind. So I gripped the counter and prepared to be punched in the face by a guy who weighed more than two hundred pounds. I shouldn't pity him, but I still did. A woman had ruined him—and he would regret his behavior tomorrow.

Then he made his move.

I grabbed his beer bottle and prepared to slam it into his head.

"I don't think so, asshole." Finn came up from behind me, spun the guy around by gripping his arm, and then slammed him down into the bar. He pinned his arms against his head and squished his cheek against the counter. "Call the cops, Freddie."

Freddie already had his phone against his ear. "I'm on it."

My heart was still pumping hard with adrenaline. I'd thought I was about to get my nose broken or, worse, get knocked out cold. But this hero came out of nowhere and saved me. I stepped back and spotted my untouched drink on the counter. I downed the entire thing.

"You alright?" Stella asked, appearing at my side with Tatum.

"Yeah, I'm fine..." I kept staring at the guy as he tried to fight Finn off, but he couldn't move an inch. Finn was way too strong, even though he didn't weight as much. I shouldn't feel bad for the guy, but I did. I knew what it was like to do something stupid in the heat of heartbreak. I'd never assaulted anyone...but I'd been pretty low.

Stella rubbed my arm. "If Finn weren't here, we would have had your back."

"I know," I said, still watching Finn keep the guy down.

Finn finally turned to me. "Baby, go sit down." His tone was clipped because he barked out the order rather than made a request. He looked at me for a few seconds before he returned his attention to the drunk man he was overpowering.

I didn't disobey.

The three of us returned to our table.

Stella kept studying me. "You sure you're okay?"

"You're oddly calm," Tatum noted.

"I guess I feel bad for the guy," I said. "He said his girlfriend left him for someone else... I know how that feels."

"You better not feel bad for him," Stella countered. "Heartbreak and booze don't give him the right to do that."

"I know," I said. "But think about how low you'd have to be to act that way. It's sad."

"I'm surprised Finn is so calm," Tatum said. "He didn't even punch the guy. He just restrained him."

"He's used to chaotic situations," I said. "He probably didn't think twice about it."

The cops came in a moment later and put the guy in handcuffs. They talked to Finn and the bartender for a while before they escorted the drunk guy out of the building and into the squad car.

Finn joined us a moment later, no longer calm and pragmatic about the situation. He went straight for me, slid into the booth beside me, and cupped my cheeks with his palms. Indifferent to my friends sitting across the table, he rested his forehead against mine. "You alright, baby?"

"I'm fine."

He rubbed his forehead against mine before he kissed the corner of my mouth. "I would have killed him if he touched you."

"Thanks to you, he never got the chance."

He kissed my forehead then wrapped his arm around my shoulders, pulling me close into his side like he was still protecting me. He rested his head against mine as he looked down at the ground. "I love you." He didn't care about the two people listening in on the conversation. Like we were the only two people in the world, he wore his heart on his sleeve.

"I love you too."

He pulled away and slid out of the booth. "I need a scotch after that..." He left the table and returned to the bar, his tight shirt showing off all the muscles of his body. His jeans hugged his ass as he walked away.

I turned back to my friends.

Stella's jaw had dropped, her eyes bulging wide. "Oh. My. God."

"He's so in love with you," Tatum said. "That was so sweet..."

"That man knows how to love a woman," Stella said. "Geez, you're lucky."

I felt like the luckiest woman in the world every night of my life. "I know...I am very lucky."

INSTEAD OF TREATING me like a fragile piece of glass, Finn loved me like everything was normal. The only difference was the devotion in his eyes, the way he hugged me a little harder, kissed me with a little more passion.

His hands sometimes shook when he touched me, when his fingers grazed my hair or touched my skin. Buried between my legs with a cock as hard as steel, he slid in and out of me like he craved me, but his attention to my eyes showed that he wanted more than just my body.

He wanted my soul.

With my legs wide apart and my ankles locked together against his back, I gripped his shoulders and felt him sink deep inside me, feeling me in a way he'd never felt another woman before. He was so thick and I was so wet, so we slid together without an ounce of friction. My body craved his so much that I didn't want to release him every time he pulled out.

"Baby." His hips slowly rocked into my body, his pelvic bone rubbing against my aching clit. Our moisture slid past each other, and he was so hard, he was about to burst at any moment, giving me another load that would sit all night long. "I would never let anything happen to you."

My hands palmed his chest and slowly rose toward his shoulders. When he looked at me like that, I felt like a supermodel with my hair perfectly spread out across the pillow. With beautiful eyes and flawless makeup, I was sexier than a porn star. In reality, I looked nothing like that, but he made me feel like I did. "I know."

He pressed his forehead against mine, his cock pushing deep inside me. His voice came out as a whisper. "I'd die before I let anything happen to you."

My thighs squeezed his hips as the surge of longing overcame me. It wasn't his rock-hard body, his tattoos, or his excellent lovemaking that made me want to come. It was the way he loved me, the way he was so vulnerable with me. "I know..." When my thighs squeezed his hips, my pussy squeezed his length.

"Because you're my baby." His mouth moved to my neck, and he kissed me, his hot breaths trailing over my skin like warm breezes. He licked my sweat then breathed against my ear. "Because I love you."

I became so tight, there was no going back. I couldn't release him, and the force made me buck against him with an orgasm so piercing that I could feel the heavens inside me. My hands gripped him hard, and I moaned as I listened to him pledge his love to me. My body exploded in a fireworks display, and I convulsed against him, having the best climax of my life.

He moaned against my ear then gave his final thrusts. When he shuddered, his cock thickened, and he released inside me, giving another groan as he filled me with a hot load that would seep out between my legs in the shower the following morning. He came when I came, probably aroused by how much I desired him.

When he finished, he brought his face close to mine, his softening dick still deep inside me. "It doesn't matter how many times I have you...I need to keep making love to you." He started to rock again, his soft cock still sliding through my channel. In no time, it would be hard again. Ready for me once more.

As much as I enjoyed staying with him, it was time for me to return to my apartment. It'd been almost a full month of practically living together, waking up to the sound of each other's alarms, having dinner together, and making love so much that we had to wash the sheets on a daily basis.

It was heaven.

But I didn't want to overstay my welcome and have him push me away because I'd crossed the line. Our relationship was so perfect, and the last thing I wanted to do was screw it up. This man filled my heart so completely that I would probably stay with him even if he never married me, even if he never wanted kids.

That's how bad I had it.

I stuffed the bag with clothes and my toiletry kit and zipped it shut.

Finn appeared in the doorway, wearing nothing but his sweatpants. His ink acted as its own form of clothing. His hands were in his pockets, and he leaned against the doorway, seeing me standing at the foot of the bed with my bag on top. "What are you doing?"

"I thought I would go home for a few days." If he asked me to stay for another month, I would—without hesitation. But I was in this for the long haul, not just a fling. I had to make the best decisions for a long-lasting relationship. "You know, make sure it's still there..." I chuckled then pulled the strap of the bag over my shoulder. "You mind giving me a ride?"

He watched me with those beautiful eyes, his expression intense but also impossible to read. Heartbeats passed, and he was absolutely still, his chest barely rising and falling. The man was never unnerved, even faced with imminent danger. The only time he lost his cool was when we had one of our fights—which didn't happen often. "Put the bag down."

I didn't want to leave anyway, so any reason to stay was good enough for me. I pulled the strap off my shoulder and set the bag on the bed. I turned to him, waiting to see if he would say anything else.

He turned his neck in the direction of his dresser. With three drawers and his iPad on top, it was the place he kept his t-shirts, boxers, and sweatpants. "There's something I want you to have. Open the second drawer."

For a man who didn't want commitment, he behaved like he never wanted me to leave. And now he wanted me to have a drawer at his place, a section where I could stow my stuff as I came and went. It was a big deal coming from him. I smiled and moved to the dresser. "You're giving me a drawer."

He crossed his arms over his chest. "Open it."

I grabbed one of the knobs and stared him, unsure why he was being so quiet. He was playful just an hour ago, but now he was dangerously serious. I turned back to the dresser and opened the drawer, expecting to find some of his clothes that he wanted me to have. He knew I loved to sleep in his long t-shirts, the cotton that was so soft against my skin. Everything smelled like him—and that was my favorite quality.

I noticed a small black box in the center of the drawer.

I stared at it, unsure what it could be.

Any woman would assume it was an engagement ring, but I knew better than that. Finn had made it clear he wouldn't be ready for that for a long time. So it was probably a piece of jewelry. Or better yet, it was one of his medals that he wanted me to have. I already had his necklace, and now he wanted me to have something else.

I grabbed the box and opened the lid.

A sparkling diamond faced me, so brilliant and beautiful, it seemed too pretty to touch. With a white gold band and rainbows in the prisms, it was a ring I'd never imagined myself wearing. The one Colton gave me was different. Full of diamonds on the band, it had been beautiful, but cluttered. This was so simple.

It took me a second to grasp what I was holding.

A diamond ring. "Finn..." I turned back to him, my eyes

moving to the door where he'd been a moment ago. But now, he wasn't there.

He was down on one knee.

I almost dropped the box.

"Marry me." He didn't give a speech about how much he loved me. It was unnecessary because he showed me every single day. He didn't even ask me to be his wife. He just told me to be. That made it so much better.

A proposal was the last thing I'd expected, so my emotions were uncontrollable. Tears burned in my eyes and quickly streaked down my cheeks. It didn't matter if this seemed too fast. It didn't matter if he was my ex-husband's brother. It didn't matter if this ended badly someday. I'd never wanted anyone more in my life, and I was ready to give my entire heart to him. "Yes..."

Without taking his eyes off mine, he took the box from my hand, pulled out the ring, and slipped it onto my left hand.

It was a perfect fit.

I wrapped my arms around his neck and kissed him as he rose to his feet, lifting me with him. With my tears dripping on his face, I kissed him, kissed the last man I would ever kiss in my entire life. The happiness in my chest was so explosive, it couldn't be contained. My whole life, I'd always felt lost, like I didn't belong anywhere. But this man made me feel like I was home.

He was home.

22

COLTON

Someone kept knocking on the door.

Knock. Knock. Knock. Knock. Knock.

It was an infinite knock, constant and irritating. It was a Sunday night, almost eight o'clock, so why the obnoxious intrusion? Tom would never do something like that. He had way too much class to be a pest.

I yanked the door open. "*What?*"

Pepper kept her hand up, her fingers balled into a fist because she'd been pounding on the door so obnoxiously. She smiled innocently, like she hadn't just been a pain in the ass. She raised her left hand, and on her ring finger was the gorgeous diamond Finn had bought for her.

My eyes shifted back to hers, and when I saw just how happy she was, all my insecurities disappeared. She wasn't hurting over me anymore. She wasn't insecure after our divorce. She'd moved on to another guy—a better guy. I put on my smile. "Congratulations."

She jumped into my arms and hugged me. "I can't believe he asked. Finn asked me."

I carried her into the apartment and shut the door, able to

hold her with one arm because she was so light. "How did he do it?"

"Oh, it was so romantic. I was packing my stuff to come back to the apartment, and he told me he gave me one of his drawers. When I opened it, the ring was sitting there. And when I turned around, he was on one knee..."

"Wow, that is pretty romantic."

"I know!" She jumped down and clapped her hands together excitedly. "I had no idea it was coming. I had no idea he would ever ask. I just stood there in shock...then I started to cry. I just... never thought this would happen. Now I'm so happy." She cupped her face then wiped away the moisture that had developed in her eyes, making sure her makeup didn't get ruined by oncoming tears.

"I'm happy for you—both of you."

"My head is still spinning a million miles an hour."

"When did he ask you?"

"A couple hours ago. I had to come over here and tell you." She grabbed both of my hands and squeezed them. "Did he tell you he was going to ask?"

"Yeah. He told me and my parents at the barbecue last month."

"Really?" she asked. "And I was in the kitchen?"

"He's risky," I said with a shrug. "Likes to hide in plain sight."

"What did your parents say?"

I gave her an annoyed look. "Come on, you know what they said. They were thrilled, babe. All of us were."

"You included, right?" she asked, slightly hesitant.

I wanted to roll my eyes to prove to her that her concern was ridiculous—but it wasn't. All these changes were hard, but it didn't mean I wasn't happy. "He asked if I was okay with it. Said he wouldn't propose without my blessing. Of course, I gave it to him. We were family before, and now we'll be family again—just in a new way."

"Yeah. Our kids will be cousins."

"Yeah, they will."

She clapped her hands together again. "I'm just so happy. I've never been this happy before."

I didn't take offense at that statement. "You guys make so much sense. My brother needed the perfect woman to set him straight—and you're that perfect woman."

"It wasn't even hard. He's just so wonderful and perfect...I'm so lucky."

"You both are lucky." I pulled her into my side and kissed her on the forehead. "I know it's Sunday night, but should we go out and celebrate?"

"No, it's late and it is Sunday. We'll get together tomorrow. I just wanted to come over here and tell you because I was so excited. You're my best friend. I tell you everything."

"Then let's have some wine." I walked into the kitchen and pulled out a bottle I'd been saving for a special occasion. I set it on the counter and grabbed two glasses.

"Hey, I recognize that." She grabbed the bottle and looked at the label. "Someone gave this to us for our wedding. Told us to open it for our five-year anniversary."

"Yeah, I remember." I popped the cork and poured two glasses. "We were saving it for a special occasion—and I think tonight is that occasion." I held up my glass to hers. "To you and Finn."

Her eyes filled with emotion as she looked at me, so happy that I was being supportive about this. She wanted both of us in her life, the two men she needed most. Having me celebrate with her made her so happy. "You'll be my maid of honor, right?"

My answer was immediate. "Of course."

FINN and I met for lunch the next day. He was off, Pepper was at work, and I was able to take a long lunch. I joined him at the table near the window, wearing my suit and tie.

He rose to his feet and greeted me with a grin. "Looking good."

"Thanks." I hugged him and clapped him on the back.

"Pepper said she had a good time last night." He sat down, approval in his voice.

"Yeah, we drank too much wine, laughed too much, and talked about the wedding. I'll be her maid of honor... Stella will be pissed."

"You aren't going to be my best man?" he asked, still smiling.

"I don't know...are you asking me?"

"I didn't think I needed to ask. I just assumed."

"Oh...I thought you'd get one of your military buddies to do it."

"I could, but I'd rather it be you. You're my brother...and my friend."

I hadn't expected him to ask me, so the question was even more meaningful. "I've never been asked to be a best man and a maid of honor before."

"That's what you get for being popular."

"I guess I'll talk to Pepper about it. If I'm her maid of honor, Stella would lose her shit anyway."

"I'm not sure how much of a wedding we'll have." He already had a beer in front of him, so he took a drink. "We'll do whatever she wants, but I thought we would have something small, just a few friends and family. She's already done this once, so I doubt she wants to do the whole thing again."

"I think she just wants to marry you."

"Yeah." He grinned. "Definitely."

"So, are you going to wear a ring?" My old ring was sitting in my nightstand where I hadn't touched it.

"No. I figured I would just get a tattoo. I wouldn't want to wear my ring to the hospital because it'd be impossible to keep it clean all the time. I don't like anything on my hands anyway." He flexed his fingers then balled them into a fist. "I doubt she'll care."

"Permanently inking your love for her on your skin? Yeah, she'll love it."

"Pretty romantic, huh?" He looked at his hands then grabbed his beer again.

"She was so happy last night, man. And so surprised."

"Yeah...she seemed it. When she looked at me, there was so much written on her face. She was overwhelmed. She didn't know if she should cry or laugh...there was a lot going on. When she grabbed the box, she didn't even think it was a ring. She thought I was giving her a random piece of jewelry. So it made it that much more beautiful."

"Wow...Finn Burke is a romantic."

"I'm a romantic for one woman—my fiancée." He grinned as he said the word, the term rolling off his tongue.

"What did Mom say?"

"You know, the usual. Lots of tears. Asked about babies..."

"That's all she cares about, huh?"

He shrugged. "I told her I'll practice making them...that's the best I can do."

I tried not to cringe.

"Come on, this woman is gonna be my wife. I'm gonna say dirty things about her."

"I know...just gotta get used to it."

Finn grabbed his menu and looked over the entrees. "What are you getting?"

I turned to wave down the waitress. "A beer, for starters."

"Even though you're going back to the office?"

"It's pretty laid-back there." I finally got her attention and ordered an IPA. Since she was there, Finn and I both ordered lunch too—salads and sandwiches. After she made eyes at Finn, she walked away.

"Hopefully, that tattooed wedding ring will keep the ladies off you."

He shrugged. "I won't get my hopes up."

"So, you're off today?"

He nodded. "I hate that Pepper owns her own business. She can't just ditch work like I can."

"Yeah, but she likes it."

"I hope she doesn't like it too much. I was hoping she would quit after we got married."

"Why would she do that?" I asked.

"I make pretty good money, and I know she lives paycheck to paycheck. Just doesn't make any sense. She could relax at home and do whatever she wants."

"If she asked you to stay at home and relax, would you like that?"

He studied my expression. "I get your point. You don't think she wants to stay home?"

I shook my head violently. "No. She would hate that. It'd drive her crazy."

"Maybe she'll hire someone else to work at the store so she can have more time off."

"Now, that is a possibility."

He looked out the window. "I guess I shouldn't have assumed she would be a housewife. I just like the idea of taking care of her. Buying her a nice car and an endless supply of lingerie."

Just when it seemed sweet, it turned sour. "She'd only stay home if she were a mom."

"Well...I guess we'll cross that bridge when we come to it."

The food arrived a moment later, and we both picked up our forks and dug into our food. Finn pulled his phone out of his pocket when it vibrated and checked the screen.

"Don't tell me it's Layla."

"No," he said with a laugh. "Pepper said something to her at the airport and got her to back off. She leaves me alone now. Still don't know what Pepper said ..."

"I do." I stabbed my fork into a cucumber and took a bite.

"You gonna share?"

"She said that when Layla falls in love someday, she'll be terrified to lose him because she loves him so much. Someone younger and hotter will come along, and she'll be powerless to keep him by her side. She told Layla she didn't want to be that kind of woman...the kind that steals someone's man. Because one day someone might steal her man away."

Finn stopped eating and kept his fork in his grasp. "That's deep."

"Pepper is a classy woman."

"Yeah, she is. When that guy assaulted her, she said she felt bad for him."

"Yeah...she's like that. Has the kind of heart that just keeps giving."

His eyes were glued to his salad as he dragged the fork through the greens, his thoughts somewhere else at the moment. "Then it's a good thing she has me. I'll keep her heart safe so no one else breaks it."

I just hoped he was never the culprit behind her heartbreak —because there would be no one to protect her. "So, it wasn't Layla? Good thing she's giving you peace."

"It was the chief. We're having a meeting tomorrow. Kind of a spur-of-the-moment thing."

"What's it about?"

He shrugged. "No idea. We don't have these meetings often,

so it's probably important. Last time we got together, it was because the Red Cross was asking for volunteers."

"I hope they aren't going to ask you to do anything else."

"I doubt it. I just did that mission, so they wouldn't ask me again so soon."

"So, if they asked you to go back to Florida, you would say no?" Pepper lost her mind when he left the first time. If he left again, especially as her fiancé, she wouldn't last another month.

"Definitely. I already did my time. Now, it's someone else's turn."

23

PEPPER

I FINISHED THE DISHES AND TURNED ON THE DISHWASHER.

Then I admired the ring on my left hand. "Wow, it's so beautiful..."

Soldier sat at my feet, looking up at me with his coffee-colored eyes.

"Isn't it pretty?" I turned my hand and showed off the diamond.

Soldier stared with the same boredom.

"Well, I think it's pretty." I never took it off, not even when I showered or did the dishes. It stayed on my hand even while I slept. Just like the military tags around my neck which I never took off. They meant too much to me to leave them on a table somewhere.

The garage door opened, and Finn stepped into the kitchen a moment later. In his scrubs and stethoscope, he walked inside and put his thermos on the counter. Soldier bolted for him and pawed at his legs. "Hey, boy." Finn leaned down and patted him down while Soldier got in a few wet kisses.

He rose to his feet and looked at me, his demeanor immediately changing when his eyes settled on my face. "Hey, baby." His arms circled my waist, and he brought his face close to mine. "I just got licked by a dog, but do you still want a kiss?"

I grabbed the front of his shirt and pulled him toward me, giving him a big kiss on the mouth. "Couldn't care less."

He squeezed my ass in my jeans then pulled away. "That's my girl." He carried his thermos to the sink then pulled out his keys and wallet and left them on the counter. "How was work?"

I shrugged. "Boring. You?"

He mimicked my movements and shrugged. "Boring."

"How was your meeting?"

He opened the fridge and took a peek inside before he shut the door. "Also boring."

"What was it about?"

"Just hospital stuff." He came back to me, most of his chest revealed in the deep V-neck shirt. His tattoos only made him sexier when he was dressed in scrubs like that. "So, I was thinking you would move all your stuff out of your apartment."

"You want me to move in with you?"

"You think I'm gonna let my fiancée live alone?" He raised an eyebrow. "Sleep alone? I gave you a diamond ring. I want sex every night for the rest of my life. So yes, I want your ass over here now."

He made something so crass sound so romantic. "Alright, you convinced me."

"There's not a lot of space for you to put your stuff, so I was going to suggest getting rid of it."

"Everything?" I asked.

"Yeah. Unless there's something you really want to keep. I guess we could put your bedroom set in the spare bedroom... even though no one will sleep in there."

Maybe bringing everything over here wouldn't make any sense. His place was already furnished because I'd helped him pick everything out. And my stuff wouldn't match anything anyway. It was all just generic things I got from IKEA after the divorce. "No, you're right. I should just get rid of it. I'll gather up all my clothes and essentials."

"We can donate the rest."

"Not a bad idea."

He leaned in and gave me a quick kiss on the lips. "I'm gonna take a shower then start dinner."

"I can make something."

"You mean, order a pizza?" he teased.

"No. I bought some stuff to make pot roast."

"Wow, you're going to be a great wife, huh?"

Wife. I never thought I'd want someone to call me that ever again. But that term fit me like a second skin—at least when he said it. This reality seemed too beautiful to be real. I wanted to pinch myself because it was too perfect. It had to be a dream. "I try."

"Well, if you don't like to cook, that's fine with me. As long as you keep giving me those amazing blow jobs." He shot me a handsome smile before he headed upstairs and into the hallway.

I watched him all the way, admiring that sexy man and every inch he possessed. That man would be my husband, the father of my children. I would live happily ever after with him, finding happiness in a way I never had before.

His phone vibrated on the counter.

He'd left it behind with his keys and wallet because he must have forgotten it.

An email popped up the unlocked screen. It looked like it was from his superior, the chief of the ER.

I knew I shouldn't look. I didn't want to have that kind of relationship, where we checked each other's phones and emails. When we had the level of trust we possessed, there was no need to look.

But the subject caught my eye.

Great to have you on board, Dr. Burke!

I couldn't read the rest of the email unless I opened it, but if I did that, he would know I'd read it.

I told myself to mind my own business and forget about it. If there were something he wanted to share with me, he would tell me. He wouldn't ask me to be his wife then keep a secret from me.

I let it go.

HE KISSED the valley between my tits, his tongue moving over the military tags that were engraved with his name. Every time he moved, the chain shifted across my skin, the cold metal touching me in different ways.

I loved it.

I loved feeling the warmth of his tongue then the coldness of the metal.

"You look so sexy wearing this." He sucked my left nipple hard, getting it between his teeth before swiping his tongue across it. "And this." He grabbed my left hand and placed it between my legs, the engagement ring visible.

My fingers rubbed my clit as he continued to suck my nipples. He'd already made love to me so many times that night, but I could always take more. I could always take another load, another kiss.

His mouth moved up my neck, and he kissed me on the mouth. "Beautiful." He sucked my bottom lip as his hand moved up my thigh. "You make me feel like a teenager getting laid for the first time."

"And you're so big, you make me feel like it's my first time."

He moaned against my mouth then sank his fingers inside me, feeling my come as well as his. "You want more, baby?"

"Always."

He spread my legs and shoved himself inside me again. Instead of making love to me good and slow like he did earlier, he fucked me hard, making the headboard tap against the wall over and over.

His arms moved behind my knees, and he pounded me into an orgasm, making my toes curl and my pussy drip with arousal and his seed. My hand pressed against his chest, and the ring caught the limited lighting, reminding me that I was, that he made me his.

He fucked me until he climaxed, giving a masculine moan as his dick twitched inside me. He released with an explosion, providing me with another pile of come to keep me warm for the night. His mouth trailed kisses along my jawline as he softened. When he was finished, he pulled out of me then rolled over. "I can fuck that pussy for the rest of my life."

"Good. Because you're going to." I kissed him on the lips before I got out of bed. "I'm going to shower."

"Why? I'm just going to fuck you again when you're finished." With his hand propped behind his head, he grinned like the cocky man he was.

"Be that as it may, I've got to shower sometime." I left the bedroom and walked into the bathroom. There were usually a few towels hanging on the rack or in the cabinet, but they must all have been in the laundry. I walked out and prepared to take the trip downstairs to where the fresh laundry was sitting on the table.

Finn was gone.

He must have left the second I entered the bathroom.

I left the bedroom and made my way downstairs.

He was sitting on the couch, his phone pressed to his ear. "No, it's not too late, Scott. You know me, I don't sleep much anyway." He listened to whatever Scott had to say.

I kept moving down the stairs. Since I was behind him, he didn't notice me creep across the tile floor to the pile of folded towels that I'd left behind.

"I haven't decided on a departure date. Still talking it over with my fiancée. We've got to get our affairs in order."

Buck naked, I stopped in the kitchen, hearing what he said without processing it. The weight of his words slowly sank in. Departure? Affairs? He hadn't talked about anything with his fiancée, because I was her, and I had no recollection of a conversation.

"I appreciate the opportunity. I understand what an honor it is. I'll get back to you tomorrow." He hung up. He tossed the phone on the coffee table then dragged his hand down his face, clearly conflicted with the commitment he'd just made and the pending conversation he needed to have with me.

I stayed behind him and considered what I might say. I could feel my blood boil even though I wasn't certain what he was talking about. Before losing my cool, I told myself to be calm. Maybe the situation wasn't as it seemed. "Are we going somewhere?"

His back stiffened as he leaned forward, shocked that I was standing behind him. He rubbed his hand across his jawline then rose to his feet. He slowly turned around, displaying the canvas of tattoos on his frame. He was just in sweatpants, the kind that hung so low on his hips that the V along his torso was more noticeable. He stopped when he faced me, the couch between us.

I forgot that I was naked. All I concentrated on was the tense moment between us, the way his eyes burned with hesitation. He wasn't the confident man who could move mountains with the snap of a finger. Now he was guarded, holding his cards close to his vest so I couldn't anticipate his next move.

"What was that about?" I pressed him again when he didn't speak.

He rubbed the back of his neck, the same movement he always made when he was stressed about something. He sighed as he lowered his hand then made his way around the couch toward me.

"Get our affairs in order? Decide on a departure date? Finn, correct me if I'm wrong, but it sounds like we're going somewhere—and not on a vacation." I crossed my arms over my chest, keeping my tone in check and not making assumptions. Would Finn really think about leaving right after he proposed to me?

He finally addressed my questions. "We just got engaged, so I wanted to enjoy that for a while before having this heavy conversation."

That didn't sound good.

"When I went to the meeting, I thought it was going to be like all the others. A group of doctors sitting around the table eating bagels from Panera. But after I walked in, I realized I was the only person coming. Scott is the chief of the ER, and he told me there was a special position available for me through Doctors Without Borders. Apparently, they asked for me personally..."

"Doctors Without Borders? Isn't that where healthcare professionals go to third world countries and stuff?"

He nodded. "Exactly."

How could Finn be enticed by that? "Finn, you just went to Florida for an entire month. You don't need to make any more sacrifices. You still help people every single day right here in Seattle."

"I know," he said with a sigh. "Normally, I would have said no. But they offered me something I couldn't turn down."

"What?" I asked incredulously. "What could possibly make

you want to go to the other side of the world for god knows how long?"

He slid his hands into his pockets. "They offered me the lead position. I would be the chief of medicine for the organization. The program was founded by the Mayo Clinic, so when my tenure there is finished, I would have a position at the best hospital in the nation... It's an honor. There's no higher level of medicine. It's a dream come true."

Maybe all of that was true. Maybe it was a great opportunity for him. But all I could think about was us. "Finn, I understand why that would be hard to turn down, but what about us? You asked me to be your wife. That means nothing to you?"

His eyes narrowed. "Of course it does. You're the only woman in the world I would have asked to be my wife."

"Then how is this going to work? Where will you be going? How long will you be gone?"

"Uganda," he answered. "Eastern Africa."

It was even worse than I feared.

"And I would be gone for a year."

A year? "You've got to be kidding me..."

"Baby, you would come with me. I can arrange all of that for you."

"Come with you?" I snapped. "And do what?"

"You could stay in Kenya while I work in the villages in Uganda. Or could come with me and help with medical supplies. We could always use more volunteers. These people don't even have clean water."

I pressed my hands over my face and sighed as I closed my eyes. "And you think I'd want to go somewhere without clean water? Maybe you don't know me as well as you think you do, but I'm not a sporty, outdoorsy kind of girl. I like to order a pizza and sit on the couch all night. It's great that you're passionate about this kind of stuff, but that's not me."

His eyes filled with disappointment.

"And what about Soldier? Where would he go?"

"My parents'." He blurted out the answer like he'd already thought it through. "And I assumed you would want to come with me. Where I go, you go. Colton said I can live the life I want with someone. I just have to share it with them. You were okay with me going to Florida, so I assumed you would be okay with this. When you were supportive about that, I realized I could make this work. I could marry someone without giving up the life I want."

My heart immediately dropped as the sadness entered my veins. "That was the only reason you asked me to marry you? Because you thought you could do whatever you wanted with me in tow?"

"No, that's not what—"

"Marriage is about compromise. You're asking me to completely give up my life so you can have what you want. I own a business, Finn. I have a life here in Seattle. I have absolutely nothing in Kenya. While you're in the jungle helping people, I'm stuck in some apartment watching TV all day, waiting for you to get home."

His hands moved to his hips, and he bowed his head. "Fine. Then I'll go, and you stay here."

Now my jaw was on the floor. "For a year? You expect us to live apart for an entire year?"

"We made it work with Florida."

I wanted to slam my hands down on the table because I was losing my mind. "That was a month, Finn. And remember how miserable we were? Remember how much we fought? We barely lasted a month, and you think we can last a year?"

"You need to give us more credit."

"No. You're really going to be faithful to me for a year?"

When his eyes narrowed, he looked hostile. "Yes. And you would be faithful to me. Our love is stronger than that."

I rolled my eyes. "A year is a long time, Finn. If you believe in us so much, then you shouldn't go. You should stay here and honor the commitment you made to me."

"I would still be honoring it while doing what I want. Pepper, the reason I never wanted to get married was because I didn't want to settle for a boring life. I didn't want to stop living when I have so much time left. I'm only thirty. You know how many more miles I have on this engine?"

"What does it matter when you're spending those miles on strangers? Those aren't real relationships, Finn. They are people you'll see for a short period of time before you're gone again. Is that what I am to you? Another pit stop?"

"You think I would have asked you to marry me if that were the case?" Now, his temper was skyrocketing like a sports car flooring it on the freeway. The vein in his forehead started to become more pronounced, and his skin tinted with the blood pounding in his veins. "I asked you to marry me because I love you and want to be with you for the rest of my life. I asked you to be my wife because you're the only woman I actually give a damn about. Jesus Christ, you're the love of my life."

It was one of the most beautiful things he'd ever said, but it was empty in that moment. "Then why would you even consider doing this? If you want to do short trips here and there, we can make that work. If you want to do humanitarian work in Uganda for a month, that's fine. I can deal with you coming and going from time to time. But you just got back from Florida a month ago, and now you want to take off again."

"That's not how it is. I was given a huge opportunity. What if I wanted to move to Minnesota so I could be a physician at the Mayo Clinic? What if I ever want to relocate? That's out of the question? We have to live in Seattle forever? What kind of life that?"

I would be able to stay in Seattle forever. My friends lived here. Colton lived here. But I would always compromise. "That's a completely different scenario. Of course, I would move with you. Honestly, I do want to stay in Seattle for the rest of my life, but I would make that sacrifice if it was important to you."

"How is it any different?"

"Because Minnesota is in America. I can live a normal life there. I can fly back and forth to see Colton when you're working all weekend. I can't fly to Seattle from Uganda all the time. Finn, it's completely different, and you know it."

He stepped back and rubbed the back of his neck. "I thought this conversation would go much differently."

"Then why did you hide it from me?"

He dropped his hand and looked at me with coldness. "I didn't hide it. I just wanted to have this conversation at the right time. I knew you wouldn't be thrilled by Uganda, but I didn't think you would be this opposed to it."

"Then you don't know me very well." It was a hard thing to admit, but it came rolling out.

His eyes darkened. "Yes, I do. I know you want me to do what I want."

"But I also expect you to compromise. I'm not going to give up my life so you can work in the jungle. If you want to keep doing humanitarian work, I will always support you. We can make it work. Even if we have kids, we can make it work. But if you want to marry me, I want a real marriage. I want us to live in this house together. I want to see you more often than not. I want to have a somehow boring life where we watch TV on the couch and go to bed. You need to give me that."

"I am giving you that. It's only a year."

"That's an eternity, Finn. Then what? You just went to

Florida a month ago, and now you're running off again. It'll never end with you. Colton was right...you can never stay in one place too long." Now I felt stupid for not taking his warning seriously. I'd assumed Finn was here to settle down, but he was anxious to keep moving. Florida was just a taste, and now he wanted more. He was a wild animal that couldn't sit in a cage. He had to be free...and always be free. "After Uganda, we move to Minnesota so you can work there until the next big offer comes along?"

"There's not going to be a bigger offer than that."

"Until you start working in the Philippines or somewhere else. Finn, you know I want a family. Did you propose to me assuming I would change my mind?"

"No." Now we were both on edge, both holding ourselves back from screaming. "I'll give you a family. I just assumed you would give me some things in return as well."

"Finn, I can't raise our kids in the jungle—"

"I'm not asking you to. But yes, we may have to move around and put them in new schools."

I didn't want my kids to live a caravan lifestyle. I wanted them to find good friends and grow up with them. I'd learned that careers weren't as important as people. Jobs came and went, but love never did. "So you want me to give up my business for yours?"

"Not in those words...but yes."

"But would you give up yours for me?"

He shut his mouth and turned quiet, probably at a loss for words. There was nothing he could say that wouldn't make him sound like a jackass. Either my business wasn't as important as his, or he expected me to make the sacrifices because I was the woman in the relationship. "Baby, all I know is, this relationship isn't going to work unless we make compromises."

"I agree. And what you're asking for is too much of a

compromise for me, Finn. I don't want to move to Uganda then Minnesota."

"Well, I don't want to have kids, but I'm willing to do that for you."

"You don't want them?" I asked, hurt. "I assumed you'd changed your mind…"

"I changed my mind about having them because it's important to you. That's a compromise. You need to meet me halfway, Pepper."

"Halfway?" My voice continued to rise as the tension escalated. "Those aren't even comparable. Having children is normal in a marriage. Moving across the world for a year is not normal."

"And I've never been normal. I assumed you understood that."

"I do, Finn." I didn't want to spend this time that should have been blissful screaming at each other, but I had to put an end to this. "I admire you for being so selfless, for always putting yourself on the line for other people. It's one of the reasons I fell in love with you in the first place. But you're asking too much, Finn. I understand, and I'm and willing to let you travel away from me and do what's important to you sometimes…a few months out of the year. But you're asking for too much…if you still want to marry me." I wanted to give him whatever he wanted to make this relationship work. I was so deeply in love with this man, I would do anything to keep him. But agreeing to something I didn't truly support would lead to resentment and then a painful divorce. I'd already been divorced once. I didn't want to be divorced again.

"So you're giving me an ultimatum." He crossed his arms over his chest, his head bowed to the floor.

"No…"

He raised his head and looked at me. "But you are. I either leave for Uganda and Minnesota without you…or I stay here and marry you. That's what you're saying. Correct me if I'm wrong."

I'd never thought I would give this man an ultimatum. I'd never thought I would make this man choose between me and his career. But what he was asking for was simply too much. "You can do humanitarian stuff. I'm not discouraging you—"

"Answer the question."

When he looked at me with those disappointed eyes, I felt so small. Like I'd committed a crime or done something unforgivable. He didn't look at me like I was the light of his life, the woman he would do anything to be with. Now it seemed like he despised me, long before I gave him an answer. "Yes..." I never wanted to stop this man from pursuing his happiness, but we couldn't have this kind of relationship and expect to last. That wasn't the kind of marriage I wanted...because I wanted one that would go the distance.

He stared at me for a few more seconds, his eyes so dark they seemed to be full of smoke. He abruptly turned away and snatched his hoodie off the back of one of the chairs. He pulled it over his head then grabbed his keys and wallet.

"Finn—"

"Don't wait up for me." He stormed out into the garage and let the door slam behind him.

I stayed rooted to the spot in the kitchen, naked with the exception of his necklace and diamond ring. Just a few hours ago, I had everything.

Now I worried that I had nothing.

24

COLTON

A FIST POUNDED ON MY DOOR AT ALMOST NINE IN THE EVENING.

Was it Pepper again?

She didn't have the strength to produce that kind of sound against the wood. I checked the peephole and recognized my brother before I answered the door. "Geez, what's with the Donkey Kong—"

"I need to crash on your couch tonight." He helped himself inside and pulled his hoodie over his head. He wasn't wearing a shirt, so it was just skin and tattoos underneath. But when he lived with me, he was nearly naked most of the time anyway, so it was normal at this point.

"Uh...why?" He and Pepper just got engaged, so I couldn't imagine him wanting to be apart from her for even a minute.

"Because." He tossed his keys and wallet on the table and helped himself to my fridge. He riffled through the cabinets until he found a bottle of scotch he'd left behind. He didn't even bother with a glass and drank it right out of the bottle.

"Because...?" I joined him at the counter. "What the hell happened? You just got engaged, and you're already fighting?"

He took a long drink then wiped his lips with the back of his forearm. "Something like that."

"You do realize she's probably going to show up here any minute."

"Then I'll go. Problem solved." He slammed the bottle down and spilled some of the booze onto the counter.

"Finn, whatever it is, you can work it out. So, unwind for a couple of hours, then go home."

He gripped the counter and dropped his head, his knuckles turning white as he sighed quietly. He suddenly straightened, his nostrils flaring. "I was offered a position with Doctors Without Borders. I would have the leading position, which is a huge opportunity and honor. After a year in Uganda, I would be given a position at the Mayo Clinic in Minnesota. It would be the biggest accomplishment of my career."

He didn't need to explain her position on the matter. She wouldn't be able to handle Finn being gone for an entire year, living in the opposite time zone so they would never be awake at the same time. Then moving to Minnesota to settle down... would be terrible for her. The only place she wanted to be was in Seattle.

"I tried to get her to come with me, but she said no."

"You wouldn't want her to come, Finn. She'd be miserable the entire time."

"Yeah, but I didn't think she would be miserable with me..."

"Come on, Finn. You're asking her to be part of a world she has no interest in. She can't even put a bandage on because she can't look at her own cuts. She barely likes to travel outside of Seattle. She's the biggest couch potato I know. You're asking her to do something she absolutely hates...and for a year."

"Then I expected her to accept my absence."

"For a year?" I asked incredulously. "Are you insane? You'd

want to have a wife living here all alone while you're on the other side of the world? That doesn't make any sense, Finn."

"I expected her to work with me. She knows I'm passionate about this."

"Which is why she supported you going to Florida even though she hated every second of it." My brother had a different perception on life than the rest of us. To him, he was always fighting the clock, feeling pressure to live life to the fullest. "And she would support you going as much as you wanted. But this is too much. I'm on her side for this."

He looked at me, slightly shocked. "Really?"

"Yes. And you know we are both right. You just don't want to admit it."

He gripped the counter again.

"You proposed to Pepper and then got offered your dream job. Now you're trying to have both when you know you can't. And you probably wouldn't have proposed to her if the offer had come first..."

"That's not true—"

"I think it is. So, what are you going to pick? Your wife or your career?"

"You told me I could have both—"

"You can have both. But this is too much. You're asking Pepper to sacrifice everything for you—which is selfish."

"Look—"

"No, you listen to me." I stood my ground against Finn because Pepper was family to me too. I would defend her against everything, even own my flesh and blood. "When you asked for my blessing to marry her, I gave it to you. I told you not to propose unless you were prepared to give her everything she asked for. You told me you loved her and wanted to spend the rest of your life with her. This just proves you didn't mean any of that—"

"Yes, I did. I love her more than anything else in this world—"

"Then turn down the job, Finn."

He stared at me, his face turning pale.

"You can't have both. You have to choose. And if you really love her, you'll walk away from this offer."

"It's the job opportunity of a lifetime—"

"And Pepper is one in a million." After everything my brother put me through with this relationship, he better make the right decision. "You asked her to marry you, Finn. That's a big commitment. You shouldn't have asked unless you would stick by her through thick and thin. You might be giving up something you think is important, but she's more important. If you don't see it that way...then you don't deserve her anyway."

FINN CRASHED ON THE COUCH, lying in just his boxers with the blanket pulled over his waist. After downing that entire bottle of scotch, he collapsed and fell asleep the second his head hit the pillow.

Hopefully, he didn't have to work tomorrow.

I sat in the armchair and felt my phone vibrate with a text message.

It was Pepper. *Finn and I had a big fight. He left the house a few hours ago, and he won't answer my texts or calls. Could you check on him?*

Of course, Pepper wasn't even mad about his childish behavior. She just wanted to make sure he was okay. *He's sleeping on my couch, actually.*

Oh, thank god. I'm so relieved...

He told me everything that happened. I'm sorry.

Yeah...not how I wanted to spend my first two weeks engaged.

Finn had fucked up the relationship so quickly. He was unable to handle commitment, so he'd already screwed up the happiest time of his life. Now he wanted to take off again.

You were right, Colton. Finn will never stay still... He'll always be on the move.

We don't know that yet. I think our talk straightened him out.

I hope so. I love him so much...but I'm not going to Uganda.

You wouldn't survive in Uganda. Without American television and food, she would lose her mind. She could barely stand staying in a hotel, let alone another country. *Finn was stupid to even ask.*

Even if Finn changes his mind, I'm worried. He's never going to want to stay still...

I was pissed at Finn for letting this happen in the first place, but I had faith in him. *Let's not forget how much he loves you. I think he'll come around and be the guy that you deserve. We just need to let him sober up first.*

25

PEPPER

I HAD TO WORK THE NEXT MORNING, SO I WENT TO THE SHOP WITH a frown on my face.

What was going to happen with Finn?

I still wore my engagement ring, the ring that meant so much to me. I was disappointed in him for his behavior, for wanting to leave when we should be planning our lives together. But I loved him so much that I wanted to just forget about it. I wanted him to say it was a mistake and he wanted to stay with me.

But what if he wanted to leave?

The day stretched on forever, and it seemed like five o'clock was a myth.

When it finally arrived, I got in an Uber and headed to Finn's house. I could have gone to my apartment, but I was hoping Finn was home. Maybe we could finally finish this conversation. He hadn't returned my texts or phone calls, so maybe he thought we were finished.

I greeted Soldier in the doorway then stepped farther inside the house. When I got to the living room, I found Finn sitting on the couch. He was in his scrubs with his stethoscope around his neck. He wouldn't still be in those clothes if he'd just gotten off work, so he must be heading out soon.

He didn't look at me when I walked inside.

The tension from the night before still filled the room, like the fight had never stopped.

I crossed my arms over my chest and stood behind one of the couches, refusing to speak first. I had no idea where his mind was at. Maybe he was about to dump me and ask for his ring back.

Soldier lay at my feet, choosing his side.

Finn finally rose from the couch, his shoulders sagging under the weight. He moved around the coffee table and came closer to me. When he was in front of me, he finally lifted his gaze and looked me in the eye. "I slept at Colton's. Don't want you to think I was out doing something stupid."

"I know...he told me." The thought of Finn going to a bar or picking up Layla had never crossed my mind. I had a much higher opinion of him than he realized. No matter how bad things got, he wouldn't do that to me. If he was faithful to me during his time in Florida, then nothing would ever break his commitment.

"I drank too much and passed out. I woke up late...that's why I didn't text you back."

"I figured." I hated this distance between us. I hated that we felt like strangers rather than lovers. I hated the fact that this relationship already felt like it was over. "I'm glad you're okay. Soldier and I were worried."

"I didn't mean to worry you... I just needed some space." He slid his hands into his pockets and swallowed the lump that must have been in his throat. When his eyes shifted back to mine, they were full of remorse. "I made a commitment to you, and I'll honor it. I understand why you don't want me to go to Uganda and why you don't want to come with me. It's a lot to ask of someone...and you've never been interested in that type of work. So...I'll turn it down." The air slowly left his lungs as he breathed out, a sigh of defeat whispering in the air.

I got exactly what I wanted—but it wasn't what I wanted at all. I got Finn to cave, to give me what I wanted. I could just take it and run, but that wouldn't be right. It would just bite me in the ass eventually. His sacrifice would lead to resentment, and that resentment would tear us apart anyway. "Finn, I don't want to be a commitment. I don't want to be a clause in a contract that you mistakenly signed. I don't want to be the regret keeping you from what you really want. If this is what you want, you should go."

He stared at me for a long time, carefully choosing his next words before he voiced them. "I do want this. It's what I was put on this earth to do. It's not just about the opportunity to advance my career. It's about making a difference in this god-awful world. But I love you, baby. I really mean that when I say it. I have two loves in my life...you and my work. I want to have both."

My chest tightened because it predicted the outcome of this conversation. I could feel the danger to my soul, the terror that would cripple me soon enough. I'd lost him once, and it shook the ground beneath my feet. Now, it would happen again...and this time, it would be worse.

"Let's try a long-distance relationship—"

"No. I want a husband who will be here with me all the time. I don't want to be married to someone who wants to be some-where his wife isn't." I'd married the wrong man once before, and I wouldn't do it again. Love wasn't enough to keep us together. Just like in the rest of his travels, I was just someone Finn had met along the way. When he got older, he would finally settle down with someone—and it wouldn't be me. I wouldn't wait that long. "I love you so much, Finn. You have no idea how much because there aren't sufficient words to express my emotions. That's why I'm ending this."

He took a deep breath, his nostrils flaring slightly.

"If you stay, you'll just resent me. We both know you're meant to drift across this world, living in different places and helping all kinds of people. If you don't do this, something else will pop up. You'll never really be happy here. Our marriage will end in divorce in just a few short years. I don't want that. And I won't come with you, so there is no other choice."

"Baby, I don't want to drift around forever. I just want to do this—"

"You just went to Florida. That was so hard for both of us, but it didn't stop you from signing up for this. Let's be real, Finn. A sedentary life isn't what you want...at least not right now. If you're honest with yourself, you'll realize that this is who you are...and you're never going to change." When he got down on one knee and showed me that beautiful ring, I thought I was finally getting my happy ending. But now I realized this was another stepping stone, another heartbreak on the long road to happiness. "I think you expected our marriage to be about me coming with you and experiencing all these things. But I don't want that kind of life. If I join you, I'll just end up resenting you. If I give up my business to live in Uganda, I'll resent you. Either way, we lose."

Finn didn't have an argument against that.

"When you proposed to me, I'm sure you meant it. I'm sure it's what you wanted. But when this offer came up, it reminded you of what you really want. It refueled those desires you have. If you hadn't proposed to me already, you probably would have broken up with me and just left."

"Baby, you're belittling my love for you. That's not how I feel at all."

"If you did feel that way, you would have turned down this offer the second you heard it. You would have known you couldn't be without me for that long and knew you wanted to settle down here. But instead, you took the offer and hid it from me. Finn, this isn't what you want. We both know that." My heart was breaking the longer the conversation continued. I knew exactly how this was going to end—and it would end badly.

"I just told you I would stay here—"

"No. You said you would honor your commitment. That's not the same thing at all. That's not you saying you want to stay with me because you can't live without me. That's some stupid contract talk. That's not what I want to hear. And as I said, you would just resent me. You were never meant to stay in Seattle. This was just something to do until you figured out your next move. Now, a new opportunity has presented itself, and you're ready to take off. I'm just one of the people you met along your journey...a memory to hold on to."

He moved his hands to his hips, the pain in his eyes.

"This is over." The words came out of my mouth, but I refused to let the tears escape. I had to be strong, to keep a straight face as this man looked at me. After fantasizing about growing old with him, this loss was so much harder. I thought I would never have to live without him. But I was so wrong. "I don't want to be with someone who wishes he were somewhere else. I don't want to be the reason you can't do what you really want. And I don't want to make so many sacrifices just to keep you. It's not fair to either one of us." I hoped that Finn would suddenly have a change of heart, that his eyes would burn with tears and he would realize he couldn't live without me. I wanted him to say he loved me so much that leaving was impossible. But

I knew that would never happen because he would have turned down the job in the first place if that was how he felt.

He took a deep breath. "I don't want to lose you…"

"I don't want to lose you either. But there is no other option."

"Baby…" His hands cupped my face and brought our mouths close together. "I love you."

"I love you too…"

He swiped his thumb across my bottom lip before he leaned down and kissed me.

But he didn't fight for me. He didn't tell me all the things I wanted to hear. So I kissed him back, but only halfheartedly.

He pulled away when my lips felt lifeless.

I grabbed his wrists and pulled his hands off my face. "I won't wait for you, Finn. If you think you can spend a year in Uganda and then come back to me, you can't. You should go to Minnesota afterward. You should sell your house and never come back. If you think in a few years we can find out way back to each other, you're wrong. When you leave, that's it for us. It doesn't matter how much I love you. I will find someone else and have the life that I want. And I suggest you do the same."

WHEN HE WAS AT WORK, I packed all of my things and stuffed them into a bag.

Soldier sat on the bed, his snout on his paws. His brown eyes watched me move, and his somber attitude told me he knew something terrible was happening. Perhaps he could absorb my sadness, perhaps he could feel the despair that lingered in every inch of the house.

Or maybe it was just because tears streamed down my face.

I zipped up the bag with all of my things and sat on the edge of his bed. My beautiful future had been destroyed by a horrible reality. There would be no white wedding dress or a beautiful dinner to celebrate our nuptials. There would be no children or holidays. Finn would be another man who broke my heart. He would be a memory—a good one and a bad one.

I thought Colton was the love of my life, but that wasn't true anymore.

It was Finn.

And I'd lost him.

Soldier shifted to my side then whined when he saw my tears. He rested his snout on my thigh then whined again, mirroring my emotions as if he really internalized everything I was feeling.

"Thanks, boy." I ran my hand over his head and down his back. "I'm gonna miss you too. But I'll still see you at Colton's parents'. They have a huge backyard, so you'll love it there. And I'll see you all the time."

Soldier whined again.

Our little family was breaking up, and it was so painful. I tried to remind myself it would have been a million times worse if we were married and had made this our house together. Ending it now was better than ending it later.

I kissed him on the forehead then rose to my feet. My ring was still on my finger, and the military tags still hung around my throat. It didn't feel right to keep those things, not when they should be given to his wife someday. The tags carried the weight of his sacrifice in the military. When enough time had passed, they would be stuffed in a drawer somewhere, a haunting memory. They deserved to be worn proudly, either by him or by the woman he loved.

I pulled the ring off my left hand and admired it for a moment longer, treasuring the fact I was still his fiancée for a few more seconds. Once that ring was set on his nightstand, it would really be over.

I would be just like the other girls—someone from his past.

I admired the diamond another minute before I gently set it on the nightstand. It made a gentle tap before it sat still. The blinds were closed and the lighting was minimal, but somehow, the diamond still shone brightly on its own.

I pulled the necklace off next and admired the tags with his name engraved in the metal. My thumb brushed over the grooves, and once the weight had been lifted off my neck, I felt off-balance. The removal of the weight wasn't freeing. The absence of the necklace somehow felt heavier.

I brought one of the tags to my lips and gave it a kiss before setting it on his nightstand.

Then it was done.

We were officially over.

I grabbed my bag and walked to the front door, knowing my Uber would be there in just a few minutes.

Soldier followed me, his ears and tail both down. He whined when I opened the door, as if he somehow knew I wouldn't come back.

Leaving Soldier was like leaving a child. He might be just a dog to some people, but he was so much more to me. I started to sob because saying goodbye to him was somehow harder than saying goodbye to Finn. I squatted down and wrapped him up in a tight hug. "I love you so much, boy." Tears streaked down my cheeks and into his fur. I held on to him for a long time because he'd become such a close friend to me. I loved him with all my heart. "I'll see you later, okay?"

He whined again, as if he knew I was saying goodbye.

I couldn't look at him again, not when I was about to leave that house forever. I grabbed my bag and turned away, making sure to close the door without looking back.

I sat on the couch and watched the light fade with the setting sun. My bottle of wine was on the end table beside me, my lipstick smeared around the rim of the bottle. As the sun disappeared, my apartment fell deeper and deeper into shadow. But I didn't care enough to get up and turn on the lights.

Everything seemed pointless in that moment.

My left hand felt so light, my ring finger so lonely. Without that ring, I felt like I'd lost a part of myself—a part that belonged to Finn. Now I didn't know where I belonged in this world. So far, I'd been existing in a fantasy world, picturing my future children and the wonderful life we would have.

Now I was back to square one.

But this time, it was worse. It hurt much more than my divorce.

Colton stepped through the door and didn't seem alarmed that it wasn't locked. He took one look at me on the couch, reading my lifeless eyes and permanent frown, and figured out exactly what happened.

Wordlessly, he sat on the couch and pulled me into his arms, protecting me against something he couldn't shield me from. The damage had been done. My heart was broken a second time —and this time, it couldn't be fixed.

My eyes were puffy from the spent tears, and my body was immobile from the shock. I left him pull me against his chest and felt the warmth of his skin. He smelled just the way he used to because he'd been wearing the same cologne for years.

He rubbed my back then pressed a kiss to my forehead. "I'm so sorry, babe..."

"I should have listened to you."

The light left his eyes at my comment.

"He'll never change...he'll never stay in one place."

Colton was truly at a loss for words while he continued to rub my back without saying anything in return. There was nothing to mask my pain, nothing to console me. Finn would never be tired of that life. He needed to be free, free until old age humbled me. Some other woman fifteen years younger than him would be at the right place at the right time. She would get a new diamond ring on her finger, paid for by the money he got from exchanging my ring.

And where would I be?

Would I be married to someone else? Would I be happy? Would I have children?

I'd gone through heartbreak twice in less than two years, and I was sick of it. I was tired of looking for Mr. Right.

Maybe Mr. Right didn't exist.

A KNOCK on the door woke me up.

I was in Colton's arms, warm because of the blanket he pulled over both of us. I jerked at the sound, disoriented by the commotion as well as the emotion that burned in my heart.

Colton woke up too. "Someone is at the door."

I knew exactly who it was.

Colton got up and answered the door, flicking on the light at the same time since it was so dark in my apartment. The open door revealed Finn on the other side, dressed in jeans and sweatshirt. He didn't seem surprised to see his brother at all.

Colton stepped around him, ignoring his brother as he vacated the apartment. With just his silence, he showed Finn how disappointed he was.

Finn stepped inside and shut the door behind him.

I sat up and didn't bother fixing my hair or smeared makeup. I could always pretend it got messed up because I'd been sleeping...not because I'd cried my eyes out on and off all day.

He stood near the coffee table and looked down at me, waiting for me to meet his eyes. "You took all your stuff."

"I didn't want to stay there anymore." I rose to my feet and finally mustered the courage to look him in the eye. My arms crossed over my chest, an extra barrier to keep away from him. Instead of holding on to him as long as I could, I wanted to let go. He'd already showed his true colors when he agreed to that trip without even mentioning it to me. Our relationship died that moment.

"I thought we could be together until I left."

Was I stupid for hoping he would come here to declare his love for me? To say that he wanted to participate in this mission, but he would much rather spend the rest of his life with me? How did I fall for this man so easily? How did I give my heart and soul to him when he didn't deserve it? I was supportive when he went to Florida because that was what relationships were about—sacrifice. But he would keep draining me of sacrifices until there was nothing left. "No." That was the best answer I could get out. I didn't want to explain my reasons, not when our last conversation had been more than sufficient.

"Then I'm going to leave in three days." Expressionless, he spoke like he didn't feel a single emotion inside that hollow chest. How could he leave me without regret? How could he decide to go when he loved me?

"Take care."

His eyes narrowed in disappointment. "Please don't be like this."

"How do you want me to be, Finn?" I countered. "You want me to keep loving you like everything is okay? You want me to pretend everything is fine? You broke my heart. Colton warned me not to fall in love with you, and he was right... He was right the whole time."

He lowered his gaze.

"Maybe you do love me...just not enough."

"Baby—"

"Just go." When Finn walked out that door, I would never see him again. He would travel to Africa then relocate to the Midwest. I wouldn't even see him for holidays. He would be gone from my life permanently—but that couldn't happen soon enough. I was tired of getting my heart broken by men who didn't deserve it. I wanted to close this chapter of my life and move on—and make better decisions. I didn't want to hug him and kiss him one last time. I didn't want to tell him I loved him. He'd tortured me when he gave me that empty proposal. He'd asked me to love him for the rest of my life. But the offer was conditional—until something better came along.

Finn didn't try to touch me. He didn't give me a goodbye kiss. His eyes were emotionless as he looked deep into mine. While I was crying a river inside, he seemed robotic. He was a strong man without deep emotion like the rest of us, but I'd still hoped he would feel *something*. "You left your ring."

"Because I don't want it. Sell it." Why would I want another diamond ring in my nightstand when I already had one? It would just be a sad pile of men who didn't really love me. Colton preferred men. Finn preferred life. I was never the most important thing to either of them.

Finn didn't try to argue with me.

"Now, go. This relationship is over, so we have nothing left to say to each other." I turned around, not wanting to watch him walk out of my life. I didn't want to see him leave me, watch him pursue his dreams. He would go back to having any woman he wanted, forgetting about me after a few notches on his bedpost. It'd be like this never happened. He wouldn't have to face his brother again because he'd been far away, so it didn't matter to him that he might have ruined their relationship. This man didn't care about anyone but himself—and I wasn't sure why I'd allowed myself to fall so deeply in love with him.

His footsteps didn't sound as he headed to the door. Instead, he came closer to me, his chest close to my back. He reached inside his pocket and felt something metal before he raised both hands above my head and lowered a necklace over my throat.

When he released, I felt the weight that had been missing since I'd removed it earlier today. The tags clanked together at my breasts, his name still right next to my heart. He pulled his hands away. "You're the love of my life, Pepper. I want you to have this...because there's no other woman in the world I would ever give it to."

Tears pooled in my eyes until they dripped down my cheeks. I did my best to stay quiet, to not let quivering lips make a single sound. I refused to show my pain, to collapse with weakness. When he walked out that door, I would give in to my grief, but not a moment sooner.

He finally turned away, his footsteps sounding against the hardwood floor. His movements were slow, like he hoped I would change my mind and ask him to stay for the night.

I continued to hold my breath until he was gone, to keep my tears in check before I was surrounded by privacy. I didn't tell him I loved him one last time. I'd spent our entire relationship showing him my devotion every single day. He was the one who decided to leave, so I refused to be pathetic and give my heart to him—again.

He opened the door, walked out, and shut it behind him once more.

When I heard the click of the door as it stationed itself in the frame, I closed my eyes and allowed the tears to stream down my cheeks. I gave in to the grief that flooded my body, and I sank to the floor, the weight of his necklace too much to bear. My bottom hit the rug, and I leaned against the couch, seeing my reflection in the dark TV screen. My arms crossed over my chest, and I gripped myself hard as the tears shook my rib cage. I broke into infinite pieces, like a shattered diamond. Dust flew everywhere, pieces that could never be put back together. Colton had broken my heart, but I'd managed to bounce back. But I couldn't bounce back this time.

This time, I was defeated.

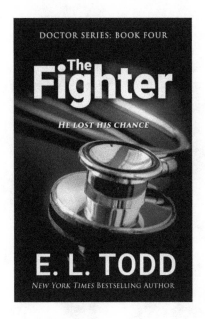

SIGNED PAPERBACKS?

Would you love a signed copy of your favorite book? Now you can purchase autographed copies and get them sent right to your door! Get your copy here:

http://www.eltoddbooks.com/